NUECES JUSTICE

THE TUMBLEWEED SAGAS

MARK GREATHOUSE

DEFIANCE PRESS
& PUBLISHING

Nueces Justice

Printed in the United States of America

10 9 8 7 6 5 4 3 2 1

ISBN-13: 978-1-948035-30-9 (Hard Cover)
ISBN-13: 978-1-948035-31-6 (eBook)

Published by Defiance Press and Publishing, LLC

Bulk orders of this book may be obtained by contacting Defiance Press and Publishing, LLC. www.defiancepress.com.

Public Relations Dept. – Defiance Press & Publishing, LLC
281-581-9300
pr@defiancepress.com

Defiance Press & Publishing, LLC
281-581-9300
info@defiancepress.com

DEDICATION

*Dedicated with love to my wife, Carolyn,
and to our two sons, Mike and Matt.*

THEME

Justice:

*The quality of being just, impartial, or fair;
the principle or ideal of just dealing or right
action; conformity to a principle or ideal.*

THE CAST

Lucas "Long Luke" Dunn – Soon to become one of the greatest Texas Ranger captains ever, Luke escapes the Great Famine in Ireland to seek his fortune on the Nueces Strip. He gains repute as an Indian fighter and respected lawman.

George Whelan – A dutiful and well-intended sheriff of Nueces County. His weakness for the ladies lands him in trouble.

Elisa Corrigan – Loses her family to frontier rigors, including fighting off Comanche. She takes over her parents' farm and soon meets and sets her heart on Luke Dunn.

Doc Andrews – The alcoholic Nuecestown doctor is the rheumy conscience of the town.

Bart Strong – "Bad Bart" Strong is a notorious killer Luke is assigned to hunt down and capture or kill. Strong seeks to add Luke as a notch on his gun.

Clyde Jones – Texas Ranger who served with Luke Dunn in the early Rangers.

Three Toes – Comanche Chief, son of famous Penateka Comanche War Chief Santa Anna and favored by Buffalo Hump. He develops a friendship with Luke that contradicts tribal ways.

Dirk Cavendish – Cav, as he's called, grows up with an abusive father and weaves a path of murder and mayhem while luring Scarlett into his web.

Carlos Perez – Cattle thief and killer embarrassed by Luke. Perez stalks his nemesis, seeking revenge. He blames Luke for the loss of his eye.

Scarlett Rose – Red-headed prostitute from Laredo who latches on to Luke Dunn for protection but hankers for black-clad mystery man, Dirk Cavendish. Her conflicted interests and bad choices of men could prove deadly.

Bernice & Agatha – Nuecestown town gossips with hearts of gold who run the boarding house.

Colonel Horace Rucker – Retired U.S. Army veteran and secessionist who becomes one of Scarlett's nemeses.

MAP OF THE NUECES STRIP

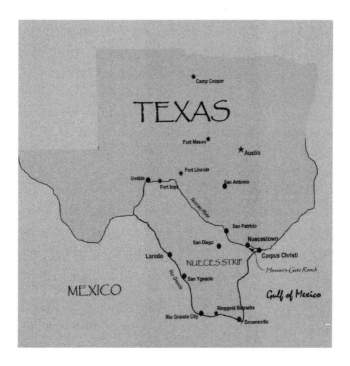

Nuecestown, established in 1852 by English and German settlers, was developed by Corpus Christi founder Colonel Henry Lawrence Kinney. It frequently serves as a setting for Tumbleweed Sagas. Thanks to being passed by the railroad, it's now a "ghost town" marked only by historical markers. All that remains is a preserved schoolhouse and the Nuecestown Cemetery.

CONTENTS

PROLOGUE

The Nueces Strip of the 1850s was mostly a vast prairie of tall grass and loamy sands stretching far as the eye could see and then some. Technically, it stretched from the Nueces River south to the Rio Grande. Occasionally among the wiregrass would spring a motte of live oak or mesquite. Mostly dry creek beds and arroyos meandered throughout, eventually feeding into Nueces Bay and…farther east… Corpus Christi Bay.

When it rained, folks were at the mercy of flash floods. The summers were brutally hot and made even hotter by the humidity. The breezes from the Gulf of Mexico didn't reach near far enough inland to matter much. The weather was about as changeable as a woman's mood.

Fauna and flora flourished in the Nueces Strip. Deer, javelina, fox, jackrabbits, armadillos, coons, and coyote were fairly common, with occasional spotted ocelots and even wolves. The harmless but ferocious-looking horned lizard or horny toad could be found in abundance. Wildflowers were plentiful, and the landscape was, at times, painted with scarlet sage, hibiscus, daisies, poppies, and lilies. Further south could be found groves of cypress, juniper, and palmetto. Of course, there was the omnipresent cactus along with yucca and agave.

No description of the Nueces Strip would be complete without mention of the Diamondback rattlesnake. The rattlesnake is part of the culture of the region and is included in many so-called Texas-isms, like, "he's so tough he'd fight a rattlesnake and spot it the first bite." Or "nastier than a nest of rattlesnakes." Bite was nasty for sure.

Most of the serious fighting of the Texas War for Independence was fought on the Nueces Strip and just north of it back in 1835 and 1836, and it was the scene of the first fighting of the Mexican-American War of 1846.

It wasn't long before the indigenous longhorn made its way into the Nueces Strip economy. Thanks to early Spanish priests setting up their missions to convert the Indians, the longhorns roamed free and bred prolifically as the missions failed one by one. Soon enough, millions of the beasts covered Texas, especially on the good grazing lands of the Nueces Strip.

By the 1850s, ranches and farms had begun to sprawl throughout the Nueces Strip. Cotton was king, and the longhorn and the all-important horse, as far as livestock went, reigned supreme. A single longhorn might need as much as five acres to stay well fed. The range was as wide open as it was beautiful. In fact, a body could swear that, on a clear night, you could actually hear the stars twinkle amidst the occasional owl hoots and flutter of bat wings.

The frontier was populating. There was still worry about Comanche, Kiowa, and Lipan Apache, not to mention the rogue marauding bandits from south of the Rio Grande. Those threats tended to remind early Texans to stay ever vigilant. It didn't take much to make the case for calling companies of Texas Rangers to patrol the vast area that comprised the Nueces Strip. The Rangers took it upon themselves to go where the military found it politically unattractive.

To say there wasn't much in terms of settlements on the Nueces Strip in the 1850s wouldn't be an exaggeration. The beginnings of settlements for stage way stations and mail service were in their prenatal stage. North of the Nueces River, there was a lot more going on. No surprise that Captain Richard King and Gideon K. Lewis would found what became the King Ranch, eventually spreading over 825,000 acres across six Texas counties of the Nueces Strip. But, other than Corpus Christi, San Diego, Laredo, Brownsville, San Ygnatio, and Nuecestown, the Nueces Strip was simply wide-open space. There was space aplenty to raise longhorns and horses, making the economics attractive despite the threats of Indians and bandits. It was those threats that brought the likes of Dunn and the Texas Rangers to the Nueces Strip.

The Nueces Strip of the 1850s was all about promise. It would be many years before it revealed all of its secrets. Meanwhile, it demanded the unbridled devotion of men like Captain Luke Dunn. Recently, he had joined about 130 men to ride with the famed James Hughes Callahan and chase Lipan Apache after their cattle-thieving attacks in Bexar and Comal Counties. Callahan had earned a reputation for gallant action in the Texas Revolution, having escaped the Goliad Massacre and fought at Victoria. Technically, the Texas Rangers had become an afterthought in some minds, given the statehood status of Texas and so-called protection of the U.S. Army. When that protection was not forthcoming following raids by the Apache, it took a concerted effort by Governor E.M. Pease to get the legislature to authorize enough money to raise the company of Rangers under Callahan.

In September 1855, Callahan and his company crossed the Rio Grande into Mexico in their chase after the Lipan Apache. About forty miles into Mexico, they were met by a force of Indians and Mexican troops, initiating an incident on the Rio Escondito in which a small number were killed and wounded on both sides, the town of Piedras Negros was looted and burned, and Callahan re-crossed the Rio Grande into Texas. Little wonder that the Mexicans took to derogatorily calling the Texas Rangers "rinches." Dunn was credited with being in the thick of the battle. He was frustrated to learn upon returning with Callahan that, while public support for another expedition was favorable, the politicians were not inclined to risk another international incident. Notably, Callahan died the following year in a fight with a fella named Woodson Blassingame.

Dunn had his horse, bedroll, armament, badge, and enough money to continue Rangering on the Nueces Strip. He figured his performance with Callahan had earned him the captain rank, and it was said that Governor Pease informally authorized it. If Dunn could eliminate an occasional Apache or some lawbreaker on his own dime, it was just fine with the governor.

It's said that the Nueces Strip never gives up its secrets. One thing for sure, justice is swift and certain. When Nueces justice is rendered, there is no question that lawbreakers are dealt full punishment for their misdeeds. It might appear that the Nueces Strip would provide a haven for lawbreakers, but the vast vistas of grassy prairie offer little or no place to hide. Nueces justice is the inevitable outcome.

ONE

The Nueces Strip

"**B**ad" Bart Strong oh-so-careful-like sighted down the barrel. The bead near the muzzle was seated neatly in the "U" of the rear sight. He'd rested the rifle in the notch of a live oak to keep it steady at such a distance. There was a strong gusty crosswind from his left, and he could see the heat dancing along the length of the rifle's blue-gray barrel. Two hundred fifty, maybe three hundred yards by his estimation. Close as he dared get and still have cover. Have to aim just a shade high and left.

A drop of sweat ran down along a scar on his wide cheek and across his lips. He ignored its saltiness, focusing on the business at hand.

Luke Dunn, Texas Ranger, kicked at the remaining coals of his campfire and looked up at the horizon. He pondered what would be a long day on the trail chasing down his quarry. He was still far enough north to keep a watchful eye out for Comanche. Nasty savages they were. Just as soon lay their victims out, scalp them, and castrate them as look at them.

A rattlesnake slithered across the clearing. Luke let it go. It belonged here more than he did.

Strong exhaled slowly. Squeezed the trigger. The barrel exploded off the live oak branch as a bullet blasted from the muzzle.

From the corner of his eye, Luke saw the grey stallion's ears perk up. He stepped back and turned. Suddenly, the tin cup in his hand exploded in shards of metal and hot coffee. Blood. Where was all the blood coming from? He looked down. His right hand was a mangled mess. He instinctively dove to the ground, shoving his good hand into his saddlebag under the tree for something, anything, to staunch the bleeding. And where was his damned pistol?

Luke found the Colt revolver in his good hand, but not soon enough to matter. He heard hooves galloping away from him in the distance. Whoever had shot at him was already running and leaving a trail that would be easy to track. Besides, he needed to tend to his badly injured hand.

"Damn!" Strong never missed. He pulled another ball and powder from his bag, but he wouldn't get a second shot. He needed to get out before he became the prey. The roan had barely stirred at the gunshot. Strong grabbed the reins and swung into the saddle. Spurs raked the roan's sides, and the outlaw was gone in a cloud of dust. No place to hide; had to run. Two days of tracking wasted.

Luke unwrapped the bloody shirt from his hand. He was lucky he was left-handed. Most of the damage had been done to the coffee cup, but its steel shards had inflicted multiple deep cuts. He thanked God that no bones appeared to be broken, but it was definitely a mess and needed medical attention. He knew he was a half-day ride from Nuecestown, and it was getting on close to midday. He needed to move.

Pulling a needle and thread from his saddlebag, he poured water from his canteen over his hand, undertook an agonizingly painful effort to thread the needle, and sewed together the two worst cuts as best he could. At least, the bleeding had mostly stopped.

When he finished his medical chore, he gingerly saddled the big grey stallion with his left hand. He slid the Colt Paterson Model 1839 carbine into its scabbard. He was one of the few in Texas to have come by one of these limited-production Samuel Colt creations. It was a new-fangled design that borrowed from the handgun by including a revolving cylinder. The age of the repeating rifle was at its dawn. He was also armed with two .44 caliber Walker Colt revolvers, one of which he carried in a holster on his hip while the other nestled in his belt. A Bowie knife, namesake of Jim Bowie of Alamo fame, completed his arsenal.

Luke grabbed the horn with his left hand and swung himself into the saddle. He appreciated the stallion in part for its ability to accommodate his six-foot, three-inch frame. In the saddle, he was an imposing sight to anyone daring—or perhaps insane enough—to take him on. No surprise that he had earned the moniker "Long Luke." It was a sort of honorific, as one of his Irish ancestors had been called "Long Larry" due to his extraordinary height. The Comanche were impressed with him enough to call him Ghost-Who-Rides.

He led the stallion in alternating walks and canters as he headed toward Nuecestown. He fought hard against the urge to go after the sonofabitch that had taken the shot at him. As a Ranger, Luke would have been expected, despite his injury, to pursue his quarry without pausing for treatment. But, on his own, Luke preferred the unexpected. It wasn't worth risking infection, and a healthy right hand could be a big asset, even to a left-handed man. With his tracking skills, he'd pick up the trail soon enough.

He was a bit embarrassed. He'd let his guard down, and the hunter became the hunted. Old Captain James Hughes Callahan, Luke's captain in the Rangers, wouldn't have been pleased to hear of it. It'd be tough enough telling Rip Ford about his run-in. John "Rip" Ford had, after all, entrusted him with this assignment. Like Luke, Ford was a holdover from Callahan's company and a veteran of the Mexican-American War. Though officially disbanded, the Rangers looked to Ford as an interim leader as they hoped and prayed the next governor would have the fortitude to reconstitute the company.

To make matters worse, the U.S. 2nd Cavalry had been transferred to Utah. This left the Comancheria, the part of Texas west of the 98th Meridian, vulnerable to Buffalo Hump's Comanche and allied Kiowa bands.

Ford had described Bad Bart Strong as the epitome of evil lawlessness. "If it lives, Strong would likely kill it," Ford warned.

The pursuit would have to wait. Luke's hand throbbed mercilessly; the bleeding had started again and wouldn't stop. He kept the big grey stallion on a northeast track and whiled away the time humming Irish ballads.

TWO

Evil Is

"Damned horse!" Bart Strong muttered under his breath. Out here on the prairie, a man was only as good as his horse. He'd ridden the roan hard, too hard. Now, the beast was breathing heavily, but managing to walk behind him.

What the hell was he trying to escape from? He knew he'd at least hit the fool Ranger. He saw the puff when the bullet hit, and he'd heard the Ranger's shout of surprise. It hadn't been a kill shot, but Dunn wouldn't be chasing him down anytime soon. Could the fool even know it was him? Yeah, he'd know. Damned Ranger always knew.

One foot before the other. It was going to be a long walk. Carrying tack and a heavy rifle would have been far tougher, especially as Strong's boots were made for riding, not walking mile after mile in the rough country. He'd barely made ten miles since the incident back at the live oak motte. But, if he could make the mail way station by nightfall, he'd at least be able to rest his feet and let the roan fully catch its wind. He cursed under his breath.

"Carlotta! I see someone on the trail headin' toward us."

Carlotta looked up the trail. "I don't see nothin'."

Zeke, the station master, was getting on in years, but still had eyes like an eagle. "Yep, see there up yonder?"

The figure came into focus. "Damn, it's that Strong fella. I can smell him."

"I see him now. He walkin' his horse?" Carlotta asked.

"Likely rode it too hard. Strong never respected horseflesh, much less humans." Zeke stepped from the doorway, extending the lantern in front of him. It cast a bit of light across the clearing in front of the station house. He called over his shoulder. "Fix up a bit of grub, Carlotta. Best stay on Strong's good side so far as we can."

The shadowy figure continued to trudge down the trail toward the station.

"Zeke? That you?" Strong's voice called from the shadows up the trail.

"Bart? Bart Strong? Slip your horse into the corral and come in for a spell." Zeke strove to be welcoming, at least as welcoming of evil as anyone could be.

Bart Strong was only about twenty, maybe twenty-two years old but, by all accounts, he'd lived a lifetime in those years.

If you needed to attach a date to when Strong's mean ways took to him, it was during one of those Texas Panhandle blizzards. The cold and snow had raged for three days. The space in the little cabin was tight and aromas were oppressively rank. His father had begun drinking early on that third morning.

"Paw, gimme that bottle. You've had enough already." Bart Strong's mother, Myrt, reached out her hand toward the bottle.

Paw squinted. His eyes began to almost squirt blood as his face turned red. The rage was coming on. "Shut yer mouth, woman!"

Bart watched helplessly. He knew better than to try to restrain his father when he was angry. His strength could seem superhuman.

Paw threw the bottle against the wall, grabbed Myrt's arm, and planted a haymaker of a punch square into her chest about heart-high, ending her life abruptly. Bart Strong's father had killed his mother in a fit of drunken rage. Bart, only sixteen at the time, witnessed it. One punch in her chest. Stopped her heart stone cold.

Paw turned to the boy. "What you looking at? Get her outside afore this place stinks more than it does."

The boy dutifully dragged his mother's body out into the still-raging blizzard. He propped her on a bench alongside the front of the house. She'd already begun to turn blue, and ice was forming on the wisps of hair across her face. He closed her eyes. The vacant lifeless stare would come to haunt him.

From that day forward, Strong's father regularly beat young Bart. He did it most every time he got drunk. He told the boy he was giving him lessons so one day he could beat others. To his credit, more or less, he would never hit young Bart in the face, as that would have left cuts and bruises and been too obvious to neighbors or anyone who might come by. The boy tried hiding the liquor bottles, but Paw would find them and then beat him for hiding them. He asked Paw why once or twice, but the answer was invariably more rage.

The only positive thing young Bart had going for him was that he learned to shoot. He became a pretty fair marksman.

One day, his father hit him especially hard. Not just with his fist, but with an axe handle planted full swing against the boy's ribs. The pain was excruciating. As Bart doubled over in pain, Paw grabbed a whiskey bottle and headed out the door and up the hill to where Myrt had been buried. He sat next to the grave and took a long guzzle from the bottle.

Bart, struggling to breathe, fetched his rifle. He stuffed a round in the firing chamber and stuck the muzzle through a hole in the door that had been put there to enable defense against Indians. This was Comanche country, so that wasn't unrealistic. He pulled back the hammer and aimed carefully. He exhaled and squeezed the trigger, placing a bullet between Paw's eyes at two hundred yards. He'd taken one beating too many. He buried the old man next to Myrt, though he nearly thought better of placing him next to the woman he'd murdered. He grabbed what he could of value from the house and headed for Corpus Christi on the Nueces Strip. It'd be a long ride, but he'd heard there were fortunes to be made in that booming part of Texas. He didn't know how fortunes were being made, but figured to work that out once he got there.

An orphan by choice, Strong quickly earned the nickname "Bad Bart." He kind of cottoned to the name. Having not experienced love since his mother died, he wasn't one to give any. It was said by those who encountered him and lived to tell about it that there was a coldness in his eyes that could turn a morning dew to frost. He seemed to be hateful to anyone who beat living things, animal or human.

It was said that he'd killed at least ten people, though three couldn't be confirmed as his victims. Two of those killed were young boys with pistols carved from wood that Strong mistook for real guns, so it was sort of self-defense. Another was a woman who tried to protect her husband from Strong's wrath. Apparently, the husband looked crossways at Strong as he was beating her, and it was interpreted as an insult. Actually, it was a twofer, as the bullet passed through the wife and killed her husband, too.

There was a price on his head, and Bad Bart knew that Luke Dunn aimed to get him before any bounty hunters. He suspected it was a matter of pride and duty for the Texas Ranger.

"Get yourself washed up, Bart Strong, and then set yourself right over there at the table." Carlotta motioned to the wash basin and the table.

Carlotta and Zeke had known Strong long enough to call him by his first name. Of course, they also knew how he'd earned the "Bad Bart" appellation and heard what happened to his mother and father.

Soon enough, a steaming dish of stew, or at least what passed for stew, was being ladled by Strong into his gaping pie-hole between swigs of hard cider. For a young, decent-looking man, he wasn't much for table manners.

"Whatcha in such an all-fired hurry for, Bart?"

Strong raised an eyebrow as he looked up and fixed his eyes hard-like on Zeke. "Better not to ask," he snarled. He caught himself. These were the only folks in the Nueces Strip he remotely cared about. They were as close to being parents as he had. "Can I spend the night?"

Zeke and Carlotta glanced at each other. "'Course you can, Bart. 'Course you can," Zeke told him. They didn't expect a rider for at least another day, so Strong was likely as safe from whoever was tailing him as could be expected.

"Maybe I ought to sleep in the stable near my horse." The implication was that he might have to leave in a hurry.

Zeke would have none of it. "It's fixin' to rain hard tonight, Bart. Likely to be a gully-washer. You can make your bed near the door. If you gotta leave hurried-like, that'll be close enough to the stable."

Strong nodded. He was growing groggy from the cider and lack of sleep. In any case, if it did rain hard, his trail would be impossible to follow.

He soaked up the last of the stew gravy with the fresh-made biscuit Carlotta had given him. About this time, exhaustion took its measure of him. A hard day of walking, a full belly, and just a bit too much hard cider had the effect of making even the hardiest soul drowsy.

Carlotta saw his eyelids getting heavy. She spread a bunch of blankets near the front door, and Strong got up slowly, walked a few steps, and barely landed on the blankets. He was passed out stone cold.

Zeke and Carlotta had been through this before. Either a fellow thug or a lawman was after him. Given his behavior, they figured it was most likely the latter. In his day, Zeke had run with a bad crowd for a while, so he could tell when someone feared the law versus his own kind. Zeke was a big man, though hunched over a bit with age and hard living. He sported a scraggly beard that mostly served as a food catcher. He disappeared with Carlotta behind a wooden divider that served as a modesty panel, sort of separating the cabin into two rooms.

As the sun broke over the horizon, Strong awoke to the smell of sausage and eggs. Carlotta knew how to care for a guest, even evil ones, though she tended to see the best in people. She'd arisen early to grab some eggs from the chickens and get some venison sausage from the cold storage.

Zeke had just returned from the stable. "Yer horse seems fine this morning, Bart." He set himself at the table in anticipation of Carlotta's cooking. "Which lawman is it?"

"You don't want to know, Zeke."

"Luke Dunn, ain't it?"

"I'm the best goddam shot around, and I missed the son of a bitch." Strong doused his face from the wash bowl. "He turned. All day tracking, an' his damned horse gave me away."

"He's the one what got yer brother, ain't he?"

"Yeah. Hung him high. And he won't be catching me. I'm gonna get his sorry ass afore he has a chance to sight his rifle on me." Strong smiled. It was the cold smile of a vengeful soul. "I know I hit him. Sure of it."

"If ya did and he's able to ride, he likely headed to Nuecestown. Wouldn't be that far for him." Zeke shook his head. He figured Strong couldn't have picked a worse enemy. "You know, he's gonna come get you. You can take that to the bank, son."

Strong began to shovel Carlotta's cooking into his mouth as though it were his last meal. She smiled approvingly. "Slow down, Bart. If he were chasin' you, he'd be here by now, rain or no rain. There simply ain't many places 'round these parts that someone on the run might take shelter." That was an understatement; the Nueces Strip was pretty much a boundless grassy wasteland. Not many places to run and hide.

Zeke pushed back from the table and lit his pipe. "Where do ya think you'll head, Bart?"

"I shan't be tellin' y'all. If you don't know, Dunn can't get it from ya." Implied was that he didn't want to have to kill them.

Strong took his time walking out to the corral. Indeed, it had rained last night, and it likely had washed out any clues as to where he might be headed. He saddled up, took some grub offered by Carlotta, and headed out. He was of a mind to eventually wind up in Laredo, but he dared not give a hint of that to Zeke and Carlotta. To avoid capture, he figured to take a route parallel to the road Colonel Kinney had cut from Corpus Christi to Laredo. It passed through San Diego, which was okay with Strong, as he'd be able to take a breather from the long journey. His only fear was that damnable Ranger getting on his trail.

Early on, Strong realized he was going to have to make ends meet. He needed to feed himself, care for his horse, stay supplied with ammunition, afford a whore now and again and, as he'd find out, ante up in a card game or two. That last thing—cards—had caught his fancy. He got himself a deck from his father's meager possessions and practiced handling the deck every chance he got. He could even shuffle with one hand. He watched card sharks at saloons early on to learn strategies. He'd even seen a man or two shot and killed for cheating at cards.

Finally, he played a few times and managed to play well enough to win more money than he lost. Most important, it was sustaining a very Spartan lifestyle. He caught on early in his card playing that the card sharks tended to dress for the part. It was as though they were actors on a stage. He surmised that it likely gave them a psychological advantage. Fancy jackets, frilly shirts with cuff links, embroidered vests, string ties, black flat-brimmed hats, grey-striped trousers, and black boots completed the typical costume. Another thing he noticed was that the "professional" card sharks generally carried a small weapon that was easy to hide in a vest pocket. Strong vowed to get one as soon as possible. He decided to be more subtle in what he wore and let his play speak for itself. His marksmanship and card playing would be the tools of his existence.

He felt a warm breeze from the northeast. He had a strange sense that something wasn't right, but he couldn't figure out what. He picked up the roan's pace just a bit. Perhaps he could find a card game in Laredo if he didn't run into that damned Ranger first.

THREE

The Live Oak Motte

A t least once a week, Elisa made the short trek to the swift-moving stream that ran past their property and dumped into the Nueces River. Now, her task completed, she began to walk back from the creek where she'd been beating her father's fresh-washed clothes on the shoreline rocks. As she beat, rinsed, and beat again, slapping the trail dirt and horse dung residue from his shirts and pants, she daydreamed about what her future might hold.

At sixteen, she was pretty much a full-grown woman. She'd been seeing and feeling changes to her body and soul. Her smooth alabaster skin was a bit prone to freckles that made her seem younger than her years. Her daydreams of a home and children of her own became ever more vivid. There were a couple of boys in Nuecestown that seemed interested in sparkin' her, but she had her heart set on a man…a real man. He was out there somewhere. Besides, she had a certain independence and feistiness about her, a spirit that demanded a man who fully appreciated those qualities.

Nuecestown wasn't much in 1856. Corpus Christi founder Colonel Kinney took kindly to the location roughly thirteen miles northwest of the city for its ferry across the Nueces River. The area was originally called Motts by English and German settlers back in 1852. Kinney had been the driving influence for developing the area. The colonel required new settlers to purchase hundred-acre tracts at a dollar an acre and at least ten cows at ten dollars a head. He even saw to it that a temporary post office was established.

The Corrigans had settled in Nuecestown, having first homesteaded a few miles west of Galveston. There, her father, Sam, had first tried his hand at farming. He had grown up in western Pennsylvania where he met and married Elisa's mother. He answered the call from Stephen Austin to come to Texas, where he fought at Goliad and San Jacinto. He had been wounded, but that didn't hold him back from having his wife join him on the new homestead. Wasn't long before Elisa was born, though it'd be several years before Robert and Michael came along.

It became clear that they needed more space to raise their family and Sam seized the opportunity to answer Colonel Kinney's call for homesteaders in Nuecestown. By this time, Elisa had reached her fourteenth birthday and was fast becoming second in command of the household after her mother. With her father and two brothers around, it was little wonder that she quickly learned to understand male ways, especially as manifest in the pranks her father taught the boys. Like as not, it contributed to her feisty nature.

Elisa Corrigan's father had literally loved her mother to death. She and her two younger brothers Rob and Mike had been playing down by the creek, when her half-naked father came staggering from the house. He sounded like a madman, crying and shouting and carrying on. Elisa ran back to the house. Sam initially tried to block her way, but she evaded his arms and burst through the front door of the cabin. Her mother lay exposed from the waist down with blood everywhere. She had already turned a deathly bluish sort of pale. Elisa grabbed her mother's shoulders and tried to shake life back into her.

"Live, Mama. Live!" she commanded through her tears. "Live!"

Sam came back inside the cabin. He'd told Rob and Mike to stay outside. "I already tried that." He pulled on his pants and boots. "You stay here. I'm gonna see if Doc is sober enough to see her."

"Papa, she don't need no doctor. She's past that, Papa."

He hung his head resignedly for a moment, and then turned and headed to the stable to hitch up the mules and wagon.

As Elisa went to cover her mother, she saw the tiny baby in the puddle of blood between her legs. "Oh, Mama." She hung her head for just a moment, feeling helpless. She'd lost her mother and a brother or sister. She couldn't bear to touch the dead baby to see what sex it was. It was so tiny, barely big enough that it might have fit in her hand. She'd heard of these sorts of things happening, but it didn't lessen the pain that shot through her. It hadn't yet struck her that she would now be the woman of the family with all the associated responsibilities.

She heard her father whip the mules as the wagon lurched down the road. She figured he needn't rush. She rightly saw it as something he felt he needed to do.

They buried Elisa's mother under the shade of a nearby live oak motte. It was a truly pretty spot with a right beautiful view of the surrounding grasslands. They'd given a fleeting thought to the new cemetery established in Nuecestown, but having her buried close by seemed vastly preferable.

That was more than a year ago. Now, she was experiencing awakenings within herself, dreams of finding a man. Her mind drifted off to such musings as she hauled the basket of wet clothes up the path toward the cabin. It was generous to call it a cabin, but her father had done the best he could on meager farming income. He'd done a fine job building the place, as there were no cracks where winter breezes might sneak through.

Elisa had pretty much taken over the woman-of-the-house duties by now. She hadn't expected to have had to learn so much so soon in her life.

It was a long walk uphill from the creek. It was far enough from the cabin that you had to holler loudly to be heard across the distance. There was a slight breeze and a quietness in the air.

As she rounded the live oak motte, the one where her mother was buried, she saw them. Horror of horrors, a big, well-muscled Comanche had just finished the grisly task of scalping her father. At least two arrows protruded from her father's chest. Mike and Rob lay unmoving just a few feet from Sam. They had taken Comanche arrows as well, and it was obvious that Rob's head had also been cracked open with a club. The warrior paused from mutilating his victim, scalp held high. "Who was this?" must have been running through his mind. He let go of Sam's head. He smiled, a cold, evil smile. His eyes narrowed. Rape would only be the beginning. A golden-red scalp would be a beautiful addition to his collection.

Elisa fought the urge to run. They—there were three of them— would have chased her down anyway. The Comanche were a fearsome sight with black war paint across their faces. Their bodies were nearly naked. The big one that stood over her father, brandishing his scalp, was closest. He took a step toward her. She felt shivers of fear coursing through her frame. Cold, unfeeling, vile, savage wickedness was moving toward her.

From under her skirt, she drew the Walker Colt. Sam had made her always take the revolver with her to the creek in case of rattlesnakes or other critters. Now, she was faced with the worst beasts she could imagine: Comanche. She'd heard from the ladies in Nuecestown about what they did to women. Mutilation would be the least of her worries. No white man would ever want her again were she to fall prey to Comanche.

The blast echoed loudly in the slow-motion silence, as the huge Comanche warrior moved toward her. He stopped, mouth open in surprise, and the wildness left his eyes as he looked down at his chest. A hole was pretty much where his heart had been. As he dropped to his knees, the other two bolted for their horses and were gone in a swirl of dust.

Elisa didn't have it in her to fire another shot. She didn't need to. The big Comanche had fallen face first in the dust not six feet from her. She snapped out of her momentary trance, ran past the dying savage, knelt in the dust, and cradled Sam's bloodied head. "Daddy! Daddy!" She stroked his face, wiping away the tears that fell on his cheeks, but it was too late. He was gone.

Minutes passed. She sobbed silently as she gently laid her father's head on the cold, hard earth and looked around. The silence was deafening. She became aware that she was alone. Not just physically alone, but truly alone. No mother, no father, her brothers…all gone.

She wiped away her tears. Grief would have to wait. She fetched the shovel from the barn and took what seemed a forever journey to the shade of the live oak motte. She began to dig next to her mother's grave. A groan stopped her. She looked back in the direction of the cabin.

Her brother's hand raised weakly and then dropped. He groaned again.

"Mike?" she screamed. "Mike!"

She rushed to her brother's side. The arrow through his ribs had broken off. He was in excruciating pain but alive. And he was breathing. Her father and brother Rob would simply have to wait for burial. She glanced at them still lying in the dust where they had fallen, but there was no time to waste on the dead.

She mustered her strength, carried little Mike to the old wagon, and hitched the mules. She prayed she'd make it to town in time…and that the two Comanche were long gone. In moments, she had the rig barreling down the trail and covering the five miles to Nuecestown as fast as the two mules could gallop.

Elisa drove the wagon around the turn into what little there was of the town, rocks and dust kicking up in her wake. She yelled as loud as she could. "Doc! Doc Andrews!"

The rheumy old man was awakened from his nap by Elisa's shouts. "What the hell?" He roused from his drunken stupor, almost fell from his chair, but managed to stagger to the door.

Elisa had brought the rig to a halt in front of Doc's house. The mules were sucking air and sweating. "Doc! My brother! Indians!"

By this time, a couple of local ladies had heard the commotion and rushed to her aid. Bernice and Agatha were lovely ladies with good hearts, well past their primes.

"Gently, lift him gently," Bernice coached. They carried Mike into Doc's parlor and placed him on a table that had been swiftly cleared of whiskey bottles and old cigars.

"Get me some hot water," mumbled Doc, sort of half-choking on the words. He craved a swig of whiskey to soothe his throat.

"You say hot?" Bernice had a bit of a hearing problem.

"Water, dammit. Just fetch some!"

Meanwhile, Elisa stripped Mike's torn and bloodied shirt from his body. He'd finally passed out from pain and loss of blood…and the wagon ride.

"Lucky. He's lucky."

Elisa wondered at what Doc was talking about. "Lucky?" she repeated softly.

"It's more a flesh wound, darlin'. Arrow passed clean through. Hold your brother still." He slowly and gently as possible pulled the arrow out. Mike awakened, went involuntarily stiff with pain, and then relaxed as he passed out again. "I'd be a tad more concerned with the bump on the back of his head. I think one of the attackers must have clobbered him."

"Will he be okay?"

"I expect so. Aggie, Bernice, help me bandage this brave young man's wound." He turned to face Elisa. "What happened?"

"I was down at the creek doing the washing and came up the trail to see my father being scalped and Rob and Mike lying in the dust. I was lucky to be carrying a pistol like my father always said to, and I shot one of the Indians as he came toward me. There were two others, but they ran off when I shot the big one. I'm thinking they looked like what I've heard Comanche to look. Black paint on their faces and all." She blurted this all out, and then collapsed suddenly in the chair next to the table. She held her hands to her face. "What am I gonna do? I need to bury Papa and Robbie. How am I going to run the farm?"

Bernice suddenly found her crystal-clear hearing. "You can stay here, sweetie." She looked at Agatha, who smiled patronizingly. She'd become set in her ways and resented changes to her life routine. Bernice continued. "At least for a few days until you can decide what you might like to do."

"Little Mike here's going to be okay, Elisa. We'll let him sleep." Doc smiled sympathetically. "Let's get the preacher from up the road and a couple of boys to get you back to your spread and take care of burying your loved ones. I'm sorry I can't help more."

There was a bit of a stir of a sudden out front of Doc's house. A horseman had pulled up alongside the wagon. He dismounted slowly, as if in pain, draped the reins over the hitching rail, and climbed the stairs to Doc's door.

Before the man could knock, Doc had the door open. "Can I help... Luke? Luke Dunn...what brings..." He looked at the hand wrapped in a bloody shirt, and then looked up. "Least it wasn't Comanche. Looks like you still have your hair."

Luke followed him inside. He wasn't laughing.

Mike had been moved to the room adjoining the parlor so, except for a little blood, the table was clear. "Grab a seat on the table, Luke, and get that shirt off."

As Luke stripped off his shirt, he noticed Elisa seated in the corner of the parlor. It was too late for any modesty, false or otherwise.

"Sorry, ma'am." He tugged at his hat. Through everything, his hat had never left his head.

"Elisa, this here's Luke Dunn. He's a Texas Ranger captain of some repute. I expect your father might have heard of him. Luke, this here's Elisa Corrigan. Her family was attacked and her father and brother killed just hours ago by Comanche."

She wanted to avert her eyes but couldn't help taking in this tall stranger with the broad shoulders and rippling muscles. Guilt edged its way into her consciousness as she found herself conflicted between grief over the loss of family and feelings of arousal over this handsome man. In Elisa's thinking, the boys of Nuecestown could never hope to measure up to Luke Dunn, this real man. In spite of all she'd been through, she felt reflexive fluttering in her chest that transcended her loss. She'd never felt those sorts of deep stirrings before.

"I'm deeply sorry for your loss, Miss Corrigan." The deepness of his voice and heartfelt honesty of his simple words served to deepen her attraction to him.

Doc caught the dynamic at play and found himself breaking whatever spell had been cast. "Let me see to Mr. Dunn's wounds, and then we'll go out to your place, Elisa. Do y'all need a casket?" He turned back to Luke's hand. "How'd this happen, Luke?"

"The guy I was chasin' nicked me, Doc," Luke told him. "Blew through my cup and shattered it."

"You got lucky," Doc said. "Scraped a bit of bone, but your tin coffee cup did more damage than the bullet. I'd guess it was from a long rifle."

Elisa wasn't paying much attention to the conversation. "Can't afford a casket, Doc, much less two."

Luke's ears perked at Doc's question to Elisa and her answer. "I'm sorry, miss. Have you lost someone?" In his own pain, he hadn't heard Doc's explanation of the Comanche attack.

"Comanche, sir. Me and my little brother Mike are the only survivors. I need to go back and bury my papa and my brother Robbie."

Luke was typically of a quiet disposition, but something about this young girl and her distress drew upon an inner vulnerability. "I'm sorry for your loss." He winced as Doc finished cleaning his wounds and started stitching. "How'd you escape?"

"I shot one."

"That's usually all it takes," Luke said, "especially with a small war party. Did they take their dead brother?"

"No. They left fast."

"Hmmm. Maybe I'd better go back to your place with Doc here. They don't like to leave their dead behind."

"I'd be much beholden, Mr. Dunn."

"You can call me Luke, Miss Elisa. I'm Mr. Dunn to lawbreakers and fellow Rangers." He looked her over, as though he were noticing her for the first time. "You're young."

"I'm sixteen, Mr. Du…I mean Luke."

Doc patted Luke on the shoulder. "We're finished here, Luke. Try to keep the wounds clean and change the dressing daily, if you can. I know you'll be back to your work right quickly, so I won't bother telling you to give it a rest. Once the cuts have healed, ball up a bandana and squeeze it regular-like so your flexibility and strength come back. You'll be back to new in a couple of weeks."

He turned to Elisa. "We'll let Mike sleep. Bernice and Agatha can watch over him."

"I'm much obliged to you, Luke, but if you've got law enforcement work to do, I don't want to be the cause of holding you back."

"It'll be my pleasure, Elisa. I want to be sure those Comanche are long gone."

Elisa, Doc, and Luke proceeded to crowd onto the seat of the wagon and direct the mules up the road and back to the Corrigan farm. The priest and one of the local boys sat in the bed of the rig. Luke's big grey stallion was hitched to the back, along with a nag for Doc and another for the priest for their return to town.

"If I may, who are you chasing after, Luke?" Elisa was curious about this Ranger. The very slight Irish lilt to his deep voice, coupled with a bit of Texas drawl, had a certain appeal, and she almost asked the question just to hear him speak again. There was something about this man.

"Fella name of Bart Strong. Some call him Bad Bart. He's a young-un, but most are."

"What's he done?"

"Seems he's killed a few folks, Miss Elisa. He's supposed to be a crack shot, so I was very lucky that he didn't shoot me square on."

"Must be a good hunter, too?" Elisa smiled.

"Yes, that could be said. He sure snuck up on me." Luke figured he really didn't need reminding of that. He wasn't about to let it happen again. It was time to change the subject. His hand throbbed as they pulled up to the Corrigan cabin. "You have a fine-looking cabin here, Miss Elisa."

"My papa built it from scratch. He was good with axe and saw." She thought about how she'd miss him. At least, it looked as though Mike would pull through.

"Think you can handle this place by your lonesome?" As Luke uttered the words, he realized it'd been a rhetorical question.

Soon enough, they were digging in the rock-hard soil alongside her mother by the live oak motte. Doc had given them some blankets to wrap the bodies in, since Elisa couldn't afford a casket.

With his wounded hand, Luke wasn't as much help as he'd have liked to have been. He was a bit distracted, as there was something strangely magnetic in the air so far as this young woman was concerned.

For her part, Elisa kept glancing admiringly at this newcomer to her life. She was barely five feet tall, so she found herself looking up to Luke. He had a broad-brimmed tan hat with a simple leather band. She wanted to reach out and touch his ruggedly handsome Irish face framed around a well-tended fiery red mustache. He wore a buckskin vest over a blue shirt with gray trousers stuffed into well-worn cowboy boots. His gun belt accommodated the Walker Colt plus plenty of ammunition. Standing out and impossible to miss was the Texas Rangers badge pinned to his shirt.

FOUR

The Comanche Way

Three Toes pulled away from his second wife behind the teepee. He felt he had to do his duty daily. He was a minor Comanche chief with three wives and about thirty horses. He was looked upon as wealthy by many, and no one ever doubted his bravery in battle. Strong as an ox and taller than most Indians go, his only defect was having lost two toes in his very first battle when an axe was dropped on his foot. It hadn't stopped him from counting three coup and taking two scalps. From that time forward, he was called Three Toes. It didn't seem to slow him down, especially since most fighting and hunting was done on horseback.

He was about to head into his teepee when he heard two horses galloping hard into the encampment.

The two young Comanche warriors pulled up not far from Three Toes' teepee. They acted as though they didn't want to face him.

"Coyote Who Runs, get over here," Three Toes ordered. He was not about to let them avoid answering to him. Coyote Who Runs and Hawk Nose walked over with their eyes glued to the earth. "Where is your brother? Where is Bear Slayer?"

Coyote Who Runs' eyes penetrated the ground. "He was killed after counting coup and scalping a white man." They were touting Bear Slayer's bravery, as if to distract from having to answer Three Toes' question.

"How did he die? Where are the scalps you took after avenging him?"

"A white woman shot him." They dared not admit the woman was a young girl. "She had a hidden gun."

"And you left him to die?" Three Toes worked to contain his anger. What had become of the young Comanche warriors these days? Where was their sense of honor? "We will talk with the Council." He waved them away. The Council would not likely result in a desirable outcome for the two. There would be some punishment. Bear Slayer had two wives and several horses. He would likely have become a chief one day.

Three Toes went inside to think. Moon Woman handed him his pipe. She was the first of his wives and exerted tight control over the other two. Three Toes was the son of the famous Comanche war chief Santa Anna. He had even come to the attention of Buffalo Hump, up to then the most notorious chief of the Penateka Comanche.

He lit the pipe and took a long draw. He contemplated the smoke as it swirled about before eventually heading upward with the draft to the vent at the top of the teepee. He caught Moon Woman's look of concern despite its being somewhat hidden by the haze created by the pipe smoke.

"You are distressed, my husband."

Three Toes appreciated that Moon Woman understood him so well. She could read his moods. It had served her well with his other wives. "They were frightened," he said contemptuously, "frightened of a woman with a gun."

"She must have been a good shooter." Moon Woman had a way of stating the obvious. "And showed no fear."

"I don't want to punish them, but I must." Three Toes puffed thoughtfully on the pipe. Finally, he put it down. "I will go for a walk and think on this matter."

He glanced at Moon Woman and smiled before lifting the teepee flap and exiting. He was lucky to have her. She had a good head on her shoulders.

Coyote Who Runs emerged from his tent at the same time as Three Toes. They avoided looking at each other. Coyote Who Runs backed away and went to tend his horse. His fellow warrior, Hawk Nose, followed. As they curried their horses, they shared furtive glances.

The two were almost like brothers. They had grown up hunting together and learning the signs of the prairie. They learned how to track all manner of game. Coyote Who Runs was the son of Mandog, a warrior of high repute, so he usually took the lead in whatever they undertook. At nearly the same time, Coyote Who Runs and Hawk Nose made their first medicine by going on a vision quest, a rite of passage for young Comanche.

Both had proven themselves in battle by counting coup. They had been given good horses, and each had found a wife. They had been mere children when Buffalo Hump made his famous Great Raid, but they heard campfire tales of the raiding, looting, burning, and killing that characterized the raid. Buffalo Hump had raided all the way to the Texas coast. The towns of Victoria and Linnville had been looted and burned by his savage horde. Not long ago, Buffalo Hump had signed a treaty with the white man and led his people to a reservation in a place called Oklahoma. But not all the Penateka Comanche followed Buffalo Hump to Fort Cobb. They'd felt deeply honored to follow the son of Chief Santa Anna. Thus, they were doubly honored when Three Toes' favorite warrior Bear Slayer had invited them on a hunt that would ultimately turn into a raid. The chance to count coup—touch an enemy—and take scalps was big medicine to the young warriors.

"We should have killed the woman," lamented Coyote Who Runs.

"She was only a girl," Hawk Nose corrected his friend. "We should not have left Bear Slayer behind."

"I wonder what the Council will decide?"

"Maybe we should go back to the ranch. We could kill the girl and bring Bear Slayer's body back."

They looked around. There wasn't much time. There'd be hell to pay if they didn't return in time for the Council. They carefully chose their best ponies and walked as nonchalantly as possible from the encampment. Once they felt it was safe, they mounted and galloped off toward the site of their ill-fated raid.

Three Toes had been standing off in the shadows of a nearby live oak motte. He watched them go. He felt he knew them well enough to give them their head, to not give immediate chase. He figured—or at least hoped—they'd do the honorable thing. The chief determined to delay the Council until they returned. He thought about simply awaiting their return. But then, he changed his mind. "Moon Woman, I'm going hunting."

She fully understood the meaning in his words. She dutifully and quickly brought him his deerskin breeches, bone vest, bow with quiver and arrows, and war lance. He'd already sent his youngest wife Dark Eyes to fetch his best pony. In mere moments, he was ready to travel. Moon Woman gave him a pouch containing his war paint and another with a little food for the journey.

Before departing, Three Toes encountered Bear Slayer's father. "Three Toes, I thought we were to hold Council." It was both statement and question.

"We will, if I return in time, Long Feathers. I must hunt some game."

Long Feathers caught Three Toes' meaning. "May your hunt go well, my chief."

Three Toes turned his horse to follow the very obvious track left by the two young warriors. Trampled grass and broken tree branches made the trail almost too easy to follow. In their haste to make amends, the young warriors had made no attempt to cover their trail. Since Comanche relied heavily on game for their sustenance, they learned early on to be excellent trackers.

Coyote Who Runs and Hawk Nose rode hard, but their ponies had limits. Soon enough, they were alternating between walking and riding. It took nearly half the day before they crossed into the outermost boundaries of the Corrigan farm. As they drew ever nearer to the house, they each instinctively drew arrows from their quivers. The tall grass provided a modest level of cover, and the yellowish hue of their buckskins tended to camouflage them.

Wasn't long before they heard voices.

FIVE

Only Fools Rush In

T he rocky soil had made for a tough dig, and Luke hung his shirt on a branch of the live oak. At last, he finished helping with the digging, at least as much as his injured hand would permit. It had started to bleed a bit, and he regretted risking the possibility of reopening the wounds. He might need the hand later when he caught up with Strong.

As he began to put his shirt back on, a faint aroma wafted toward him. He thought a moment and then recognized it as buffalo dung. Strange. Buffalo had pretty much been hunted out of these parts. Longhorns and wild horses far outnumbered them. He finished buttoning his shirt, still just a tad troubled by that whiff of buffalo dung.

Doc and the boy from town helped Elisa wrap her father and brother in the blankets. The young boy from Nuecestown was just old enough to be a bit titillated by the bit of cleavage revealed by Elisa's dress as she bent to wrap her brother. She caught his eyes and gave him a scowl. This wasn't the time nor place, and certainly not the situation. Besides, this boy was just that, a mere boy. His name was Dan, and he took good care of the livery stable in town. Luke Dunn, on the other hand, was a man.

They soon laid the bodies in the graves next to Elisa's mother under that shady live oak motte. Doc held his hat in both hands below his belly and nodded to the boy to do the same as they prepared to pray. Luke doffed his hat as well out of respect.

The priest was about to say a few words when Luke shushed him. He stood upright, scanning the near horizon. There was that hint of buffalo dung in the air, only stronger now. He picked up his Colt rifle.

"Keep praying, Reverend," he whispered. "We've got company. Just act like we don't know." He put his hat back on and then slowly edged his way from the motte. As he stealthily moved away, he ensured that there were rounds in the rifle. It was fully loaded.

He sniffed the air. Upwind, the breeze was still sending that telltale smell of buffalo dung his way. This was a habit Comanche used so as not to spook the buffalo they were hunting. It would be innocuous enough if there were buffalo around and, if there weren't, there was the possibility of the dung being smeared on Comanche warriors hunting human prey. Thus, it served as an unnecessary camouflage.

Luke looked over at the body of Bear Slayer. Could be that the Comanche simply wanted to retrieve his body. It didn't take much to do the math.

Luke scanned the tall grass. He was irritated that his hand was throbbing from shoveling. He should have let the boy do the work. Then he heard a faint rattle and stepped quickly aside to avoid a rattlesnake that had been lurking under the prairie grass beside him.

In that moment of avoiding the snake, he heard a whoosh as an arrow whizzed by. He turned to face the direction the arrow came from to find himself face to face with Hawk Nose. The young Comanche couldn't avoid Luke's bullet. By this time, Coyote Who Runs had nocked an arrow, pulled back the string and was set to let it fly, when a shot from another direction blasted the bow from his hands. Luke followed with another round from the Colt rifle. Coyote Who Runs collapsed in the dust.

Elisa emerged with her Walker Colt in hand. "He was one of them," she said matter of factly.

Luke was surprised. "You're a brave young lady, Elisa Corrigan. And a helluva good shot." He reckoned she'd likely saved his life. To cover the uneasy feeling that gave him, he bent down to be certain the Comanche were dead.

The sound of his complimentary words and his physical nearness, coupled with the reality of what had just happened, made Elisa a little giddy. Her heart fluttered a bit as she watched Luke bend down to be certain the Comanche were dead. She could see his muscles flex under his shirt.

With the gunfire, everyone came running. They came to a sudden halt as they entered the clearing and saw the dead Comanche.

About that time, the happenings of the day were finally combining to create emotions that apparently began to work their way into Elisa's thoughts. She shook involuntarily and tears welled up as she began to cry, for the first time since her father's and Rob's deaths.

Luke, standing closest to her, was caught completely off guard as she threw herself sobbing into his chest. He looked over at Doc with an expression of helplessness. Elisa's sobs only lasted a couple of minutes, but it seemed like forever for Luke. Besides, she was just a young girl, and he thought it unseemly to have her clinging so tightly to him. It aroused feelings he wasn't prepared to handle, especially in this situation. The men all slowly made their way back to the graves with Elisa walking beside Luke, her hand draped over his good arm.

The brief little funeral done, Luke and Doc saw to dragging the Comanche bodies off into the brush. Luke had enough of digging, so wouldn't be doing any burying of these heathen. He tried to be as respectful as possible, even though they were heathens by his or most any measure. His Irish upbringing, heavily influenced by his father's strong Catholic beliefs, had taught him respect for the dead, regardless of their sins. Disposal completed, Luke fetched his horse, retrieved the saddle from the wagon, and threw it on the big grey. Soon enough, he was ready to go chase after Bart Strong.

"Will you be coming back this way, Luke?" Elisa asked softly.

"I expect so, Elisa…from time to time," he said.

"I'd be looking forward to that, Luke." She turned to the doctor. "Thanks for your help, Doc."

"You're gonna come stay in town, Elisa." Doc rightly figured that keeping up the farm would be a huge challenge for a sixteen-year-old girl with a little brother barely standing above waist-high to a grasshopper.

"I'm thinkin' I'm gonna make a go of it, Doc," she told him.

Doc remained concerned. He was a sort of conscience for Nuecestown. Colonel Kinney had lured him to Corpus Christi a couple of years back. As the city was growing, it needed a doctor to look after the sick and injured. The one thing Kinney hadn't counted on was that Doc was often passed out drunk. He needed someone more reliable. He had a heart-to-heart talk with Doc and persuaded him to move up to Nuecestown to be available for travelers using the ferry. Kinney then promptly brought in another doctor.

Doc understood, but he couldn't help himself. He was addicted to the booze and helpless to stop drinking. He tried several times, but something would invariably come up and he'd find himself back into the bottle. Often, he'd go off the wagon when thoughts of his wife were triggered. He'd loved her more than anything in the world and blamed himself for her passing. His health was starting to fail, thanks mostly to demon whiskey. Still, the folks in Nuecestown loved Doc and appreciated his sage advice and talent for curing the sick and injured, even when he was inebriated.

Luke was up in his saddle. He made an imposing figure on the big grey stallion.

"Horse have a name, Luke?" Elisa asked him.

"I call him horse, but some have called him Ghost. Others call him Shadow." He gave an aw-shucks grin. "I hope you do well here, Elisa. I'll stop by and check on you next time I'm up in these parts."

It was as close as Elisa was going to get to a promise to return for her.

Luke turned the horse, and walked him off into the late afternoon sun.

Three Toes watched from a distance. The girl and the man had killed three of his warriors. It wouldn't do for a mere girl to kill Comanche, but the Texas Ranger was big medicine. Should he follow the Ranger? Should he wait and then come back to see to the fate of the girl? Should he go back for reinforcements? Dealing with the girl would have to wait and getting reinforcements would delay his following the Ranger's trail. He decided to pursue the Ranger.

He planned to use a strategy his people had found very effective. Rather than risk a head-on confrontation, he'd steal the Ranger's horse at night, leaving him vulnerable to attack. The Comanche planned to simply follow Luke's trail and wait until nightfall. Might take a day or two, but time was on his side. There was certainly plenty of cover in the tall grass, and he needed to hang a couple of hours or so behind. He noted that the Ranger apparently was tracking someone. It might do to see whether he could satisfy his vengeance on two or more white men.

Luke headed southwest, from whence he'd been attacked. Soon enough, he realized that the area had been deluged with rain the night

43

before. There'd likely be no clues to track, so he decided to head toward a mail station to the south.

SIX

Tracking Human Prey

Three Toes watched Luke ride out of sight. Soon enough, the girl and the man rode away on the wagon, back toward Nuecestown.

The chief gathered Coyote Who Runs' and Hawk Nose's ponies and rode into the clearing where his warriors had fallen; they weren't there. He hadn't seen Luke and Doc move the bodies, so had to do a little tracking to find where they'd been deposited. The drag marks in the dust made it fairly easy. Soon enough, he came upon them.

He was appreciative of Luke's attempt to lay the bodies out respectfully. It wasn't the Comanche way, but the white man's care was duly noted. Because of this, he might only kill him, sparing him any torture.

Three Toes thought about tribal custom. Traditionally, he'd wrap the dead warriors' bodies in blankets, place them on horses behind riders, and then ride in search of a burial place like a secure cave. After burial, the bodies would be covered with stones. The riders would return to the encampment, where the tribe would burn all the deceased warriors' possessions. He sighed. There simply was no time. He'd have to satisfy the spirits by covering the bodies right where they lay, uttering songs and incantations appropriate to the spirits of the dead, and be on his way. Three Toes would pay his respects later to Long Feathers and others of the tribe.

It took Three Toes more than an hour to cover the bodies of Bear Slayer, Coyote Who Runs, and Hawk Nose and to offer chants to the spirits. He knew that the Texas Ranger on the Ghost horse would not be too hard to track.

Soon enough, he reconnoitered the area and picked up Luke's trail. The horse and rider left an easy track in the sandy soil, though the hoof prints didn't form well, given the nature of sand. In a few days, the tracks would be gone, either blown or washed away.

Strong bid farewell to Zeke and Carlotta. He pointed the roan east, knowing that he'd ride on a few miles out before turning south. He gave some thought to heading north toward Nuecestown, but decided that would be a bit too bold, even for someone as trail-smart and confident as himself. No, he'd go south toward Brownsville a bit and then take a turn toward Laredo. Maybe he'd feel up to taking his chances in Mexico. "*Porque no?*"

The roan seemed to be traveling just fine with no hint of whatever ailed him the day before. Zeke had been good enough to replace two of the roan's shoes. Strong didn't expect he'd have any difficulty so long as he kept a steady pace. There'd be some rough patches of landscape ahead, and he couldn't afford to have his horse fail him.

He found himself occasionally looking over his shoulder, scanning the horizon for the Texas Ranger, though he knew the lawman was at least a day behind.

Strong would look for a place suitable to set an ambush. He needed a high place with a field of vision affording a view across a wide vista to perhaps three or four hundred yards. Ideally, he'd be sheltered enough to build a small fire and fix a bit of coffee. Carlotta had been good enough to pack him a bit of jerky, so he wouldn't be hungry. In any case, he was anxious to seize the tactical advantage and once again become the hunter rather than the hunted. He reveled at the thought of adding a well-known Texas Ranger to his list of kills. This was how legends were made on the frontier. He might even get into one of those little magazines the hucksters were selling.

Other than stopping for a quick cat nap, Luke had moved under the light of the moon. It was nearly bright enough to be mistaken for daylight. About all he could hear were the thuds and clops of his horse's hooves and an occasional hoot owl. Far as he could tell, he was pretty much alone. Early in the afternoon, he caught sight of smoke rising from Zeke and Carlotta's mail station. He rightly figured the station would be a logical place for Strong to stop. Blessedly, Luke's hand had stopped throbbing.

As he drew closer, it struck him that there was an awful lot of smoke for a chimney fire. He quickened his pace. Soon enough, the station came into view. It wasn't a pretty sight. The station itself had been burned to the ground, though the stable and corral still stood. The horses were nowhere to be seen. They must have been totally surprised. He rode past Zeke's rifle laying in the dirt. The hammer was still pulled back. He'd never even fired the thing.

Passing the stable, he finally caught sight of Zeke staked out spread-eagled in front of the burned-out station. He'd been scalped and his private parts cut off and stuck in his mouth. This was what Comanche did. Luke wondered where Carlotta might be. Hopefully, she wasn't kidnapped. He hoped against hope that they'd spared her. He dismounted and hitched the stallion to the rail that still stood in front of the station. He heard a noise from the stable. As he approached, a chicken ran out across his path, clucking madly. He heard the noise again, almost a groan, then a whimper of pain. He took a cautious step into the stable.

Carlotta was in the corner, hanging by her tied-up hands from one of the stall support beams. She'd been stripped. Her eyes looked vacantly at Luke, but she didn't see him. They'd cut off her nose and likely raped her repeatedly. From the look of the station and number of arrows, Luke figured there were at least a dozen of the heathen Comanche.

Carlotta moaned. It was barely audible. Luke moved across to her. He cut the rope suspending her from the beam and let her down gently. He left her to get his canteen. As he approached his horse, a gunshot shattered the air. He ran back to Carlotta, but she was dead. One of Zeke's pistols had been close enough for her to grab it and finish what the Comanche had failed to do.

Luke dutifully picked up one of the shovels, went out to a nearby motte, and began digging. He was having his fill of digging graves, and his hand was throbbing again. The graves would necessarily have to be shallow.

Luke finished burying Zeke and Carlotta. There wasn't much of anything else he could do. When he eventually got back to Nuecestown or Brownsville or Laredo, whichever came first, he'd let the mail folks know they were short one station.

Luke had a sense of being followed, but had no idea by whom. He climbed back up onto the big grey and stood tall in the stirrups a moment, scanning the horizon. Nothing moved. He saw Strong's track heading east, but figured that was a ruse to throw him off the trail. Common sense pointed west.

He knew that if he continued south, he'd soon be in King Ranch country. This was the huge spread that Captain Richard King had founded. Nobody messed with King's *vaqueros*, so he suspected that Strong would likely turn from a southern track. More importantly, for Strong, there'd be more cover if he headed west.

Luke set his reckoning on Laredo. Between the mail station and the Laredo settlement, the prairie was even more sparse of any tree cover. The only settlement was in San Diego, and the road from there to Laredo was pretty good. He felt it likely that Strong might rest there, but not linger long. With only a couple of dozen families comprising San Diego, it wasn't really a place where someone on the run could hide. Other than arroyos and occasional live oak and mesquite mottes, there would be good line of sight for hunter and hunted. Overall, the elevations would rise as he traveled further from Corpus Christi and the Gulf.

He'd have to be extra careful. He had already experienced Strong's shooting expertise at a couple of hundred yards. Now his challenge would be picking up Strong's trail. He looked around the station for clues, and his practiced eyes soon spied a couple of horseshoes that seemed out of place. It was as though they hadn't been put away. It was a fair bet that Strong's horse was sporting some new iron on its hooves.

Luke's hand had swelled a bit from the shoveling. It made the bandages tighter, so he took a moment to change his dressings, as Doc had recommended, before moving on.

Three Toes was downwind several miles behind and heard the gunshot. He doubted that the Ranger had found his quarry just yet, but recalled that one of the white man's mail stations was along the trail they were following.

When he caught up to the Ranger, the Comanche watched Luke bury Zeke and Carlotta. From the blood and the absence of horses, it was clear that his people had struck effectively. He held back quietly and waited for Luke to leave.

Three Toes finally got close enough that he could see Luke's hat as he began to follow a trail leading west of the station. The Indian pulled up in a nearby dry creek bed behind a live oak motte to allow Luke to get some distance on him. It wouldn't do to be discovered this early.

It took just a few minutes for Three Toes to reach what remained of the mail station. His people had apparently done well, as there was evidence of the torture they'd inflicted. He assumed they'd taken scalps. The raiding Comanche were surely Penateka, but he couldn't be sure which band they were from. They could have been some of Buffalo Hump's people, but didn't appear to be from Three Toes' own band.

SEVEN

Respite?

It didn't take long for Doc to drive the wagon the five miles back to Nuecestown. Still, they weren't in much of a hurry at this point. They finally made it to the town, and he pulled the wagon up at the livery stable. Bernice saw them and came out to greet them. "Elisa, are you all right?"

The girl nodded, but she was worn out. It was dusk and pretty much obvious that Elisa wasn't returning to the farm that night. Doc went about unloading a few of Elisa's personal effects and some fresh clothes for Mike. He extended his hand and helped her down from the wagon.

"Dan," he told the boy, "take the rig down to the stable, unhitch the mules, and give them some feed." He then turned to Bernice. "We're all right, Bernice. Elisa here could use some rest."

Bernice paid Doc no never-mind. "Why, Elisa dear, you're welcome to spend tonight with us. Mike awakened for a bit earlier but went back to sleep. The poor dear is still weak from his ordeal."

Elisa chewed on that reference to an ordeal and had a ready retort but held back in deference to the woman's kindness. "Thank you,

Bernice. You're right, I sure could use some shut-eye. It's been a long day."

"You just come up the way a piece when you're ready, dear. Aggie and I would be pleased to fix you a dinner. Doc, you're most welcome to join us."

"Thanks, Bernice. I'll check on little Mike and be by in a piece." Doc took Elisa's arm, and they walked toward his house to check on her brother.

As they reached the porch, Elisa stumbled. She was more tired than she'd thought. Thankfully, Doc was fully sober by now and had a firm grip on her arm. It had been a day of emotional ups and downs. She'd lost family, saved family, killed a Comanche, buried her kinfolk, met a real man, and was faced with life decisions not of her choosing.

"Excuse me, Doc." It was a deep male voice. Sheriff George Whelan had gotten back to town after a couple of days in Corpus Christi at the trial of a horse thief. Amazingly, the thief had managed to avoid the hangman's noose by turning himself in and begging for mercy. Despite Sheriff Whelan's testimony and recommendation to hang the man, the judge had decided to be lenient and sentenced the lad to three years in prison. It was unusual and caused quite a stir in the city.

The sheriff had stayed the night in case they needed help in Corpus. Fearing a lynch mob, they'd put the thief in jail pending his being sent to prison. Folks didn't cotton to horse thieves. The horse, after all, was the primary mode of transportation through most of the territory. It almost had citizen rights. It had been tough enough fending off horse-thieving Comanche and Apache in recent years. Even some Mexicans had gotten in on the thriving business of rustling horses.

Sheriff Whelan wasn't actually the Nuecestown sheriff. The town couldn't afford one. He was based in Corpus Christi and assigned by Colonel Kinney to keep his eye on the region surrounding the city.

That included Kinney's interests in Nuecestown.

"George, you've missed all the action." Doc wasn't exactly a big supporter of Sheriff Whelan. Whelan invariably seemed to show up after any danger had passed. Likely a coincidence, but it happened a lot. "We had to deal with Comanche. Also, Captain Dunn was here, but he's long gone on the trail of Bad Bart Strong."

Whelan raised his eyebrows to acknowledge Doc's news, then turned his attention to Elisa. "Is this Elisa Corrigan?" Whelan moved his eyes from her head to...well, he noticed she was growing up.

That was another thing Doc took issue with. Whelan was always leering at the ladies. He figured the sheriff had kept the ladies of ill repute busy last night in Corpus Christi.

"She's had a rough day, Sheriff." Doc held his temper. He figured a drink would be about right at the moment...maybe the whole dang bottle.

About this time, Bernice stepped up and took charge of Elisa. "Pay the sheriff no never-mind, dear. Let's check on little Mike and then get you over to my place for that dinner." She gave Whelan a sideways glance that reeked of disapproval. It was a *she's-only-sixteen, put-your-eyeballs-back-in-your-head* look.

"I've got some business at the jail." Sheriff Whelan took the none-too-subtle hint, turned, and started walking his horse to the stable. He walked slowly but heard no dinner invitation. He was quite tired from being on the road from Corpus and figured he'd just as well find out more from Doc in the morning. He was a bit worried about how close this most recent Comanche raid had been.

On the desk inside what pretended to be a sheriff's office and jail, Whelan saw a couple of new wanted posters. One was for this Bad Bart Strong that Luke was chasing, and the other was for a fellow named Dirk Cavendish from Montana Territory. Both were mean and had serious bounties on their heads. Strong was a skilled marksman, while Cavendish preferred a knife. It was almost tempting enough to lure him away from Corpus Christi to track them down.

Luke was set on heading to Laredo. He realized, as he rode west from San Diego, that there was plenty of cover on the trail from which Strong could set an ambush, but it was likely that his man hadn't yet figured he was so close. He'd stopped in San Diego just long enough to inquire as to whether Strong had passed through. He wanted some assurance that his man was indeed headed to Laredo. He was.

Luke had closed the gap by riding through most of three nights under what was called a Comanche moon. That moon hung in the night sky nearly as bright as the sun. Luke didn't realize his non-stop travel was also a source of frustration to the person tracking him, Three Toes, who coveted Luke's horse. At least, Luke's hand had stopped throbbing and the swelling had gone down. He figured he might be nearly healed by the time he reached Laredo.

He thought back to his last trip to Laredo shortly after the Callahan campaign had ended. Other than the U.S. Army with its post at Fort McIntosh, the population was nearly all Mexican immigrants. After the Treaty of Guadalupe-Hidalgo, there had been a brief but ill-fated attempt to cede the property back to Mexico. A few unhappy Mexicans had moved across the Rio Grande to Mexico and established Nuevo Laredo. With the predominantly Mexican population, Strong would stand out like a sore thumb. He'd be despised as well, given he was an Anglo. He would be wise to keep his stay short, stopping just long enough to refresh, tarry with some old acquaintances—Luke was pretty sure the outlaw had no friends—and move on.

Three Toes kept his distance a couple of hours behind Luke. He was patient.

He was glad that Moon Woman had packed him some jerky but, on the third day, he'd shot a jackrabbit. He decided against a fire. The jackrabbit was tasty and the blood quenched his thirst.

He'd also seen a few dozen buffalo, lots of wild horses, and about twice as many longhorn cattle, but to kill them would have been a waste of meat, time, and arrows.

He'd bide his time and eventually catch the Ranger.

Luke had purposely shied away from two other mail stations between Corpus Christi and Laredo, taking a wide arc around them. Partly, he didn't want to deal with the outcome of another Comanche attack. It was going to be rough enough ahead, as there could still be horse-thieving Lipan Apache roaming north of the Rio Grande and there was no love lost by Mexicans as concerned Anglos, especially those that had ridden with Callahan.

About this time, Luke figured he'd become too predictable and decided to double back in case Strong circled around to trick him again. He headed east, following along the meandering course of an arroyo. This kept him partly covered from sight by tall prairie grass and an occasional live oak motte. By chance, he stopped to reconnoiter.

He slowly stood upright in the stirrups to scan the horizon. Something was moving toward him, perhaps a hundred or so yards up the dry creek bed. As it drew closer, he realized he was seeing the business end of an Indian war lance. He slowly and as quietly as possible dismounted. He slipped the Colt rifle from its scabbard. In what seemed like an interminable minute, a horse and rider rounded the bend in the arroyo, and Luke found himself face to face with Three Toes.

The Comanche chief was fully taken by surprise as he came around the bend in the dry creek bed. This was not a good situation. How could he have been so careless? The hunter had suddenly become prey.

The two stared at each other. Sworn enemies standing eyeball to eyeball. What next?

Luke had the rifle trained on Three Toes' chest. From so close a range, he couldn't miss. He motioned Three Toes to dismount and drop his weapons. "You speak English?"

He watched as the warrior assessed the situation, noted the point when he decided it would be suicide to attack the white man. He dismounted, keeping his eyes warily on Luke.

"Some," he replied slowly. "You are the one they call Ghost-Who-Rides." Three Toes' English was halting, but intelligible. Luke almost felt flattered. He'd earned a Comanche nickname.

"How long you been tracking me?" He kept his gaze and rifle riveted on Three Toes.

"Three days."

"Those your warriors at the farm?"

Three Toes nodded. "They were foolish to be killed by a woman."

Clearly, the Comanche was not happy with the prowess of his young warriors.

Luke replied, "The two boys were too young. The attack was foolish." He tried to help Three Toes save face.

"Girl killed Bear Slayer."

Luke thought on that one. "He was careless, crazed with lust." He was careful not to mention the slain Comanche's name, as that might have been taken as disrespectful.

Three Toes nodded. A frown crossed his brow. Perhaps he himself was acting rashly. There must have been some greater reason the spirits had allowed him to ride into a trap.

Now, the two found themselves awkwardly staring at each other, momentarily at a loss for words.

Finally, Three Toes broke the ice. "You tracking someone?" It was a rhetorical question. The Comanche no doubt knew the answer.

Luke was about to respond when a horse and rider appeared from behind him. He prayed it wasn't Strong. If it was, he'd likely already be dead. He tried to keep an eye on Three Toes as he glanced over his shoulder.

"Clyde? Clyde Jones? Dang, it's been a long time, partner." He thanked God it wasn't Bart Strong.

"Whatcha got here, Luke? A Comanche redskin? A chief no less."

Three Toes' expression had changed from uncertainty to just a hint of fear. The Ranger's medicine was strong. Not only had he surprised the chief, but now he had reinforcements that magically appeared. He began to hum a spirit song, as he sensed death was near.

Clyde had ridden with Luke under Callahan's command on the Rio Escondito. "Dang, Clyde. Your timing couldn't be better." Luke had the drop on Three Toes, but reinforcements were a huge help.

"What do you mean, Luke?" He looked at Three Toes. "You want help disposing of the chief here?"

Luke remembered Clyde's habit of saying wrong things at wrong times. He lowered his voice, so Three Toes couldn't hear him. "This Comanche understands English, so watch what you say. As to his fate, I was just parlaying when you showed up. Now, if you truly want to help, let me talk with him."

Clyde nodded affirmatively and eased back in the saddle.

Luke turned back to fully face Three Toes. "Chief, I'm Luke Dunn. This here is Clyde Jones. We're Texas Rangers." It was about time to make formal introductions, if for no other reason than to show mutual respect. For the Comanche, it was important that all people have names.

Three Toes was increasingly curious. If the Ranger was going to kill him, why was he making introductions? "I am Three Toes, a chief of the Penateka Comanche."

"Ah, you are with Buffalo Hump."

"He has gone to the white man's camp." Three Toes referred to the reservation where Buffalo Hump had taken most of his people under a treaty with the U.S. government.

Luke cocked his head. "You no longer follow Buffalo Hump?"

"When my chief is free, I will follow him again. I must lead my own people."

Luke didn't like where this was going. It was time to change the subject. "You seem like an honorable man, Chief. You've tracked me for three days, but haven't attacked me. Why?"

"You respected the spirits of my warriors. It did not feel right to kill you out of revenge." Three Toes, hesitating at first, extended his hand to Luke. "You could have killed me. Let us make truce."

"There's no reason to kill you, Three Toes. I have no quarrel with you. Back in Nuecestown…well…people died…your people and my people. It's time to stop fighting." Luke grasped Three Toes' hand. "Clyde, show your friendship with the chief."

Jones hesitantly took Three Toes' hand and forced a smile. The truce was uncomfortable, but a truce nonetheless. This went against Jones' instincts, but he'd seen Luke's performance with Callahan and thus respected the Ranger's judgment.

The chief relaxed a bit. Luke's respectful treatment of his dead warriors and now his effort to make a mutually beneficial truce were appreciated. "Three Toes has come a long way. I would like to return to my people with a good story. I would help you find your prey." The implication was to kill, not capture.

"So how'd you get your name?" Luke asked. It was a personal question aimed at establishing more of a friendship.

"Battle wound." Three Toes smiled.

Luke decided to not press it further. "Well, now that there's three of us, we should have an advantage over Bad Bart."

They were less than a day out from Laredo. Nuecestown and the mail station were long behind them now. Luke found himself thinking about how that young girl he'd helped was making out. Her having taken on Comanche had impressed the veteran lawman. He was nearly twice her age, but he'd noticed how pretty she was. He remembered how she'd hugged him in her grief and felt her young body pressed against him. But he also was impressed with her seemingly steel nerves as she shot the Comanche that was about to release an arrow at him.

He figured she'd manage to care for her brother and rebuild a life on her dead folks' spread. A hundred acres should be manageable, and her little brother would grow up fast helping her out. What was her name? He thought a few moments. "Elisa," he whispered to himself. "Yes, Elisa Corrigan."

EIGHT

Making a Texas Ranger

Luke hadn't had the easiest childhood himself. He'd been born in Ireland back in '34. As a nineteen-year-old, he'd heard about some of his cousins from County Kildare going to the United States to a wild place called Texas. Luke's impression of the United States was colored by his admiration of their having gained independence from the hated British. He wished there was an ocean separating Ireland from England, as such a physical barrier might have helped with the various Irish uprisings.

Luke's grandfather's brother was a fine fellow in County Kildare named Lawrence Dunn, and four of Long Larry's five sons had already immigrated to the Corpus Christi area of Texas. One had set up a smithy establishment in the city and the others were ranchers and farmers. The first had even fought with General Zachary Taylor in the Mexican-American War back in 1845. Luke found it ironic that he'd garnered a family nickname of Long Luke, not unlike his own grandfather's brother.

On a visit to Long Larry, Luke got to read a couple of the letters his cousin Matthew sent from Texas. It whetted his appetite in a big way. So, through back-breaking farm work as a teen, he mustered the financial resources and persuaded his father and mother to let him follow his cousins to America. They didn't protest overmuch, as the famine caused by the potato crop failures had left them destitute. His mother had even miscarried, due mostly to inadequate nourishment. Her body simply wasn't up to supporting a pregnancy.

As part of his motivation to escape Ireland, Luke found himself allied with some kinsmen in Killeigh who were planning to revolt against the British oppressors. While that revolt never materialized, he was able to develop and practice fighting skills that would prove handy later in life. The combination of the Great Famine, fueled by potato blight and the rumor of a price being placed on his head by virtue of word having leaked out about the rebellious plans of his kinsmen, weighed heavily in Luke's decision to head to Texas.

Despite the potato blight and seemingly ramshackle agricultural system, crop rotation somewhat mitigated the effects of the famine around Kildare. However, to the western regions of Ireland came horror stories of starvation and disease. The mighty potato had been attractive largely because its farming was not labor-intensive, as compared to raising oats and barley and livestock. But the famine reached far beyond only farmhands. Its heavy shadow touched the population at large. Rare was the day when there weren't poor souls starved to death by the side of the roads. The desperation that had driven Luke to join a rebel group and earn a price on his head was widespread among the clans and sects. He preferred living, if at all possible. Living in freedom would be ideal.

Luke was impressionable, but he was headstrong. It could be said that his body, at well over six feet tall, was developing far faster than his brain. One evening, as he headed home from dining with some of his cousins, his path was blocked by three British soldiers. They were drunk, and one had vomited over the front of his red tunic. He stunk to high heaven.

"Hey, Mick, where you think you're going?" They used the

derogatory nickname applied to the Irish.

The passage was narrow, so Luke had no choice but to face the soldiers. The stench from the sick soldier in the damp confines of the passageway was nearly overwhelming. The others were so drunk that they apparently did not notice. "I'm headed home, sirs."

"Look, sergeant, he's one of them rebels we've been warned about."

Luke knew they'd have no way of knowing his affiliation. They were guessing. "Do I look like a rebel, sirs?"

The largest of the three placed his hand on his sword as if to draw. "Methinks he's a brassy lad."

The third soldier, the least drunk of the trio, held him back. "Lads, it's not a good evening for a fight. We've got that duty in the morning."

He held back the sergeant and the sick soldier so Luke could pass.

It had been far too close for comfort. Luke was having to grow up way too fast, and lingering in Kildare was going to eventually get him into trouble. In the innermost reaches of his young soul, he saw the conflict between Irish and British as an issue of justice. He was deeply offended at the injustice perpetrated by the British against his kinsmen. Freedom... justice...opportunity. He sought a life featuring the confluence of those values. The next morning, he went to Long Larry's home and received his uncle's blessing to go to America.

Long Larry made no bones about what Luke should do. "Lad, you've read your cousin's letters from Texas. Methinks it's the place for you. Kildare will only hold trouble for a lad as spirited as you."

Luke managed to find passage to England, then found his way north to Liverpool. He was hired for work on a sailing ship heading from Liverpool to New Orleans. He didn't see much of the ocean while working in the bowels of the ship, but he managed to avoid seasickness. From New Orleans, it was an easy journey to Corpus Christi and connection with fellow Irishmen carving new beginnings on the Texas frontier.

On arrival, he soon learned of the challenges of frontier life, some of which made the oppressions by the British seem like child's play. They could be viciously evil and terribly sadistic with their torturing, but deeds of the British paled in comparison to the Comanche atrocities he soon heard about. Another threat came from south of the Rio Grande, where there was still a lot of resentment to the treaty that ceded the Nueces Strip to the United States. The twin threats weighed on Luke's conscience. He wondered what sort of justice might be found.

He found a small room to live in Corpus Christi and hired out for odd jobs. As it happened, he ran into a man one evening at a local market. He could tell the man was of some importance and found out from a passerby that it was in fact Colonel Kinney, and he was credited with being the founder of the city. Notably, Luke recalled that the man had befriended one of his cousins, the one who'd fought with Taylor, giving him a place to live, purportedly in exchange for minding the colonel's fighting cocks. Luke decided that boldness was in order, so he walked so his path would intersect that of the colonel. He brushed Kinney as their paths crossed.

"Excuse me, young man."

"Sorry, sir, I meant no offense." Luke's Irish accent came through quite clearly. "Pardon me, but aren't you Colonel Kinney?"

Kinney was uncharacteristically thrown a bit off balance. "Yes, and you are?"

"My name is Luke Dunn. I think you may have known my cousin, Matthew."

"Yes, a hard-working family man. I'm a friend of Matthew's." Kinney had a suspicion by now that this meeting had been purposeful. "May I help you?"

"To be straight, sir, I arrived in your fine city from Ireland just a couple of months ago. I've been working in the port but am looking for something with greater purpose for my skills. I'm concerned about the threats Texans face on the frontier and am looking for a way to make peoples' lives safer." He could see that he'd grabbed Kinney's interest.

"Do you have a sense of the law?"

"If you mean am I of high morals and can I fight when necessary, yes, sir, I am."

"A few of my friends are joining me at the cock fights on Sunday. It can get a bit unruly. I'd be willing to try you out to help keep order. After that, we'll see about the future." Kinney smiled and extended his hand. "See you at your cousin's place?"

Luke shook Kinney's hand. "Yes, sir, I'll be there."

Kinney looked at Luke's waist and belt. "Do you have a pistol?" Obviously, he didn't. Kinney gave him two dollars. "Get yourself one, Mr. Dunn. You might need it." He turned, then added, "Look for George Whelan."

Following the meeting, Luke promptly purchased a .36 caliber Colt 1851 Navy single action percussion cap revolver. He purchased several rounds of ammunition and decided that in the future he'd learn to make his own. It would be less expensive, and he'd be certain of the load. Now, however, he needed to learn to use the Colt. Back in Ireland, the weapons of choice had been claymores and flintlock pistols. Technology had come a long way, and some inventor named Samuel Colt had been changing the face of weaponry.

As it was Wednesday, he determined to practice enough with the Colt to be reasonably familiar with it by Sunday.

The first acquaintance Luke made at the cock fights was the George Whelan fellow Colonel Kinney had mentioned. Kinney had appointed Whelan as *de facto* sheriff of Nueces County. It would be official a month later.

"Mr. Dunn, it's a pleasure to meet you." Whelan looked at the Colt jammed into Luke's waistband. "You know how to use that piece?"

Luke nodded affirmatively.

"You been to cockfights before?" Catching Luke's nod, Whelan went on. "The cocks have the easy part. They use their talons to fight each other to the death. It's the crowd that's of concern. They are betting their hard-earned money on their favorite fowl. There are inevitably sore losers, and they can get nasty. Sometimes, they're drunk and can't control themselves. That's pretty much it. Our job is to protect Colonel Kinney's interests."

"Do we shoot anybody?"

Whelan smiled. "Hope not."

Nothing like a couple of armed guards to keep emotions under control. At the end of the day, Luke thanked Whelan, received a dollar from Colonel Kinney, and headed back to Corpus Christi.

The experience had intrigued him. Luke had never seriously considered guarding or law enforcement as a profession. It appealed to his inner sense of morals and honor, coupled with the inbred traditions of clan loyalty and protection he'd grown up with in County Kildare. The maintaining justice part was particularly intriguing. That resonated well.

At this time, the opinion of Texas folk in general was that the federal government had pretty much failed to live up to the protections that were supposed to be part of statehood. With Mexicans and Lipan Apache the major challenges to the south and the Comanche to the northwest, Texans felt the threats needed to be pursued, hunted, and killed. It was that simple. With federal troops mostly moved to conflicts outside of Texas, there was a widespread view that Texas Rangers should be the hunters and executioners of these threats. For all intents and purposes, the Texas Rangers were not much more than wishful thinking. It wasn't until the Lipan Apache problem arose as a major threat that money would eventually be designated to raise Callahan's company of Texas Rangers. But that hadn't happened just yet.

Luke accepted a role as a deputy sheriff under Whelan. He mostly patrolled the region on his own, as Whelan preferred hanging back in Corpus Christi where he could have his fill of local ladies of ill repute. In fact, he found it an annoyance that Kinney would send him up to Nuecestown once a month to check on the ferry and make sure all was mostly peaceful.

One day, Luke found himself riding about twenty miles south of

Corpus Christi. It was an unusually cool day for the Nueces Strip in July. It was normally brutally hot and humid this time of year, with only light sea breezes coming in from the Gulf if you were close enough to the shoreline. The soil was sandy and the footing fair for his mount. He'd been riding eastward in a dry creek bed, keeping a low profile. Impulsively, he decided to turn south. Horse and rider climbed out of the arroyo and onto the prairie.

"*Carlos, mire!*" The man pointed in Luke's direction. There were four of them riding slowly perhaps five hundred yards away from him. All four riders stopped and searched the horizon in Luke's direction.

"*Caramba!*" The leader saw the threat and decided to hustle along away from Luke. They waved their hats and ropes, and it became clear that they were driving a few longhorns southward.

Luke saw that he was outnumbered, and he'd already lost the element of surprise. His suspicion, driven by their actions in hustling along rather than engaging him, was that these men were probably cattle thieves.

By this time, Luke had added a second revolver and a rifle to his weaponry. The revolver was a .44 caliber Walker Colt, an impressive piece that could be reloaded at a gallop. He continued to head south, paralleling the men's route. The sun was sinking ever lower on the horizon, and it would be sunset soon enough. He might have a better chance at night. With the heavy humidity and virtually no moonlight, he could sneak up on them. He headed in the direction of what turned out to be Mexicans. He heard animated discussion about stopping for the night, but the men were fearful of whomever was lurking in the prairie grass. Luke was glad he'd learned some Spanish, although he spoke the language with a bit of a brogue.

At last, night fell, and the men encamped. Luke dismounted and grabbed his rifle with scabbard, slinging it over his shoulder. He checked the loads in his revolvers and, perhaps most important, drew his Bowie knife. If he could disable a sentry, he'd be evening his odds a bit more. It wasn't long.

The man, now judged by Luke to be a cattle rustler, stood about a hundred feet from the encampment. His three companions stupidly kept up a lot of noisy chatter, probably a bit nervous. Luke was about a step behind him when the sentry realized someone was close at hand. Too late. Luke's height advantage played well and the man's throat was slit before he could utter a sound.

The talking from the encampment stopped for a moment. "*Luis, qué pasa?*"

"*Es bien,*" Luke responded. Apparently, it worked as the rustlers returned to their chatter. They'd grown over-confident.

It was time for action. There'd be no reinforcements and no second chances. One of the men stood to relieve himself, and he made a silhouette against even a darkened sky. Luke aimed carefully. The report of the rifle echoed through the night. Startled wildlife scattered. The man fell where he stood. There were shouted curses as the other two men tried to saddle their horses in the dark. Luke chambered a second round, drew a bead, and fired. He apparently hit something, because there were more curses. "*Andale, Carlos!*" There was panic in the voice.

Soon Luke heard hooves galloping off to the south at breakneck speed. By those thieves' reckoning, whatever was hunting them in the prairie grass wasn't to be messed with.

Once he sensed the thieves were far enough away, Luke walked into the encampment. The man who'd stood and was shot first had been relieving his bladder. He lay in the sand bleeding out from his wound. A horse lay fallen but alive nearby and had apparently been the victim of Luke's second shot. A bullet to the head put it out of its misery. Luke made out a few head of cattle and at least two horses. The escapees were sharing a mount. Luke poured himself a cup of coffee from the rustler's pot and enjoyed a bit of the jackrabbit they'd been cooking for dinner. He'd take a full inventory at first light and head back to Corpus Christi.

Whelan greeted him next day as he rode to the outskirts of the city. He had eight cattle and two horses with saddles occupied by dead cattle thieves.

"Damn, Luke," exclaimed Whelan." That's impressive. Sam Wright will be pleased to have his longhorns back."

"Two of them thieves got away." Luke smiled. "They were likely peeing in their pants. They even rode double. Call it Nueces justice, George."

"Colonel Kinney's got some sort of opportunity you might find interesting. When you get into town, be sure to look him up," George told him.

Luke nodded, waving the cattle onward with George outriding to help keep them headed in the right direction.

Turned out that the colonel had a letter from the Texas governor to form up a company of Texas Rangers to chase a bunch of horse-thieving Lipan Apache out of the Nueces Strip.

Texas Ranger. It had an appeal to Luke. He'd heard of their brief exploits a few years back after the Mexican-American War. He didn't hesitate to sign up.

When the Callahan campaign ended and the company was effectively disbanded, it left a big hole in Luke's psyche and his employment. He'd rapidly learned to love the camaraderie with fellow Rangers, and he'd had enough of patrolling Nueces County by himself while Whelan dallied. Callahan intimated to several of the more accomplished Texas Rangers that they might consider being sort of lone wolves until government finances caught up with popular public sentiment. Luke seized on Callahan's charge. Being unmarried and with few obligations, he'd saved enough to enable him to patrol on his own for a couple of years, if necessary.

He handed in his resignation to Whelan, who feigned annoyance but Luke thought he saw a hint of admiration for his lofty purposes.

Now, after a couple months of patrolling the Nueces Strip, Luke found himself on the trail of a notorious killer. He'd received the informal assignment from none other than Captain Rip Ford, a well-respected former Ranger-turned-politician, and a newspaperman who had the ear of the Texas governor.

Up to now, Luke had broken up some hiders, been wounded by Bad Bart Strong, fought off a small Comanche attack, returned to tracking Strong, and subdued a Comanche chief. By sheer chance, another Callahan veteran, Clyde Jones, had found him on the trail and joined him along with their new friend, Three Toes.

Bernice and Agatha prepared a fine dinner for Elisa and Doc. Bernice was chatty as ever. She'd lost three philandering husbands, one to yellow fever, one at Goliad in the Texas fight for independence, and a third who was shot by an angry husband who found him in bed with his wife. The last one was no loss to Bernice. Doc believed Bernice's constant chatter and bickering manner led her men to stray. In any case, she had plenty of advice for Elisa. She'd seen the way Whelan looked at her, as well as the way Elisa looked at Luke. Couldn't have been more opposite emotions.

"You keep a watchful eye out for that sheriff, dear." Agatha had observed the same dynamic. "Let him seek his satisfactions in Corpus Christi." The intimations weren't lost on Elisa.

"Pay her no mind, Elisa. The sheriff is a good man but for that one transgression. Remember, our Lord Jesus had prostitutes around him during his ministry." Bernice blushed as she said the words. "Not that He partook, dear, but He was forgiving."

After some further inconsequential conversation with much advice about Elisa moving to Nuecestown, Doc at last pushed back from the dining table. "Bernice, Agatha, that was a magnificent dinner. I'm much obliged." In the back of his mind, he was feeling blessed to not have choked on the overcooked roast. "I do suggest that Elisa get to bed early. She'll have a big day ahead of her."

"I'm gonna keep the farm, Doc." Elisa's words were very firm.

"You think carefully on that. It's quite a responsibility."

Bernice caught Doc's drift. "You're welcome to stay here for a couple of days, dear. It'll give little Mike more chance to rest from his ordeal, too." She looked over at Agatha and nodded as if to have her reinforce her own advice to the girl.

Elisa was determined. She returned to her home the next day, despite the attack and the funeral being fresh in most folks' minds. She felt a need to immerse herself in farm work as she struggled to fight back the sense of grief that clawed at the edges of her emotions.

Her brother Mike still had a bit of a headache, but he was young and would recover quickly.

She'd managed to avoid Sheriff Whelan. She waited until he made his departure for Corpus Christi. She wasn't up to dealing with his leering eyes again. She thought he might even have drooled.

In the inner recesses of her mind, she held out hope that Luke would return, and it would be for her. She had felt his kindness and sensed that he just might have some sort of feelings for her. She was young and hadn't experienced any of these sorts of emotions before. Bernice, three times widowed, and Agatha, who'd lost her only husband, tried to teach her some of the ways of courting rituals.

They also told her that all bets were off as concerned men on the frontier. They tended to be unable to show feelings, would escape whenever possible for days on end, and lovemaking was strictly a biological urge that never took the woman's heart or physical needs into account. Agatha told her that men who hung around close to home tended to be what she called "clingy." They wouldn't give a woman any space. In any case, they described men in rather extreme and not especially complimentary terms.

Elisa began to take inventory of her situation. The cabin seemed spacious with three fewer occupants. As she began to go through her parents' belongings, she found her mother's mirror. She couldn't help but look at her reflection. She could see her face and shoulders, but wished she could see her whole self. What was it that men found so attractive? Her long reddish-blonde hair needed washing, and she determined to go down to the creek the next morning. She'd need to look right for Luke's return, whenever and if ever that might be.

Mike was finally waking up and would have lots of questions as his senses came around. She dreaded explaining to him what had happened. She wanted to teach him to be grateful to the people who'd helped them during the disaster and to not harbor a hatred for the Comanche.

NINE

Lucky at Cards

"Ante up, my friends." The card shark scanned the men around the table, caressing his own cards. He peeked at the corners. The hand was terrible. He'd have to bluff, fold, or cheat.

He'd noticed something threatening about the plainly dressed young man across from him and sensed that it might not do to cheat. The fellow was hard to read, even by an accomplished card shark like Bronson Smith. He mostly won, losing just enough to keep the hopefuls coming back to play. It irritated Smith that he didn't know the kid's name. He had already won two large pots, and the evening was young. The losses irritated Smith, given that he himself had become a fixture at the table over the past several months.

Another young man, an itinerant named Oscar, and Bronson were the only other Anglos in Texas Jack's Saloon. There were two Mexican locals in the game, and they talked now and then between themselves in Spanish.

The other players tossed their antes onto the felt-covered card table. The air was thick with the aromas of smoke and whiskey. The lighting was dim as candles flickered in the oxygen-deprived atmosphere.

As bets were placed, Smith took up a little chatter. "You're new here, my friend," he said to the kid. "Got a name?"

"Yeah."

Smith didn't take kindly to rudeness. "Can you share it with us?"

"Don't matter."

Smith was getting ever more annoyed, and it began to affect his judgment. He decided to improve his hand.

"I wouldn't do that, mister." Strong had seen the card start to travel toward Smith's sleeve.

"You accusing me of something?" Smith barked.

"Only if that card goes any further." Strong had already seen the pearl handle peeking from under Smith's armpit. He locked his eyes on Smith's. "Don't be foolish."

Oscar pushed back from the table. The two Mexicans did likewise. There was total silence. It had grown about as quiet as a prairie grave. Had the young man without a name actually had the temerity to challenge Smith? Would Smith back down? Everyone knew that he cheated, but no one had ever called him out.

Smith's left hand quivered a bit, then he dropped the card on the table. Meanwhile, his right hand started toward his hidden pistol.

"You really don't want to do that." Strong's voice was commanding for one so young.

Smith looked at him inquisitively.

Strong caught the unspoken question. "Because, if you do, you'll be digesting a .44 caliber bullet deep in your intestines."

Smith raised his hands. He'd never encountered anyone like Strong. He stood up from the table and began to turn. As he turned, he reached inside his coat for the pistol. The sound of the shot was loud in the near-silence. He was dead before he hit the floor.

Strong holstered his revolver, scooped his winnings into a bag, and left a fair amount for Oscar and the Mexicans. As he strolled from the table, he gave the barkeep a couple of dollars for Smith's burial. He turned to face the saloon patrons as he reached the door. "If a Texas

Ranger captain named Long Luke Dunn stops by here lookin' for me, tell him I'm waitin'." He pointed south.

As he exited, he caught the eye of a pretty, red-headed young woman at the end of the bar. He gave a hint of a smile and tipped his hat. "I'll be back." Be back with a bigger than life reputation was what went through his mind.

He rightly figured it was a good time to get out of Laredo. No lingering and certainly no time for whoring. No telling how close Luke was by now, and he needed to find an appropriate killing ground for an ambush. He still regretted missing Luke back near Nuecestown. He'd forced that shot. He needed to be patient; he knew better than to force a shot.

No one paid him any never-mind as he walked to his hotel to gather his belongings. He hadn't expected to have to shoot the card shark, but there didn't seem to be any displeasure over what he'd done. Strong gathered he must have rid the town of a problem. He saddled the roan and took the trail south toward San Ygnacio. There were plenty of places along that route where he could lie in wait for Luke. So long as the folks at the saloon in Laredo would tell Luke that he could find Strong by heading south, that would work just fine.

As Strong headed out of town, he passed a lone rider on a big black horse. The man was fully outfitted in black and armed to the teeth. He tipped his hat to Strong as they went by each other. Strong felt as though it was some sort of professional courtesy. There was that sort of sense among men running afoul of the law.

Strong was so focused on heading south that he didn't figure to get acquainted with any newcomer. There was something rather ominous about the man he'd passed, though Strong was so into his own evil that it didn't especially bother him. He kept his horse headed south out of Laredo.

Dirk Cavendish had traveled from the Arizona Territory through New Mexico and the heart of the Comancheria. He managed to waylay a couple of mail riders along his route and even robbed a train single-handedly.

Turning due south, he'd soon found himself wending his way along the Rio Grande, traveling mostly at night despite his unfamiliarity with the territory. He was of a mind to eventually explore opportunities on the Nueces Strip as far as Corpus Christi. From what he'd heard, it was a place where he felt he could lose his past. It was his past that weighed on him. Everything might be right, if only he could put it out of the dark recesses of his soul.

Cav, as he was called by friends and enemies, had been born and raised in the broad ranch lands near the Absaroka Range of the Rocky Mountains up in the Montana Territory. His mother was part Sioux and his father, the son of a trapper known as Bear Man Cavendish for his inclination to take on the beasts with naught but a hunting knife, tried his hand with moderate success at raising horses and cattle. If skill with a knife was genetic, Cav inherited the genes. He loved working with knives. He even learned to throw knives with unerring accuracy. Both knives and guns fascinated him, but he much preferred the former.

One summer, when Cav was only fourteen, his mother passed away in childbirth. It wasn't uncommon on the frontier where medical help was limited at best. She was likely just a bit too far past her prime to be having babies. Cav would have had a brother. He had two teen sisters, Cora and Belle. The girls were as wild as the mountains they were raised near, and they made a habit of flirting with about any man who came near the ranch, or on rare trips to Bozeman.

With his mother gone, Cav's father began to inflict himself on his daughters. Cav learned to knock before entering, as his father and sisters might be romping naked among the blankets in the only bed in their cabin. In fact, Cav mostly took to sleeping in the stable, even in cold weather. The arrangement didn't seem morally quite right to Cav at the time, but he really didn't know any better. He simply had never received any teaching in such things. Aside from day-to-day ranch chores, he whiled away the hours with knife and gun. He became so good with blades that any knife became an extension of his hand. They were like part of his body.

He could just about hear the faint giggling, grunts, and cries of pleasure emanating from the cabin most any night. Occasionally, he heard his father lay a whip on the girls. That was one of his new deviances, apparently designed to lend excitement to their play. They screamed, much to his father's delight. Cav noticed welts on his sisters' arms and on their wrists from being tied up. It hurt him to see them hurt, but neither complained. Likely as not, they were fearful of what might happen were they to refuse their father's advances.

One evening, Cav had just settled in among a couple of blankets, when Cora appeared in the stable doorway.

"Cora?" Cav whispered.

"Where's your clothes?" she gasped.

It was a warm night, and Cav slept with next to nothing on. He sat up as Cora approached him.

"I've waited so long for this, Cav."

What was she saying? This seemed so wrong, but his own teen physical urges had already begun to come into play. He was confused and conflicted. It was wrong. It was terribly wrong.

She stood over him. Waves of her seductive charms were sweeping over him. Her aroma was alluring. He felt guilt, but it was tainted with a testosterone-heightened urge. He strove to resist. Cora was about to make Cav a willing victim.

As if on cue, Cav saw the silhouette of his father standing in the doorway to the stable.

"What do you think you're doing, you no-good sonofabitch?" his father yelled.

Cav had never seen his father this angry. With one stroke from the back of his hand, his father swept Cora aside. She tumbled helplessly across the floor. Cav's father lifted him by his throat and slammed him to the ground. He began kicking the boy. "You pervert. Don't you ever touch your sisters." He kicked Cav again.

Cav had no idea what pervert meant. He tried to get up, but his father laid him out with another punch. Notably, Cav was taller than his father by a couple of inches, but he didn't have the body strength to match the man.

Cora had stood to one side, naked and horrified. Cav's father turned to her and leveled her with another punch. The strong odor of cheap whiskey hung in the air. "What you lookin' at, you little whore?" He prepared to hit her again, only this time he'd grabbed a shovel. He raised it high.

Cav was in a panic. He feared for Cora's life. In a heat-of-the-moment thing, Cav grabbed a pitchfork and, with all his strength, shoved it deep into his father's back. The prongs shoved clean through to his chest. It was like a stabbing with a handful of knives. Cora gasped. Cav's father's eyes bugged out as he crumpled forward into a heap, pretty much killed instantly. He slumped in a spreading pool of blood on the straw-and-dirt-covered floor of the barn.

Cav tossed a blanket at Cora. "Cover yourself. Get to the cabin and tell Belle we're leaving." He left his father there, the pitchfork still protruding from his back. He paused to think about what to do next, then followed Cora to the cabin.

"What are we going to do, Cav?" Cora had already run inside and shared the not-so-tragic news with Belle.

"I can't stay here. They'll hang me sure as shootin'." In the emotion of the moment, he was trying to be realistic about their circumstances, especially his own. "You two can't take care of this place by yourselves. You must leave. It doesn't mean anything to us anymore."

"But where do we go?"

Cav was trying to sort out his own next move. He'd begun gathering travel essentials, especially his father's guns. He took special care to pack his knives and wore one in a sheath on his belt. He threw extra clothes, venison jerky, coffee, and his all-important whetstone into his saddlebags. He'd travel light. Most important, he knew where his often-drunken father had stashed what little there was of the family fortune. He pried up a floor board and pulled out an old leather sack.

Cav poured the contents on the table and divided the lean bounty equally among the three of them. "Look, I'll guide you up to Bozeman," he told the girls. "There ain't much to the place, but I hear it's growing."

The girls started packing while Cav hitched up a couple of horses to the decrepit but serviceable wagon gathering dust behind the stable. He tied his father's best three horses behind the wagon and threw the tack in the wagon bed, along with his saddlebags and his sisters' bags.

Within the hour, they were on the rough trail to what there was of Bozeman, Montana. It took better than two days, but they made it. Cav saw to it that Cora and Belle were put up at the only boarding house in the town. Little did he know that the place doubled as a brothel. The weather was getting chilly, so he decided to spend a bit of his birthright on some clothes and a warm coat. He was partial to black, so he bought a black shirt, vest, bandana, and some black trousers. He already had a black hat.

After settling his sisters in, Cav stopped by the local saloon. He sidled up to the bar and ordered a whiskey. He'd never had whiskey before and was taken aback by the burn in his throat. He noticed the barkeep smile, as he likely often did when someone drank their first whiskey. Through whiskey-burned vocal chords, Cav asked advice. "If I was looking for opportunity a long ways from this place, where might I go?"

The barkeep was used to this. Normally, he'd advise going to the gold fields of California. He sensed a different sort of earnestness in this young man. "You're Cavendish's boy, aren't you?" He made eye contact. "Okay, you're leaving. If I were you, I'd head south to Arizona. You've gotta watch for savages, but that's just how it is. Oh,

NINE | LUCKY AT CARDS

and I'd get a deck of playing cards and learn how to play."

"Much obliged." Cav threw a coin on the bar.

"Your old man's all right, isn't he?"

"He's not well. Maybe someone could check on him after I leave."

Cav bid farewell to the barkeep and headed to the boarding house. His sisters were seated in the dining area. "You are going to be on your own now. I'll write to you when I can. I'm headed south to a place in Arizona. They call it Tucson. When I get settled, I'll send for you."

Somewhere deep inside, he doubted that would happen. It really wasn't in his constitution to be a caregiver. He'd especially avoided any emotional intimacy since his mother had passed. Cav loved his sisters, but only because he was supposed to. Besides, he'd witnessed their depravity with their father, and that tainted his feelings with a sense of pity.

Cora and Belle, at age sixteen and fifteen respectively, were quite comely young ladies and they'd be able to take care of themselves. It wouldn't be long before they'd be servicing the population of miners, hunters, and trappers, plus an occasional Crow Indian.

Cav knew what the girls would do. He could hardly blame them for the life choice they'd made. Maybe they'd find happiness with one of their customers.

He'd taken what he could of value from the ranch. Given that he'd murdered his father, the authorities would soon be looking for him. He didn't exactly cotton to jail time or possibly a hangman's noose, so he'd be heading far to the south. Tucson sounded increasingly attractive. As he looked outside at the turning leaves and hints of winter's onset, he rather looked forward to a warmer environment. Yes, Tucson would work.

He had taken the three horses from the ranch. Somehow, as he rode south, he managed to avoid the Arapahoe, Crow, and Lakota Sioux indigenous to the region. He had plenty of time to keep his knives sharp and to become fairly dexterous with the card deck.

He still had some of the money from his father's modest savings, but was concerned that he'd need more when he got to Tucson. It was while he was thinking about his need for more money that Lady Fortune took him across the path of a stalled train. He'd never done anything illegal other than kill his father, but this was an opportunity to quickly solve an immediate problem.

He calmly walked his horse along the tracks until he reached the train. It was then that he noticed the passengers were milling about outside and were in some distress. Seems they had been robbed. The train crew lay dead, along with a couple of passengers. Three others were wounded.

Cav pulled up to the group. "Howdy. What happened?"

"We…we was robbed. They blocked the train and rode down hard on us shooting and carrying on." The women were crying, and one was cradling the body of a man who apparently had been her husband.

A coldness swept over Cav. "Did they get all of your valuables?"

"No. But nearly so."

Cav drew one of his pistols. "Sorry for your misfortune, but I'll be happy to relieve you of the rest." He almost couldn't believe he was doing this. Yet it seemed natural to him, as though it were in his bones.

The passengers were incredulous, but too weary with the shock of what had already happened to them. They gave up what little they had left. Cav took their money, but left the watches and necklaces they offered.

One of the men decided he'd had enough. He inched over to one of the dead railroad men whose rifle lay beside him near the tracks.

Cav caught the man's movement out of the corner of his eye. "Don't!" Too late, the man reached for the rifle, and Cav put two bullets into him. He hadn't bargained for having to kill anyone. He'd become a train robber and now a murderer twice over in the span of a mere month's time.

It took him nearly three weeks, but he made it to Tucson, Arizona, which was part of an area that had recently been ceded to the United States from Mexico. There was a lot happening in Tucson, as it had become a gateway to the California Gold Rush and an important stage station on the San Antonio-San Diego Mail Line. He didn't hang there long, however, as he heard of riches to be had in the silver mines around nearby Tombstone. He had to watch for Apache and bandits roaming the area, but he found his way to the burgeoning town.

Tombstone was already the stuff of legend, as it had become a haven for reputed gunslingers and gamblers looking to make a quick fortune.

It was in Tombstone that Cav began to forge his reputation. It began one afternoon at a friendly card game. Cav had learned the rudiments of poker fairly quickly and enjoyed games with small pots. He didn't win a lot of money, but most folks could keep their tempers in check when the stakes weren't especially high.

Then it happened. One afternoon, Cav found himself sitting at a game with three other gentlemen. Early on, he sensed that the three knew each other but were pretending they didn't. It raised an alarm in his brain. They were all grizzled and disheveled, apparently from hard days on the trail.

Cav won a couple of hands, and then began to lose. After about a dozen more hands during which he'd lost about four dollars, a handsome sum at the time, he paused.

"Is there a problem, son?" The oldest of the three growled the question with a nearly toothless smile. He took a swig from a bottle of whiskey. He'd nearly finished the contents. Even watered down, the whiskey was likely potent.

Cav noticed these men were carrying impressive personal arsenals. Each had one or more pistols, and at least two of them had what appeared to be Bowie knives. "By chance, you fellas know each other?"

"Would that be a problem?"

Cav looked around the saloon. A couple of men at the bar had paused in their lavishing of affections on a scantily-clad woman to pay attention to the obvious discomfort that seemed to be brewing at Cav's table across the room.

"Just asking." Cav felt the handle of his own Walker Colt pressed against his ribs. Both of his hands were on the table. There was no way he could pull the gun quickly enough to take on one of these men, much less three.

"I'm not sure I like what you're implying."

Out of the corner of his eye, Cav saw the hand of the man on his left move toward his pistol.

"Let's not do something we might all regret later, gents." He slowly pushed away from the table. "Y'all have won quite a bit. Let's call it a day." He kept his hand above his waist to show he wasn't going for his gun as he started to stand.

The oldest of the three began to rise. He turned away and was slightly bent over, concealing his hand going to the gun in his waistband.

By this time, Cav's raised right hand dropped and his throwing knife found its way into the man's throat. With his left hand, he pulled the Colt from his holster. The other two men were slower to react and found themselves staring at the business end of Cav's Colt.

Cav carefully bent down and pulled the knife from the man's throat. There was an awful lot of blood. Cav had severed the man's carotid artery. He wiped the knife on the dead man's shirt. "I think we're done here. Y'all take your friend and git."

A deputy sheriff walked in just about the time the action was winding up. He had a shotgun in hand and leveled it at Cav.

"Put your gun down, son. You're under arrest."

The shotgun muzzle was no more than three feet from Cav. The other two card players backed away cautiously.

Another gunshot broke the stillness when Cav put a slug into the surprised deputy's chest. The lawman crumpled to the floor, flinched reflexively for a moment, and then bled out in the whiskey and sawdust.

"No one aims a gun at me." The words flowed natural-like from Cav. He holstered his Colt, sheathed his knife, and headed for the door. A man made a move to block his escape, but Cav stared him into retreating. Soon enough, he had saddled his horse, grabbed his remaining spare horse, and was heading out of Tombstone. He'd contributed significantly to the town's reputation and lore as the scene of much gambling and many gunfights. He rode slowly past the O.K. Corral, which would one day become legendary.

He headed east through Apache country. Amazingly, Cav avoided at least two war parties. His Sioux blood likely wouldn't have been worth a tinker's damn to an Apache or Comanche, or even a Kiowa, for that matter. He had the good sense not to build any fires, despite the cooling temperatures.

He managed to waylay a mail carrier by setting up a trip line. The horse and rider tumbled but were not seriously hurt. The pickings were slim. There was nothing of value in the letters Cav bothered to open. He considered killing the rider, but thought better of it. The man was already scared to death. All told, Cav rode away with about ten dollars. He decided that robbing mail carriers wasn't worth the trouble.

Soon enough, he'd made it through the rugged mountains of eastern New Mexico and arrived in El Paso. After finding a place to spend the night, he penned a letter to Cora and Belle. He assumed they were still in Bozeman. It was his usual chicken scrawl, as he'd not really learned to write properly. He basically let them know that he had left Arizona and was still alive. He sincerely hoped his sisters were doing well and that they might have found men to change their lives for the better.

He'd heard there were opportunities in Corpus Christi, as it was becoming a port of some repute. Consequently, after a few uneventful and profitable games of poker in El Paso, he soon found himself tracing the Rio Grande toward Laredo from whence he could strike a trail due east to the port city. He'd been a bit uncomfortable in El Paso when he saw a wanted leaflet posted at the mail station with his name on it. It showed a $200 reward for the murderer of a deputy sheriff in Tombstone. Cav was impressed that anyone would risk life and limb to chase him for that much money.

As he entered Laredo, he waved friendly-like at some man leaving hurriedly. He couldn't know that he'd passed a man with an even greater price on his head. Cav wound up at a hole-in-the-wall place called Texas Jack's Saloon. It had just about the right sort of pass-through clientele to help him sharpen his card playing. Laredo was okay, but he wanted more. He wasn't certain just what he was seeking, but he sensed he wouldn't find whatever it was in this town.

TEN

A Wild Card

Strong decided to slow down to permit Luke to close the gap on him. He didn't want to have to wait too long once he'd set his trap. Ambush was his style, after all. He stayed away from any ranches and homesteads such as they were along the route toward San Ygnacio.

San Ygnacio was originally a Mexican pueblo founded by settlers from nearby Guerrero, Tamaulipas in Mexico around 1830. The town had suffered frequent Comanche and Apache attacks that necessitated the use of stone architecture for defensive purposes. San Ygnacio earned notoriety in 1839 as the place where plans were laid for the short-lived and failed revolution of the Rio Grande Republic.

Bad Bart knew he had a price on his head, having seen the poster at the post office back in Corpus Christi. The reward was likely to have increased by now. In fact, it was plausible that the Texas Ranger captain wasn't the only one chasing him. There were some folks who made a living bounty hunting, whether collecting animal varmint pelts, Indian scalps, or lawbreakers on the run like Strong.

He had no intention of getting so far as the town itself. He finally found the perfect location for an ambush and hunkered down to wait for Luke. The place was high enough to afford him a view out over a couple of miles of prairie, and the natural rock outcropping offered enough cover to build a small fire without being detected. The grasses were tall, but not so tall that you couldn't see a rider on the trail.

He bided his time. He'd have to be patient, and that would likely only last so long as his food held out.

Luke and his entourage of three rode within sight of Laredo. Three Toes stayed at a small encampment they set up to the east of the town. It wouldn't do for him to be seen in Laredo, what with the locals' sensitivity to Comanche. The Penateka had raided Laredo and its outskirts several times in past years, killing settlers and stealing livestock. The Comanche even had the audacity to try to sell the stolen cattle back to their former owners. In any case, Three Toes would stay clear. He recalled that his pony was one of those stolen from a Laredo rancher a year earlier.

Clyde rode beside Luke. They gave off little doubt that they were Texas Rangers. There was simply a commanding "we're the law" look about them. Most town folk were pleased to see them, despite issues the previous year over the Callahan matter. Most of the citizens who had an issue with that incident had moved across the Rio Grande to Nuevo Laredo.

Luke and Clyde pulled up in front of Texas Jack's Saloon, dismounted casually, and tied their horses to the hitching rail. Luke felt in his bones that Strong had been there but was likely gone. He had a sense for these sorts of things.

They climbed the steps and strode into the saloon. Luke went to the right and Clyde to the left as they scanned the space. Clyde did a quick check of the room. There was a man dressed in black playing cards at a table at the back of the room. A trio of Mexicans closer at hand were drinking and laughing at crude jokes. Their table had one shorter leg and tended to rock during their fits of mirth. Two cowboys were seated on stools at the bar, sipping whiskey, and flirting with some sexily clad women. The wooden walls were permeated with odors of alcohol, sweat, and sex.

Clyde stopped just beyond the door and stood rear guard just in case. Luke eased over to the bar. He swept his duster back a bit so his badge and Walker Colt showed clearly. He tipped his hat to two cowboys standing at the bar.

"How are you gents?"

It wasn't usual for people to be poking their noses into other people's business without being asked, so Luke's question was unexpected. The two cowboys nodded and turned to the bar away from Luke.

Luke persisted. "My name is Captain Luke Dunn. I'm a Texas Ranger, and I'm looking for someone."

One of the cowboys slowly turned to face Luke. "Something in it for us?"

"Depends on how good your information is." Luke at least had the cowboy's attention. "I'm looking for a man named Bart Strong."

The cowboy leaned back, and the second cowboy joined in. "Shucks, Captain, you missed that murdering thief by a day. He killed one of our finest citizens and then killed the deputy sheriff."

Luke shook his head over the loss of the lawman but was pleased he'd made up enough ground to be only a day behind Strong. "Much obliged. When I collect the reward, I'll be sure to share it."

"How about sharing now?" The words were blurted out in a tone that suggested a challenge.

Luke stepped back from the bar and threw two bits on the counter. "Consider that a down payment, boys. Enjoy a drink on me." Trouble was the last thing he wanted.

The two looked quizzically at each other, trying to decide whether to continue to challenge Luke.

"You guys look to be too smart to start trouble for trouble's sake. Again, my name is Luke Dunn. I'm good for my word."

The two decided that discretion was the better part of valor. They nodded to Luke, wished him luck finding Strong, and turned to the bar to enjoy newly poured drinks.

"Clyde, let's go." Luke wasn't going to waste time hanging in Laredo if Strong had already left town.

They took one more look around and headed out the door to their horses. As they reached the hitching rail, Clyde paused. "Luke, did you see that fella in the back dressed in black? I think I read something about him. He might be that outlaw Dirk Cavendish."

"Well, he was gone when we left. Must have slipped out the back door. I suspect he'll still be around after we finish up with Strong." Luke seemed at least outwardly unconcerned. "Let's get back to Three Toes. We'll get started after Strong in the morning."

Clyde shrugged. Long Luke could just as well have been nicknamed Quiet Luke so far as he was concerned. The man didn't waste time with idle conversation. They rode in silence to their little encampment just outside of Laredo.

Three Toes had a fire going and was cooking up what appeared to be deer. A bit of venison sounded right good to the Rangers.

"Good news in Laredo?" Three Toes wasn't exactly a conversationalist either.

"Strong's headed south toward San Ygnacio."

"Not good. Plenty cover for ambush." Three Toes stated the obvious.

Luke appeared to ponder that for a moment. "He won't go so far as the town. We'll swing wide east and then circle back to approach from the south. He won't be looking for us from that direction."

"Dang, Luke, that makes sense." Clyde figured Luke had been conjuring up some sort of plan during the short ride from Laredo to their camp.

Three Toes said, "We should divide and conquer. It's an old Comanche way."

Luke smiled respectfully. "I like that, my friend." He unsaddled the big grey and placed the saddle on the ground near Three Toes.

"Clyde, you're goin' to be bait."

Clyde's expression turned. He wasn't smiling at Luke's strategic genius. "You want me to be what?"

"I want you to come in from the north and kick up a bit of trail dust." He understood Clyde's hesitation. "You're a Texas Ranger, Clyde. You can handle this."

Clyde was all too aware that Strong was known to fell a target from as far as five hundred yards out and didn't even have one of those new-fangled telescope sights on his rifle.

"We'll be on him afore he draws a bead on you, Clyde," Luke assured him.

Three Toes lifted the spit from the fire. The venison sizzled and dripped just a bit of blood. Tearing off chunks of meat for Luke and Clyde, he grinned broadly. In a way, he didn't miss the responsibility of dealing with a tribal council and keeping his wives happy. He could enjoy much-anticipated spirited sex with them after he was finished with this new-found adventure. Besides, he appreciated the opportunity to learn a bit more of the white man's way.

"Three Toes head west to big river, then follow trail south." He was telling Luke that he'd parallel the road to San Ygnacio. The escarpments that would afford cover for Strong tended to be west of that road. Everyone nodded approval. A plan to get Bad Bart Strong had evolved. They'd capture or kill, depending on Strong's resistance. Either way, the outlaw would likely wind up a dead man.

Strong kept watch in between naps and stoking a small fire. He was about five hours' ride south of Laredo, so figured Luke would show up soon enough. Other than brewing coffee, chewing on jerky, and occasionally leaving his roost to relieve himself, he was resolved to simply wait for his prey. The trail that Luke would likely take was within two hundred yards and at a lower elevation. It was an easy shot for an excellent marksman like himself.

ELEVEN

Ambush

"*Donde nos dirigimos, jefe?*" One of the bandits asked where they were headed.

Carlos Perez leveled his remaining eye on the men. He scanned the eight bandits that rode with him. "*Quién dijo que?*" he responded with great irritation. Who had the temerity to speak without being asked?

No one owned up.

"*Tenemos una puntuación que resolver, amigos.*" Perez reminded them that they had a score to settle. Implied was the command to simply follow unquestioningly.

Nine bandits plus spare mounts and a couple of pack mules made for a serious entourage. There was no question they were looking for trouble. They'd crossed the Rio Grande down near San Ygnacio and headed north. Perez had heard their quarry was headed to Laredo, and he had revenge on his mind. He hadn't forgotten the incident in Corpus Christi. A ricochet bullet from Luke's shooting at him had cost Perez his left eye as he'd made his escape. The wounded horse and lost member of his band were but collateral damage. He wore a black patch as a constant reminder of his loss.

From his vantage point hidden behind the saloon, Cav watched Luke and Clyde leave. He breathed a sigh of relief. His plan was to head due east in the morning. In a few days, he'd arrive at Corpus Christi and seek further fortune. That assumed all went well. There was no telling what manner of difficulty he might encounter along the way. Now that he was a wanted man, he'd have to be alert for bounty hunters. They could be right mean.

Meanwhile, with the Texas Rangers gone, he figured to have a few hours to kill before heading out. Cav went back into the saloon and scanned the local ladies. There was still a young lady flirting with the two cowboys at the bar, and another teasing an older man at a table in the back. Some would consider her a ravishing beauty with her high cheek-boned classic facial lines and long red hair. Yep, she was right attractive. As Cav bellied up to the bar, he tipped his hat to her.

The young lady was intrigued by the man in black. Something about him pulled at her. There was a mystery that seemed to surround this man. Maybe it was the black, maybe the thin mustache, maybe the look in his eyes.

Cav turned to the bar as if to ignore her.

Of a sudden she was next to him. "What you up to, mister?"

"Care to join me for a drink?" Cav asked.

"Sure. My name is Scarlett." She gave him her sexiest smile. "You just here to drink?"

"Been on the trail a long time. What do you have in mind?" Something about her reminded him of his sister Belle. There was a toughness borne of too many men but also a vulnerability.

The barkeeper slid a key toward Scarlett. As was often the case, he likely took a cut of whatever she earned by her trade. Barkeeps often as not were pimps as well as bartenders.

Scarlett tugged gently at Cav's arm. "Come along, big guy." She yearned to learn more about the stranger, but first things first.

Upon entering the room, she'd barely had time to close the door behind them when Cav had her nearly stripped naked. It's what Cav knew. He'd seen his father do it to Cora and Belle. Scarlett liked to play a little rough, so Cav's technique worked for her. He lowered her onto the bed and slid on top of her between her parted legs. Soon enough, he had completed his business and began to get ready to leave.

"Where you going? What's your name? You gonna be in Laredo long?" She earnestly wanted answers.

Cav looked her over, taking her in almost dispassionately. It brought back the memory of Cora trying to slip into his bed. He had an urge to hit Scarlett, but held back. "You don't need to know my name or where I'm headed. It'll likely be to hell anyway."

She was taken aback. Sex with Cav had been intense, not much tenderness but tremendous passion. She loved it. Now, he seemed aloof. He wasn't like other men she'd had, the young ones meeting raw biological urges or older ones trying to recapture long-lost youth. There was a sense of mystery that intrigued her, that pulled her toward him. "You can spend the night here, if you like."

He paused to consider her offer as he finished buttoning his shirt. "I'm heading out to Corpus Christi first thing in the morning." He took in her nakedness, barely covered with a silk sheet, and shrugged. He leaned over and began to pull on his boots, but then pulled them back off. "You gonna let me sleep?"

Scarlett laughed quietly. She didn't want the ladies in the adjoining rooms to think she was having too much fun. "Sure, you can sleep, so long as you pleasure me again in the morning."

"My name is Cav." He laid down beside her and went to sleep.

Luke knew Clyde would wait about an hour for Luke and Three Toes to get well ahead of him before starting on the trail to San Ygnacio. He sure didn't like the idea of being bait. He'd be in the line of fire if he ran into the expected ambush before Luke found Strong's hiding place.

Luke had ridden south, taking a path that was far to the east of the road. He judged that Strong wouldn't go too far to lay his trap. It was terribly hot. His bandana was soaked, and his shirt was so wet with sweat that it stuck to his back. His wounded hand was overheating from the bandage. He decided to lighten up the dressing. It had been several days since Doc had stitched him up, and he figured it was getting close to healed.

He unwrapped the bandage and was momentarily taken aback by the damp, wrinkled-looking skin. Drying out in the fresh air would do it good. As he thought about turning west to pick up the trail that would take him north back toward Laredo, Three Toes appeared seemingly from thin air. Luke was momentarily startled by the chief showing up so unexpectedly. "Three Toes? I thought you'd be west of here."

"Found Strong." Three Toes smiled with pride, as if he'd found a sweet and enjoyed sucking on it. "Was too easy."

"Where is he?"

"Hiding in rock cave to north. Not far." It was the chief's usual cryptic response.

Luke was pleased, but immediately concerned for Clyde's safety. He hadn't really expected Strong to still be so far north. He wished he could warn Clyde, but that wouldn't work without giving away their advantage. "Let's stay west of the San Ygnacio road but within sight of it. You lead the way, Chief."

They spent the next half hour dismounted, keeping the horses at a walk and the dust to a minimum. Slow and careful was essential. The only surprise they sought was the one they'd spring on Bart Strong.

As he stepped around cactus and clumps of prairie grass, Luke couldn't help but think on what had brought him to this place in time. He and Three Toes necessarily remained silent so as to minimize sound. He'd even removed his spurs and stowed them in his saddlebag. Back as a mere boy in Ireland, he could never have dreamed of this life in Texas. His sense of propriety and yearning for justice had turned him to becoming a lawman, a person to help keep the world a morally straight place. He'd become wed to the wild lure of the Nueces Strip. Now, he'd begun to have a hint of feelings for someone. It was a new sensation.

He stole glances over at Three Toes to be sure they were moving at a similar pace. They stayed ever alert. Falling into a Bart Strong ambush was not an option. Strong's nearly successful attempt up near Nuecestown remained fresh in his mind.

Mid-afternoon, Bart Strong saw a bit of dust kicking up nearly a mile off. It was a clear day. If Luke Dunn was kicking up that dust, he'd be a dead man inside the hour.

Not too long later, Strong saw that tell-tale Texas Ranger-style hat emerge from the trail dust. He assumed it was Luke. He stood and rested the barrel of the rifle on a rock shelf at shoulder height. There was no wind, and the distance was near enough to require very little adjustment. The target was moving very slowly. He took aim about a foot and a half below the hat, and inhaled deeply. He exhaled, squeezing the trigger. He saw the target fall from the saddle and disappear behind the tall grasses. The horse emerged and walked around aimlessly.

Strong was dying to know who he'd shot and whether the man was dead. He was concerned that he didn't see a big grey horse like Luke's, but his quarry could have switched mounts back in Laredo. Not knowing gnawed at Strong. He simply had to be certain of his kill. So far as he knew, Luke was traveling alone. If it was the Texas Ranger, he'd not only be safe; he'd have established himself as a legend on the frontier.

He cautiously poked his head from the escarpment and looked around. Revealing a hiding place in this country could prove fatal. He had no way of knowing there had been three pursuers. His curiosity outweighed caution. If it was Luke Dunn that he'd shot, he'd have no concerns. He had to know.

Near bursting with curiosity and sweating in the summer heat, he cautiously climbed out of his hiding place and carefully headed down the slope. He saw a riderless horse walking in circles. Soon enough, he was standing over Clyde's inert form. "Damn!" Bart thought.

Clyde was still breathing. His breathing was shallow from the lung shot, and he'd likely soon bleed out. He twisted with pain and looked pleadingly at Strong. The outlaw threw caution to the wind, aimed carefully, and put a bullet in the Ranger's head. It was a touch of mercy from somewhere deep within Strong's perverted soul.

Once Strong realized that this was a Texas Ranger but not Luke Dunn, he headed back at a run toward his lair. It was a fair bet that this man had joined up with Dunn, and the Ranger could be lurking somewhere nearby. Bart feared it could have been a trap, with the man he'd shot as the unfortunate bait.

Moving uphill was slower and made more difficult by the rocky terrain. Sweat kept getting in his eyes. He swiped his face with his bandana. Just a bit of panic was setting in. His shots would have given away his position. If Luke was anywhere in the vicinity, Strong would now be vulnerable. He needed to get to the relative security of the cave. It had been stupid to check on the man he'd shot. A sixth sense had told him it wasn't Luke. He should have stuck with his instinct. Now, he was in great danger. Luke couldn't be very far. He strove to stay low and moved as quickly as he dared. He'd almost reached the relative safety of his hiding place when a voice stopped him cold in his tracks.

"Halt!"

Luke and Three Toes had heard what was clearly a rifle shot ahead of them and not that far off. Luke prayed it wasn't a shot at Clyde. Strong could have killed him just for sport, or even mistaken Clyde for Luke. They quickened their pace to more rapidly close the distance.

The two were soon close enough to tie the horses to a mesquite tree and move forward at a running crouch. According to Three Toes, they should be about two hundred yards south of Strong's roost. The breeze, such as it was, wafted down from the northwest, so they'd be downwind. They ran north, staying roughly twenty feet apart. Three Toes pulled an arrow from his quiver and nocked it to his bow. Finally, he pulled up and signaled Luke to slow down.

Then they heard the second gunshot. Now Luke feared the worst for Clyde. It was from a pistol, and that was a sign of a finish shot, to be certain of a kill. They stayed low but moved at an even more hurried pace.

"Halt!" the Ranger said again.

Damnable luck. Bart began to turn toward the sound.

"Bart Strong, I do believe." Luke had a bead drawn on him with the Walker Colt held steady in his left hand. His right was still too tender to handle firing a virtual cannon like the Colt. "I'm Captain Luke Dunn, Texas Rangers, and you are under arrest."

Strong held his revolver at his side. At shoulder level to his right was the rock outcropping he'd used to steady his rifle for the shot at Clyde Jones. Slowly, ever so slowly, he turned to face Luke. The veins on his neck bulged from heat, exertion, and stress. The Ranger had him dead to rights.

"Don't move a muscle, Strong." Luke saw what Strong could not.

Strong didn't realize Luke's command was more than a warning not to shoot. He sneered with venomous hatred, cocked his head, and raised his own Colt. At the precise moment of the upward movement of his revolver, the rattlesnake on the rock outcropping struck him full in his neck. The fangs penetrated deeply into Strong's throat, straight into the carotid artery. The full load of rattlesnake venom was released.

A look of sheer horror swept across the outlaw's face. He fired one shot wildly into the sky as he swept the rattler away with his free hand. He had become a dead man standing. The blood seemed to drain from him as he dropped to his knees with the realization that he couldn't be saved from his fate.

The last thing he saw in his consciousness was the snake slithering away. It had lost its rattles. There had been no warning. The venom acted far more swiftly than if it had been a bite in a leg or hand. The toxins in the bite worked quickly to begin to destroy Strong's circulatory system as he began to hemorrhage internally. The venom was already working to immobilize his nervous system. He was racked with involuntary seizures. His breathing turned to shallow, rapid gasps, and then stopped as if he had been choked to death. He fell face first into the dust.

Three Toes had moved beside Luke to watch the venom work. Going through the Comanche's mind was how strong Luke's medicine was that a serpent had been sent to destroy the evil-doer. Indeed, this was a powerful sign.

Soon enough, Strong was finished. In the end, he'd not even been able to say anything, much less fire his gun at Luke. His vaunted marksmanship didn't matter. It was an ignominious finish for a craven killer.

Luke shrugged, took another long look at Strong's body, and walked down the hill to see to Clyde. Three Toes helped himself to Strong's scalp. Luke wasn't pleased with that but tried to be understanding.

He reached Clyde's body. As he'd suspected, Strong's first shot had knocked Clyde from the saddle and immobilized him. It was a lung shot just below and to the right of his heart and had apparently continued clean through, partially severing his spine. The merciful finish had been a shot to the head. Clyde's horse now stood idly nearby.

Luke and Three Toes buried Clyde out there on a rise in the escarpment. They covered the shallow grave with rocks to discourage scavengers. Luke said a brief prayer, placed Clyde's personal effects in a saddlebag, and threw the bag behind the saddle of his big grey stallion. They took Clyde's and Strong's horses in tow, having slung the outlaw's body over one.

Strong's body was already beginning to swell from the toxins. They headed north back toward Laredo, where Luke could deposit Strong's body and get credit for the bounty. He could send a message by courier to Captain Ford that his mission had been accomplished. Luke hoped the news might inspire some action in Austin to reconstitute the Texas Rangers.

As they began to depart, Luke pulled up. "Three Toes, you don't have to go back to Laredo with me. Go in peace back to your people and tell the story of your adventure." Luke knew it would make for a great tale when shared around a tribal campfire. He pretty much figured that Three Toes would properly embellish the story. It was as though the Comanche had just a touch of what the Irish might call blarney. Luke handed Three Toes the lead to Clyde's horse. "Take this horse as a gift of thanks for your help."

"I have been honored to ride with you, Luke Dunn. You have strong medicine. I will tell my people to protect Ghost-Who-Rides. Go, and ride with the spirits." Three Toes then turned his pony eastward toward his Penateka Comanche encampment and moved off with Clyde's horse in tow. His adventure with the Texas Ranger had far exceeded his expectations.

Luke began the trek to Laredo to turn in Strong's body. By now, it was an ugly, blackening, bloated mess. The venom had done its work quite efficiently. While he was saddened by the loss of Clyde Jones, Luke felt blessed to have avoided further bloodshed. He figured he'd spend the night in Laredo and head back east toward Nuecestown in the morning.

When he got to Laredo, he pulled up in front of Texas Jack's Saloon. He tied the big grey to the rail and then walked the fifty feet or so across the street with the roan behind him carrying Strong's now grossly deformed body. The horse had become skittish, likely as not from the pungent odor of Strong's remains.

Luke banged on the door. "Sheriff Stills, I've got a very special present for you!"

Stills opened the door and stepped out on the little gallery across the front of the building. "Why, Luke Dunn! Whatcha got there, Ranger?" He peered past Luke at what was draped over the roan. He could smell it from where he was standing

"This here's a fella named Bad Bart Strong. He ain't so bad anymore."

"Holy crap, Luke. He don't even resemble the fella in the wanted poster description." Stills held a bandana over his nose and examined the body from a distance. "Where's his hair? Don't look like you had to shoot the varmint." The corpse reeked so that the sheriff's eyes were beginning to water.

"Rattlesnake will tend to mess a body up, Sheriff. I had Strong in my sights, but the rattlesnake did the job. As to his hair, I had a helper who wanted a souvenir. You won't find any bullet holes in his sorry carcass."

"Shoot, Dunn, what was he? Apache? Comanche?" Sheriff Stills had a thing for how the various tribes scalped their victims. Some took strips of scalp, others took bigger pieces. This looked suspiciously like a Comanche scalping.

"Close, Sheriff. Let's just say he was a big help and deserved a reward." Luke was tired and the bit of banter that Stills was throwing at him wasn't all that humorous. "Sheriff, I lost a Texas Ranger on this manhunt. I hear you lost a deputy a bit ago. I just want to turn Strong in for the record so I can collect the bounty."

Sheriff Stills rightly judged that he'd better end his game of feigned doubt as to Strong's identity. He'd heard of Luke's reputation when he got seriously irritated. In fact, it was apparently a trait with the man's entire family. These Irish immigrants only joked around when they drank.

"You've hit the jackpot, Luke. The bounty on Strong was upped to three hundred fifty dollars just yesterday." His voice was slightly muffled, owing to keeping his mouth and nose covered with the bandana.

Luke handed the roan's reins to the sheriff and strode back across the street to Texas Jack's Saloon.

There were about a half dozen men inside and half of those were Mexicans. Four young ladies were receiving a lot of attention. One, a redhead with a freckled face, was right pretty. Luke tipped his hat to her as he sidled up to the bar. Soon enough, she left the table where she had been seated while enjoying the attentions of a couple of cowboys and sashayed across the room to check on the big hunk of a man that had just walked into the saloon.

Luke was not exactly aromatic, but then, neither were the others in the saloon. He ordered a whiskey. He rarely drank but figured he'd earned this one.

"Hi, my name is Scarlett. How are you, mister?" The little redhead was no shrinking violet. "You lookin' for love?" She got right to business.

Luke looked at her and took a deep breath. The images of Clyde lying dead in the dirt and the bloated body of Bart Strong weighed heavily on his soul. His just wanted to sip the whiskey and find a reasonably comfortable bed to catch some shut-eye before heading out to Nuecestown in the morning. It had been a long time since he'd had a woman, and that had been someone back in County Kildare that truly mattered.

"Sweetheart," he said, "you are indeed a pretty little gal, but I'm really not up to whatever you're offering."

She feigned insult. "Why, you sonofabitch, did you think I'd go to bed with you?! I ain't no two-bit whore!" She placed her hands on her hips and slinked back to the gaming table.

Luke turned to the bar. She wasn't worth arguing with. Turned out the pretty little thing had a trash mouth, anyway.

The saloonkeeper leaned toward Luke and handed him a brass key. "Up the stairs and first door on the left, sir. Should be pretty quiet tonight."

Luke didn't waste any time. He took a scan of the bar to be sure there was no trouble brewing, went upstairs, and plopped himself in the bed. He did give a passing thought to that man in black that Clyde had pointed out. He'd have to check on that one. He thought he'd go right to sleep. He certainly was tired enough.

He wondered how that little lady he'd helped in Nuecestown was making out. Was she working the farm? Had she had any more problems with Comanche? How was her little brother? Why was Luke even thinking about her? She was only sixteen. He simply didn't need thoughts of women on his mind at this time in his life. It was inconvenient.

When he awakened in the morning, he headed downstairs to a nearly empty saloon. Only the barkeeper was around. He had gotten up early to clean up a bit.

"Where can I find some grub this morning, barkeep?" Luke asked.

The barkeeper pointed him to a place across the street. "The lady that owns the boarding house across the street can fix some great bacon and biscuits, Mr. Dunn. I'll be heading over there myself shortly. That was fine work you did with Mr. Strong."

Luke didn't quite know what to make of the barkeeper addressing him by name. Apparently, he was building some sort of reputation as a lawman.

TWELVE

Nuecestown

It had been a couple of weeks since the Comanche attack on her farm. Elisa was working at picking up the pieces of her life. Every now and then, she'd succumb to a crying spell as grief overwhelmed her. But these episodes became fewer. Eventually, she found the need to head to Nuecestown for a few supplies.

Doc had come out once to check on her and Mike. Her brother was healing well, and the bump on his noggin had all but totally disappeared. In fact, Mike was becoming a solid helper with chores around the cabin. Elisa even started to teach him about the rifle and how to aim and shoot it. They were low on ammunition, so they didn't do a lot of actual shooting.

Her nights had been difficult mostly. Despite young Mike being around, there was a palpable loneliness. She struggled with getting the image of Bear Slayer out of her mind. She finally found that the only thoughts that gave her peace and drove the fear and sadness from her dreams were of Luke Dunn. Would he return? Would he be attracted enough to see her as more than a young girl? Would he realize that she was a woman, not a girl?

She recalled standing against him after the Comanche attack at her father's funeral. She dreamed of what it might feel like to hold him truly close to her and what might a kiss be like? She'd never kissed a man on the lips before. Nor had any man deigned to kiss her. The boys in Nuecestown were a bit wary, even intimidated, by the strength of this teenage woman who'd fought off Comanche and was running a farm single-handedly.

She hitched the wagon and boosted Mike into the seat. The mules seemed to understand where they were headed and needed very little urging. The five-mile trip into Nuecestown was uneventful except for chasing longhorns off the road once or twice.

Bernice was first to see her enter the town. She waved at Elisa as the girl drove the wagon on by and pulled up in front of Colonel Kinney's little general store. By little, it was just that it didn't feature a huge inventory. It offered only the most basic necessities of tools, food, cloth, and the like. Occasionally, something special would be sent, like ladies' dresses or men's cowboy hats or some sweet-smelling bath salts.

Elisa climbed from the wagon and helped Mike down. "You can come inside, but don't go touching things."

She encountered Doc as she was about to climb the steps to the general store.

"Good day, Elisa. I see Mike's getting back to his old self. How's your farm these days?"

"Thanks, Doc. I finally had to come into town to pick up supplies. I did manage to sell some feed to the neighbors." She paused for a moment. "Have you heard anything from Captain Dunn?" She tried to be nonchalant, though her heart was beating madly with hope of good news.

"Word has it that he brought that Strong fella to justice, if that's what you mean."

Elisa's facial expression said it all. She was pleased with the news. Doc understood these things. "In case you're wondering, I have heard that he's headed back to Corpus Christi. Likely, he'll come through Nuecestown."

Her heart felt like it was about to burst from her chest. "Thanks, Doc. Thanks so much."

She distractedly went into the general store to shop. She'd want herself and her farm to be at their very best when Luke Dunn came to pay a visit. That bolt of pretty blue cotton fabric could be turned into a lovely dress that might turn Luke's head. She decided to splurge and bought a couple of yards. She had her mother's sewing needles and plenty of spools of thread.

Dirk Cavendish was gone from Laredo by the time Luke returned with Strong's carcass. He decided to ditch his all-black attire, as it was attracting far too much attention. It was even part of the description on his wanted poster. He decided a lower profile was in order. He even shaved off the mustache.

He'd managed a final roll in the bed with Scarlett before he departed. He was a bit put off at what seemed to be a certain attachment to him. He didn't need a woman in his life at the moment.

He decided to take it easy, switching mounts every ten miles or so. As it was, the journey would take the better part of a week if all went well. He'd have to be vigilant for Comanche and Apache, not to mention Mexican and Anglo bandits. He figured there likely wouldn't be many lawmen on the prairie. He thought about following the road from Laredo to Corpus Christi, but feared running into the law. He took a parallel route a mile or so to the south. It was rougher terrain, but he felt it made for safer travel.

Cav hoped Cora and Belle had received his letters up in Bozeman. He lamented that he wasn't there to protect them, though what common sense he had recognized that they'd made their own choices.

He couldn't know that young Belle had already met her end, caught in the crossfire of a saloon gunfight. Moreover, Cora had gotten herself pregnant with some itinerant cowboy's contribution. The sisters had grown up far too fast. All of the Cavendish kids had matured faster than most; that is, if it could be called maturity.

Bozeman, Montana was a hellhole by any description. Trappers, miners, whores, and cowboys pretty much defined its population. Poor Belle Cavendish was trying to give up her whoring ways and had taken up with a miner named Pete Wickers, who'd made a modest strike and offered promise of a good life for her. Likely, the promise was made for the base purpose of getting into her bed, as he had a family back east in Philadelphia. Unfortunately, he liked to gamble at cards. One night he clumsily tried to cheat. Belle had seen the man opposite him at the table take offense and pull a gun. She stepped in front of Pete and took the bullet meant for him.

Cora sought escape, too. Despite the tragic ends that many whores met, she felt she'd found her man. He claimed to have a spread on the other side of the Absaroka Range, though no one could confirm that. He had his way with her, got her with child, and then excused himself to take care of some ranching business. He promised to return before the birth. Whether he was telling the truth about returning would never be known, as he was killed by a Sioux hunting party a mere two days from Bozeman. Cora wouldn't find out until weeks later, when his personal effects were brought to town.

Cav pushed on toward Corpus Christi, oblivious to the fate of his sisters. They were the only humans in his life that he cared about, and he was losing them as surely as he'd lost his own soul.

He had learned to be ever more trail-savvy, as the trek from faraway Montana demanded much from any man. Aside from wolves, bears, and poisonous snakes, Cav learned to be on the lookout for Indians, lawmen, and bounty hunters. He traveled light, eventually even selling off one of his two spare horses at a mail way station. He kept his knives sharp, his pistol loaded, and his cards at the ready.

It made for an interesting confluence of purposes that Luke, Cav, and Perez and his gang would all eventually be simultaneously following the trail to Corpus Christi, yet unaware of each other's presence. Such was the vastness of the Nueces Strip and the vagaries of fate.

Perez rode into Laredo a few hours after Luke had started down the trail back to Corpus Christi. With eight men in his gang of bandits and flush with money from the sale of stolen cattle, he was feeling especially cocky and ready to relax and have some fun before heading east.

Perez's gang rode straight into town and went directly to the livery to stable their horses. Next stop was Texas Jack's Saloon. They didn't even pause to clean up from the dusty trail. Whiskey and women were first and foremost on their minds.

Scarlett and the other women were not enthusiastic about their new visitors. They hated whoring with most Mexicans. This bunch hadn't even bothered to clean themselves up, so the ladies would be suffocated by the trail odors of horse manure, sweat, and damp leather.

Scarlett thought about sneaking out the back door. Perhaps she could catch up with Cav. Perez saw her and would not tolerate her leaving. Now, she recognized him from months earlier, when Captain Callahan had chased him and his gang through town. He'd taken her for the proverbial quickie, and it was clear that he remembered her and was now aiming to repeat his previous dalliance.

"*Yo, pelirrojo. A dónde vas?*" He stood with his slightly bowed legs wide and hands on his hips. He motioned the pretty redhead to join him at the table with two of his gang. As Scarlett reluctantly moved toward him, he poured two whiskeys. "*Rápido, aqui. Beber.*"

Scarlett moved toward him as he asked, and took the glass of whiskey he offered. She figured she'd need more than one to endure this man. She felt his ugliness ripple like a shudder through her body. The black eye patch only added to his repulsiveness. He'd lost most of his teeth, so his smile was like the opening of a black maw surrounded by thin dark lips. The barkeep brought another bottle and slipped a room key to her.

A couple of drinks later, Perez excused himself, grabbed Scarlett roughly by the arm, and pulled her along up the stairs. There was no question of his intentions or his drunkenness. Perez hurried her along, staggering drunkenly. He was rough and stunk to high heaven.

Once inside the room, Perez wasted no time. He had just enough to drink that he had trouble getting aroused. Nevertheless, he threw back her petticoats and unbuttoned himself. He stood over her, looked at her, and then looked down at himself. Nothing was happening. The room seemed to spin around him.

Scarlett knew what she needed to do, but didn't want to do it. It would be especially disgusting.

Perez pointed to his privates. *"Béseme!"* He smiled and puckered his lips. *"Béseme ahora!"* He thrust his flaccid member toward her while teetering in his drunkenness, as the whiskey began to have its full affect.

The thought of kissing that thing was even more repulsive. But, as Scarlett reached for him, she watched with relief as he passed out and crumpled to the floor. A chill of loathing coursed through her. She was determined to be far away from Laredo when he awoke. She hoped to catch the early stage to Corpus Christi.

Scarlett still had the man in black on her mind. Few of her customers left any lasting impressions, but Cav had. Perhaps she could catch up with the man in black. She began to stuff personal effects into her satchel. She needed to get away fast.

Having gotten all the supplies she needed from the general store and the information on Luke she'd hoped for, Elisa hustled Mike back up onto the wagon and headed back to the farm. She felt uplifted and hopeful that her feelings for the Texas Ranger captain might be reciprocated.

She had to focus for the present on reaping a small but profitable harvest. Fortunately, Sheriff Whelan hadn't visited. In fact, no one in Nuecestown had seen him for a couple of weeks. Elisa figured he must be keeping the ladies of Corpus Christi satisfied.

She pulled the rig up in front of the cabin to facilitate unloading supplies. Mike was just big enough to be of some help. His arrow wound had just about fully healed, though the poor child was still having nightmares about the Comanche attack. He definitely missed his mother and, try as she might, Elisa was simply no substitute there. Mike would need a father, too. Elisa could hope.

As she began to lead the emptied rig back toward the corral, she noticed a saddled horse tied to one of the corral posts. When did that arrive and where was the rider? She stopped and went back to the house to retrieve her Walker Colt. Upon her return to the rig, she was faced with none other than Sheriff George Whelan. She let out a small but audible sigh of resignation at having to deal with the sheriff.

"Miss Corrigan. I'm glad to see you doing well. I thought I'd stop by and be sure you are okay."

"Thank you, Sheriff. All is indeed quite well. I appreciate your concern. I think I'm able to take care of the farm by myself." She hoped he'd get the veiled hint and vamoose.

"Anything I can do to help?"

"Thanks again, Sheriff, but little Mike and I have everything under control. We appreciate your offer." She wondered how she might get rid of Whelan without totally alienating the man. "I understand that Captain Dunn was successful in his pursuit of Bart Strong, and now he's headed back this way."

Whelan's expression changed. He now realized that he had a very serious rival for the young lady's affections. He decided not to push his luck. "Well, Miss Corrigan, if you ever decide you'd like some help around here, please don't hesitate to give me a call. I'm never that far away."

She thought on that last phrase. It was good news and bad news from her perspective. "Thank you, Sheriff. We'll keep that in mind." She was careful to respond as "we," since Mike and she were family and it sounded stronger. She saw that it wasn't just about her and her needs. Whelan was likely a capable man, but hardly what she had in mind as a father figure to her brother. In her eyes, only Luke Dunn could fill that role.

THIRTEEN

On the Trail

Luke rhythmically squeezed the bandana in his palm as he strove to strengthen his hand back to where he could effectively fire a gun and apply whatever other uses he found necessary. He'd pointed the big grey stallion east from Laredo. There was no special hurry, and the riding was easy. In any case, he thought he'd stop in Nuecestown, figuring he might as well check up on that charming young girl. He hoped and prayed she wasn't having further problems with Comanche or any other folks of ill intention. She seemed to be a sweet girl but frontier-tough, too, and Luke couldn't get her out of his mind. He especially liked her spirit.

He hoped that Three Toes' travel back to his village was proceeding incident-free. Luke wished he could be at Three Toes' council campfire as he told the story of his travels with the Ghost-Who-Rides. The thought brought an involuntary smile to his lips.

He decided to travel a fairly straight route, avoiding the twists and turns of dry creek beds. The arroyos offered cover, but were not especially efficient for quickly getting from place to place. He'd have to be a bit more watchful. He hummed some Irish ballads. At least, he thought he was humming, though his voice was actually loud enough to spook any wildlife within hearing.

A loud voice, a familiar voice, startled him. "Ghost-Who-Rides, you chase away game."

He turned to see Three Toes. Only, it wasn't just Three Toes. Clyde's horse had been joined by half a dozen more of the four-legged beasts. Apparently, Three Toes had been diverted in his journey back to his village.

"Dang, Chief, you've been busy." Luke smiled. "Do I need to arrest you for horse thieving?"

Three Toes smiled broadly. "These are Apache ponies."

Luke couldn't help but be impressed. He noted that two fresh scalps hung from Three Toes' lance. The Apaches were surely fair game out on the Nueces Strip. Scalping was a grisly practice, but folks who dealt with Comanche, Apache, Kiowa, and the like necessarily got used to it. "The sun will set in an hour. Let's share a campfire."

They rode a way further until they found a suitable spot to camp. Luke gathered enough dead live oak branches to make a small fire, and they feasted on some venison that Three Toes had also managed to steal from the hapless Apache.

"Where are you headed, Ghost-Who-Rides?"

"Somewhere between here and Corpus Christi is a killer named Dirk Cavendish. I hope to catch up with him and bring him to justice."

Luke thought on that last word a bit. What would justice really be for someone like Cavendish? What had led the young man to his choice, and his inevitable fate? Was he a product of a tough life, as Bart Strong had been? Why did an immigrant from Ireland who also had life challenges take the right side of the law, while men like Cavendish and Strong chose a life of evil?

"Are you headed straight back to your people, or do you hope to find more Apache?" Luke laughed.

"Seven horses plenty, my friend. I think my people may be wondering what became of me. Maybe there's a new chief." He chuckled, but actually feared that might happen. There were certainly Comanche that coveted Three Toes' position.

They made small talk for another hour after the sun had fully dropped below the distant horizon. Out on the vastness of the prairie, it seemed like a setting sun was drawn to the horizon like iron to a magnet. The pinkish-orange sky boded well for a beautiful next day for traveling. There was little so awesomely inspiring as a sunset on the Nueces Strip.

Before retiring for the night, Three Toes left the camp to check on his string of horses. When he returned, Luke was already sacked out and snoring. The Indian noted that the white man made much noise when he rode during the day as well as when he slept at night. He was afraid that his new-found friend wasn't being as careful as he needed to be on the dangerous prairies of the Nueces Strip. Three Toes decided he'd have to take first watch.

She saw the campfire light in the distance. Scarlett had talked the stable boy into selling her a usable nag for the trip to Corpus Christi in lieu of waiting around for the stage coach and the risk of encountering Carlos Perez. She'd already heard that Perez's men had passed around a couple of the ladies from Texas Jack's Saloon to their pleasure. She felt lucky to have avoided that fate. Now she wondered what she might find at the distant campfire. The attraction was like a mosquito to a hot flame, perhaps the heat of a dangerous flame. She wasn't familiar with travel in such rough country.

This wasn't the life Scarlett had dreamed of growing up in Richmond. Her parents died in a flash flood from a rainstorm when she was a toddler, so she was raised by her mother's elderly parents. She'd become bored. She had dreams of adventure. As a fifteen-year-old, Scarlett found herself swooning over a soldier home on leave from some duty station out west. He worked his charms on her and persuaded her to leave Virginia and run away with him. They made it as far as a riverboat on the Mississippi River, when she discovered she was pregnant. It scared her soldier nearly to death and he took off, leaving her alone on the boat.

There was no going back to Richmond. A gambler on the boat befriended her and accompanied her to New Orleans, taking advantage of her along the way. It turned out he owed some folks money and was on the run. She followed him to Texas and eventually to Laredo, where he was shot dead after a game of poker gone terribly wrong. Scarlett then had the fortune, or misfortune, to miscarry her baby. So there she was, alone and vulnerable, a stranger in a small Texas town on the Mexican border. She made fast friends with some ladies who turned out to be prostitutes. Given her increasing familiarity with men and having no marketable skills other than her outer beauty, she took to whoring.

Now, she found herself on a wild chase across the Nueces Strip, following a man who likely didn't know or care that she existed.

It took Scarlett about an hour to close the distance to the campfire in a darkness lit only by the light of the stars and a nearly half-moon. She'd also acquired a revolver, but prayed she'd never need it except to take her own life if attacked by Comanche or Apache. She didn't feature ever being a sex slave to some savage.

She finally drew close enough to see horses. She made out a big grey in their midst. She vaguely recalled that the Texas Ranger back in Laredo rode a horse like that. But the ponies had symbols painted on them like those she'd seen on Apache ponies. She was now in a quandary as to whether to approach the camp.

"You looking for something, ma'am?"

She'd heard that voice before. "Mr. Texas Ranger?" She certainly hadn't heard Luke sneak up on her.

"Scarlett, I recall?" He smiled reassuringly as she turned to face him. "Our little camp is safe, if that's your concern. My friend Three Toes is a Comanche chief, but he is my friend. You are welcome to spend the night without worry of being attacked."

At another time, she might have been wishing Luke would be interested in attacking her in a different way than he was referring to. "Thank you. Excuse me, but we were never properly introduced." She reached down from her horse and offered her hand. She incidentally nearly thrust her ample chest in Luke's face.

"Oh, I'm Captain Luke Dunn, Texas Rangers. Let me help you with your horse. Don't pay Three Toes no never-mind." He ignored her cleavage.

Three Toes was fast asleep as Scarlett entered the camp. She'd had the forethought to grab a blanket and her satchel before Luke hobbled her horse for the night.

Luke returned soon enough. He whispered, "Rest easy. I'll keep watch."

Scarlett wasn't used to traveling any distance on horseback and, combined with the emotion of having had to deal with Perez, she was dead tired and went to sleep quickly.

Luke stared at her. Pretty girl to be so messed up, was his thinking. Why did so many young girls find their way to the whoring life? Was it the same reason that young men turned bad? He thought back to his days as a teen in Ireland. He recalled that Dublin had its share of prostitutes. At least, that was how his father described them. Like these ladies of the frontier, their desperation drove them to selling their bodies to men who should have known better.

Luke saw the evil and destructiveness inherent in the wasted lives. Most men and women who chose these paths died very young, or at least younger than those with productive, seemingly righteous lives and families. Luke recalled being told by his father about a Bible story in which Jesus forgave a prostitute. Maybe, Luke thought, he should be more understanding of this woman who was seeking the protection of his company. At least, he felt empowered to protect her, though he had no way of knowing that his prey was her passion.

Just as the sun was about to break over the eastern prairielands, Three Toes awoke to see the interloper in their camp. Luke was asleep, though he was sitting upright and apparently had tried to be a sentry. He nudged Luke and whispered, "Ghost-Who-Rides, who is this?"

At the sound of Three Toes' voice, Scarlett awakened. She was momentarily horrified to see a Comanche standing in the camp at first light, much less one that was heating coffee, cooking venison, and speaking English.

Three Toes smiled. "No fear, red-haired one. I'm not interested in your scalp." He laughed at his own early morning humor.

Luke was awake by now. Sleeping in a sitting position did him no favors, and he stood with stretching and groaning appropriate to such an undesirable slumber position. "Good morning, Miss Scarlett. I hope you slept well."

"Excuse Texas Ranger manners, miss. I am Three Toes, war chief of the Comanche."

Scarlett was befuddled. She wondered what on earth a Comanche chief was doing sharing camp with a Texas Ranger? "Um…pleased to meet you."

"Ghost-Who-Rides, I must head north. I hope your new companion is no trouble in your hunting."

Luke understood Three Toes' need to get back to his people. "Don't worry about me, my friend. Let your people know they have a friend in Luke Dunn."

"What is it with you two? How come you're not trying to kill each other?" Scarlett was dumbfounded by the friendship between Luke and the Comanche chief. It seemed civil enough, but was counter to what she'd been led to believe about the white man and the savages.

Luke finished his coffee and helped himself to the last of Three Toes' venison. "Let's just say we have mutual respect, Miss Scarlett."

Soon enough, they had broken camp and were saddled and on their way. Three Toes headed north with his string of ponies, while Luke and Scarlett headed east.

★

Cav was well along, likely at least a days' ride ahead of Luke and Scarlett. Thus far, he hadn't encountered anything that might slow him down. As the temperatures warmed, he was pleased that he'd decided to not wear the black shirt and trousers. He noted how the black seemed to absorb heat. It hadn't been a problem in cooler, higher-elevation climates. It didn't hurt that not wearing it would also make it harder for bounty hunters and lawmen to identify him.

He still had his sisters on his mind. That little red-haired whore back in Laredo preyed on his mind, especially the resemblance to his sister Belle.

He was still a couple of days of steady riding from Corpus Christi. He hoped that his posters hadn't found their way to the sheriff there. He wanted to start over, build a new life. With any luck, he might even be able to lure Cora and Belle to Corpus Christi.

Perez was beside himself when he awakened alone in the room in Laredo. He stormed down to the bar at Texas Jack's Saloon and demanded to know where the red-haired whore had gone. *"Dónde está la puta pelirroja?"*

"Sorry, Carlos. The bitch headed out at first light. Hell, and she owes me money."

Perez grabbed the shot glass on the bar and threw it across the room, narrowly missing one of his gang members as it shattered against the wall. *"La mierda!"* Death and vengeance constantly preyed on his mind.

There was stunned silence in the bar. Apparently, everyone had gotten their satisfaction with the whores of Laredo, except for Perez. This was not good. A raven-haired Mexican prostitute stepped forward seductively. Perez slapped her across the face and then sent her tumbling. He wanted the red-haired one. Only she would do. Now his price of vengeance had doubled to include Scarlett. He did not take kindly to being embarrassed, especially as it involved his manhood.

Perez grabbed the barkeeper by his shirt. *"Adónde iba?"*

"Corpus Christi, I think. She's following after some gambler in a black hat."

Perez released the barkeeper. Had he known that Luke had been there mere hours before, he'd have been boiling mad.

"Vámonos, hombres!" Perez headed out the door. His gang followed reluctantly, as they looked longingly at the easy women they were suddenly leaving behind. Such was the fate of those who chose to ride with Carlos Perez. It appeared to them that they were headed into a period of forced celibacy.

Soon enough, they were saddled, provisioned, and heading east toward Corpus Christi. Perez almost wished he was traveling alone. He could make better time. On the other hand, dealing with marauding Comanche, rival gangs, or even soldiers might require numerical superiority. They slowed him down, but the gang would likely be more beneficial than not.

Perez rode silently in the lead. There was an aura of evil, a darkness, that now surrounded him. His men were even fearful of talking among themselves.

Ironically, all the travelers, Cav, Luke, and Perez, kept pretty much the same pace. It was as though some pre-destiny on the trail would keep them from overrunning each other.

FOURTEEN

Comanche

It was close to dusk when Cav first saw them. Looked to be about eight or ten. They were all mounted, and he guessed them to be maybe half a mile away and upwind. From what had been described to him, and despite the ever-dimmer daylight, they appeared to be Comanche. He'd never dealt with Comanche. Cav had fought some Arapahoe once, and Sioux. The Sioux were nasty, but he understood they were as nothing compared to the Comanche. Even their name portended what they existed for. In the Ute language, *kimantsi* meant enemy. Comanche were everyone's enemy.

Cav couldn't know that these warriors were those of Long Feathers.

With the death of his son Bear Slayer and his growing impatience waiting for Three Toes' return, Long Feathers had decided to take matters into his own hands. He had headed southwest from the encampment toward where they thought Three Toes had gone. Along the way, he was on the lookout for enemy.

Long Feathers had struck the Smiley ranch just that morning. He and his warriors rode their ponies hard into the clearing in front of the cabin, whooping and hollering as they attacked. Jason Smiley was tending the field not far from his wife and children. He watched in horror as Long Feathers descended on his home. The children, a boy and a girl of no more than ages six or seven, were killed immediately by Comanche lances.

Smiley grabbed his rifle and ran as fast as he could toward his family. Long Feathers' warriors had bound his wife to a corral post. By the time Smiley reached the clearing perhaps a hundred yards from the house, the Comanche already had her stripped naked and were raping and cutting her. She screamed, so they cut out her tongue.

Smiley caught his breath long enough for one shot. The bullet ripped through his wife's bloody chest, wounding a Comanche warrior on its way out. The wounded warrior turned toward the sound of the rifle.

Long Feathers was on Smiley almost immediately, delivering a mortal wound with his lance and scalping the farmer while he was dying. As Smiley lay on the ground, another warrior pulled off Smiley's trousers, cut off his privates, and stuffed them in his mouth. The poor man suffocated to death before he bled out. It was the Comanche way.

The Comanche set the house afire and stole the family's two horses.

Cav had no idea that he was facing a war party flush with the pride and invincibility that comes with victory. He dismounted to create a lower profile and made both of his horses lie down, kneeling beside the nervous beasts, and keeping his head just high enough to see what the Comanche were up to. If all went well and they continued on their chosen course, they should pass him at a safe distance.

Now, he found himself confronted with a new problem. About a dozen feet away, he spied a coiled rattlesnake. Beads of sweat formed on Cav's forehead and trickled down his face. He tried not to move a muscle. He dared not risk a gunshot. He drew one of his knives. He could throw a knife with great accuracy, but a striking snake could be a challenging target.

He saw the snake bring back its head as it prepared to strike. At that instant, a rabbit walked between them. The rattler had his dinner a split second later. Cav breathed a sigh of relief and turned his attention back to the Comanche. They were still about the same distance from him.

He started to look over at where the rattlesnake had been when he heard a noise from the direction of the Comanche. He strained his eyes to make out what was happening. The setting sun wasn't any help toward figuring what was going on. Best Cav could tell, someone had joined the Comanche war party.

It sounded like some sort of reunion, as there was much chatter in a language he couldn't make out. In any case, they seemed happy and distracted.

Three Toes was overjoyed to have chanced upon Long Feathers and his warriors out in the middle of the Texas prairie. He showed off the string of ponies he had captured, while Long Feathers boasted of counting coup and fresh scalps. The two nags he'd captured from the Smiley place didn't compare to the ponies Three Toes' had stolen from the Apache.

They moved off toward the northeast in the direction of the Comanche village. Three Toes kept quiet about his adventure, letting Long Feathers' warriors boast of their exploits. There would be many stories to tell the next night at the council campfire.

Cav waited until he felt they were a safe distance off before letting his mounts stand. He decided to take a more southeasterly direction to be certain he kept a safe distance from the Comanche.

After a long day's ride in the hot sun, Luke and Scarlett decided to rest in the evening and cool off for a few hours. She still was oblivious to Luke's mission, seeing him strictly as a means of safe passage. He obviously had no interest in her, at least none of a sexual nature.

Luke hobbled their horses, removing the saddles to let them breathe. "Here's a blanket, Miss Scarlett. Grab some shut-eye while you can. I'll keep watch."

A chill had begun in stark contrast to the heat of the day. "Can we build a fire?"

"Well, I expect we're not the only ones out here, Miss Scarlett. Best I can do is share my spare blanket."

"Do we have anything to eat?"

Luke handed her a canteen and a piece of smoked venison.

Scarlett felt like pouting, but realized that tactic would not likely have much of an impression on this Texas Ranger. She decided to be uncharacteristically gracious. "Thank you, Captain Dunn."

At what was likely near midnight, Luke finally crawled over near Scarlett, rested his head on his saddle, and fell asleep. During the night, she cuddled closer to him for warmth.

Luke awakened at first light, startled by a distant sound. The ground vibrated a little. He made it out to be horses and longhorns, likely a cattle drive. He nudged Scarlett. "We'd best get up and get going unless you're up for company."

He saddled the big grey stallion, then Scarlett's horse, and got her seated. Once he was mounted, he could see off in the distance that he'd been right in judging the noise to be from cattle being driven to market. It appeared to be a fairly large herd so it was unlikely that they were stolen cattle.

Luke turned their horses eastward, making a perfunctory friendly wave of his hat at the drovers not more than a quarter mile off. He could just about hear them yelling at the herd. Their voices were the expected mix of English and Spanish typical to Nueces Strip ranches.

He and Scarlett headed their mounts off at a brisk walk, trying to put distance between them and the herd.

"Thank you for the extra blanket last night, Captain Dunn." She smiled as she looked in his direction. "I appreciated your warm body, too."

Luke blushed and strove to make light of it. "It's part of a Ranger's job to make citizens feel safe, Miss Scarlett."

They relaxed and enjoyed a bit of a laugh.

"Maybe we can make a small fire and heat some coffee soon."

Carlos Perez had left Laredo with three missions. The first two involved that damnable red-haired woman and the man she was chasing after. Perez was trying hard to control his anger at her affront, lest it affect his judgment. The rival for her affections was peripheral damage so far as Perez was concerned. The leader of the *Caballeros Negros* also hadn't forgotten about that Texas Ranger that had embarrassed him near Corpus Christi and cost him an eye.

It could be said that he had a full platter of revenge in mind. No matter that revenge could be said to be feasting on a very sparse meal for the one doing the revenging. There was generally no satisfaction to be found in these sorts of endeavors. As Perez saw it, though, both his livelihood and his manhood had been threatened. It was an intolerable truth to his way of thinking.

The woman would be no problem, but neither of the men could be taken lightly, even though Perez had them outnumbered. He gazed off into the horizon with his good eye. The damned woman had laughed at his temporary impotence. This was a killing offense, but only after he'd proven her wrong.

Perez no longer thought of his days growing up in Matamoros. His father and two older brothers had died twenty years ago fighting for Santa Anna at Goliad and San Jacinto. As a teenager, he wound up caring for his mother, who took to plying the streets of Matamoros to whore away her grief. His bitterness had generated deep hatred of the

Tejanos. His mother soon died of complications from some venereal disease, likely syphilis.

While fueling his hatred, Perez also began to build friendships with like-minded fellow disenfranchised Mexicans. He emerged as their leader if for no other reason than his passionate hate for the *Tejanos* transcended that of his *compadres*. He led them on regular forays into the Nueces Strip to rustle cattle, skin them for their hides, and leave the carcasses to rot in the sweltering heat of the prairie. He even set up a sort of outpost, a cluster of small homes for the families of hiders that were loosely referred to as ranches. They'd sell the hides in Matamoros to buyers from Brownsville, who would in turn sell them to meet needs for cheap leather goods in eastern U.S. cities.

Perez's *Caballeros Negros* became a steady nuisance on the Nueces Strip. They stole just enough cattle from enough different ranches to be annoying, while not causing any initiatives to be mounted to stop them. The northern limit of their range was the road that ran between Corpus Christi and Laredo. They weren't like the Lipan Apache that stole larger herds and ran them south into Mexico, grabbing the attention of the leaders in Austin who eventually sent the Texas Rangers after them.

His run-in with Luke had been a fluke. He only had three of his *Caballeros Negros* with him that day, and had swiped a mere handful of cattle. His encounter was pure chance, pure fate. The deputy sheriff was not hunting them that day; he simply came upon them. Every time Perez thought about it, he regretted his carelessness, and that would make him remember the loss of his precious eye.

In the subsequent time, he'd discovered a perverse pleasure in striking fear in the minds of the *Tejanos*. The gang had killed a couple of people in Nuevo Laredo, and word got out about their deed. He was a wanted man for murder in Mexico and for cattle rustling in Texas.

If sheer numbers mattered, traveling with his eight *Caballeros Negros* at least gave him a sense of confidence.

Three Toes, Long Feathers, and their band were drawing ever closer to the Comanche village. They'd ridden all night.

It was simply fate that the mail rider crossed their path. One of Long Feathers' sons shouted the alarm, and the chase was on. This was easy prey. The warriors mounted fresh ponies from Three Toes' string. It had almost become a sport. In any case, it was a contest to see which Comanche would count coup and then bring down the mail rider.

Panic born of the Comanche reputation drove the rider to whip his horse. Inevitably, the horse broke down, hurling rider and mail satchel to the ground. The Comanche were on him in a heartbeat.

The mail rider stood shakily, firing wildly with his pistol. Three warriors disarmed him, pinned him to the earth, and bound his hands behind him. The sheer panic in the man's eyes told of such extreme fear that his heart was in danger of exploding from his body. Two other warriors began to dig a hole. Soon, it was deep enough and they slid the mail rider's upright body into it. They filled the hole such that only his head was sticking above the ground. They scalped him, then waited to be certain the ants had found him and his bleeding open wound. The crushing weight of soil on his chest prevented him from screaming loudly enough to be heard by anyone close enough to help. The Comanche left him to die.

Long Feathers' son brandished the scalp and led the mail rider's hard-ridden but serviceable horse. Three Toes complimented the young warrior on his bravery and resourcefulness. It almost was enough to forget about the loss of Bear Slayer.

Three Toes took the moment to share his admiration for Captain Dunn. Within hearing of the other Comanche, he briefly shared the strong medicine that the Texas Ranger had shown, including respecting the dead Comanche, setting a successful trap to catch Three Toes, and calling the snake to strike Strong. He especially embellished the story of the rattlesnake, describing how Luke had summoned a snake that had no rattles to warn the victim. He told them that Luke controlled the snake with his mind. "Ghost-Who-Rides is strong medicine. He is a friend, and I have promised his safety among the Comanche. He is not to be harmed by our people."

The Comanche were impressed with Three Toes' tale and promised to keep his word for Luke's protection.

The Comanche passed the old burned-out mail station on their way back to the village. No one was around, but a new structure was already being constructed nearby. The mails would continue despite the Comanche attacks.

Three Toes took careful note. The white man was ever encroaching on the land of his ancestors. He knew from first-hand experience that not all the Anglos were honorable. Just as the Penateka Comanche traditionally did battle with surrounding tribes, so they would continue to take on the white men and the Mexicans.

He wondered about the black men that he'd occasionally see. Some appeared to be free, but many were apparently slaves. He hadn't fully figured out how the white man thought. Of course, the Comanche enslaved captive women, so he could understand them in that context. Having slaves certainly eased the workload, though getting them to accept their fate was a challenge. While the Comanche simply disfigured their woman captives, the white man was more inclined to use whips and chains. He guessed that both ways were effective. At least the Comanche had no need for keeping male captives.

The chief also knew that the white men and the Mexicans both worshipped some sort of Great Spirit, but the meaning of that escaped him as well. He understood that they practiced a variety of rituals, but he'd seen little or none of it. The closest he'd actually gotten was when they'd get on their knees and plead with their Great Spirit for mercy when faced with Three Toes' knife. He resolved to learn more so as to better understand these interlopers to the Comanche way. It led him to wonder what Luke Dunn's feelings might be. Did he practice any of the rituals of his fellow white men? More important, he wondered whether the white man's Great Spirit was the same as the one he meditated to? After all, how many could there be?

FIFTEEN

The Unexpected

The drovers had the cattle settled down for the night. They posted a watch. No reason to believe they couldn't get this herd to market with little or no trouble.

The sun rose to reveal a clear day on the south Texas prairie. The Nueces Strip was displayed in all its boundless beauty.

Cookie began fixing victuals for the men before they headed back on the trail north. They hoped to reach the Shawnee Trail in about four days.

Carlos Perez was feeling especially grouchy. As he aged, the ground made for an ever-less-pleasant bed. At only thirty-five years old, this was already a sad state of affairs.

The *Caballeros Negros* broke camp and resumed their journey eastward. Imagine their surprise when, having gone but five or six miles, they found themselves closing on a large herd of cattle. Hiders' heaven loomed before them. Were there enough hides to tempt them to delay their travels?

Perez gazed longingly at the herd. The drovers had not yet seen the hiders. But, if he attacked, he'd be stuck with cattle that would further slow his travel.

Perez' contemplations were rudely interrupted by a single shot from the direction of the drovers' camp. One of his *Caballeros Negros* dropped from the saddle. Half his head had been blown away. Perez turned his horse away from the herd. *"Rapido, vamos!"*

Whoever was shooting had a buffalo gun, knew how to use it, and had no love for heavily armed Mexicans looking like they were up to no good. The .50 caliber Sharps was the weapon of choice for buffalo hunters and had a devastating effect on human targets. The shooter had made Perez's choice for him. They'd give the drovers and their cattle herd a wide berth. Perez rightly figured it would be better to live and fight another day. Besides, he'd likely as not stolen some of their cattle at one time or another.

Sound carries a long way on the broad expanses of the Nueces Strip prairie. Luke heard the faint sound of the Sharps off in the distance. It was from the direction of the drovers they'd seen the day before. He picked up their pace. Whatever had been targeted might not be something or someone he wanted to encounter.

"What's your hurry, Captain?"

"Just a hunch, Miss Scarlett. This is rough country."

"Indeed," she agreed. "So what drives you to roam the prairie mostly alone searching out lawbreakers?"

No one had asked Luke that question before, and he hadn't given it much thought.

"Where are you from? Your voice doesn't sound much like a Texan."

Now, he had two questions to deal with. He wasn't done thinking about the first. "Born in Ireland, Miss Scarlett. County Kildare. Came here a couple years ago to escape trouble from the British." He was still pondering the answer to the first question. He wasn't prone to lengthy answers. "I guess the open spaces give me a sense of freedom. Upholding the law and protecting folks gives me a purpose. It's about justice. Yeah, that's what drives me."

Scarlett thought on that. She rather admired Luke for his answer. She could tell that he was earnestly committed to protecting her, so it lent credence to his reasoning. "Do you have a woman?"

Luke wasn't sure he appreciated her prying. Her question was quite personal. "Nope." He said it with a finality that indicated he was done with such prying. He made a loud chucking sound and gave the big grey stallion a slight kick of his heel to put a few feet of distance between himself and Scarlett.

Scarlett smiled to herself. She'd chew on that for a while. She had the protection of a Texas Ranger for the present.

Cav decided to turn slightly to the northeast. He'd heard about Nuecestown and thought to rest there before moving on to Corpus Christi. He also figured he might learn something useful about opportunities in the city before venturing into it.

Half a day later, he found himself riding into the sleepy town. It still benefited from the commerce generated by Colonel Kinney's ferry crossing. He'd passed numerous farms and ranches and liked what appeared to be a settled family atmosphere. He had no appreciation for the sorts of threats places like Nuecestown periodically endured from Indians and desperadoes, other than himself. He noted the small general store, a sheriff's office, a town livery with a respectable stable and corral, and what appeared to be a boarding house.

The sign on Doc's place caught his eye. Someone was sitting on its front steps. Actually, the person was more lounging than sitting. Upon closer inspection, the man had considerable facial stubble and disheveled clothing.

He pulled up in front of Doc's place. "Excuse me, sir. I'm passing through. Y'all have any sort of rooming house? Perhaps a saloon?"

Doc looked up at the man through his rheumy eyes. "Nope." And he went to sleep and began snoring.

Cav was none too happy. He thought of dismounting and shaking an answer out of the old drunk. Thinking better of that and not wanting to stir up any trouble, he crossed the street to the sheriff's office. He dismounted and knocked on the door.

"Sorry, young man. The sheriff is in Corpus Christi today." Bernice seemed to invariably be the eyes of Nuecestown. She'd seen him ride in and simply bided her time until Cav drew close enough that she could talk without raising her voice.

Cav smiled at this apparently sweet elderly lady. "Do you...?"

Bernice interrupted. "Agatha and I run a boarding house around the corner. Can you pay?"

It was a rather presumptive question, but he took it in good spirit. "Yes, ma'am."

"You can call me Bernice. Now, go check your horse at the livery, then git back here so we can feed you."

Cav did as he was told. Far as he could tell, Bernice ran the town. There was no sense messing with her. "Yes, Miss Bernice. Oh, my name is Cav." He'd long ago stopped using the given name that was on the wanted poster.

Cav was feted with one of Bernice's overcooked pot roasts. He could endure her cooking, especially if she had information about Corpus Christi that he could use.

"Thanks for the fine dinner, Miss Bernice." He sought to ingratiate himself only so far as necessary. "I'm headed to Corpus and would be deeply appreciative if you know of labor opportunities for a strong, motivated person such as myself."

It was about this time that Bernice thought this man had a familiar face. She couldn't remember where she'd seen it. "What sort of work are you looking for, Cav?"

"I've got a few talents." He didn't want to share his abilities at card playing and killing. "I'd like to be involved in commerce."

"There's plenty of that, young man." Then it struck her. This man's sketch was on a wanted poster in Sheriff Whelan's office. She'd need to be careful.

Cav noticed a very faint expression of recognition in Bernice's face. He wouldn't want to stay in Nuecestown very long. In a bigger city like Corpus with its couple of hundred residents or so, he might hide from his reputation.

"I expect I ought to be grabbing some shut-eye, Miss Bernice, ma'am. I plan to travel to Corpus tomorrow." He pushed back his chair.

"You do that, young man. Have a sound sleep." Inside, she was praying that Whelan returned sooner rather than later.

The bed was likely the most comfortable Cav had ever slept in. He'd been in some comfortable beds, but not for sleep. He awakened to shards of sunlight streaking in through the room's lone window. He pulled himself up and out of bed to look out onto the street. He was anxious to see this Nuecestown in daylight.

His eyes grew wide. Standing hitched in front of the Doc's place was a big grey stallion. Next to it was a smaller horse with a woman's embroidered bag hanging from the saddle horn.

Back in Laredo, he'd heard rumors of some lawman that rode a horse like that. Whoever rode those horses apparently had business with the doctor. He decided it might be a good course of action to avoid any possible trouble. He could stay hiding in his room or sneak over to the livery and quietly walk his horse out of town. He also considered the possibility of the local sheriff returning to the town. It was a dilemma for sure.

"Doc, good to see you." Luke and Scarlett had let themselves in, as the door was ajar.

Doc was lying on top of his *de facto* operating table just about passed out from the whiskey. "Huh?"

"Just wanted you to check out my hand. It feels good...a little tender in parts."

Doc shook the cobwebs out. "Damn, Luke. It ain't been that long." Then he realized there was a young woman with Luke. "Pardon, ma'am. I didn't notice you standing there all quiet-like."

"Don't mind me, Doc. I'm headed to Corpus Christi soon as we can get back on the trail."

"Well, you don't have but another twenty miles to go, young lady." He gave her the once over. He figured the men of Corpus would likely chew her up and spit her out. "Not too safe for a young woman traveling alone, ma'am. It's rough country."

They were interrupted by a noise outside as a rickety old wagon pulled up at the general store across the way. As fate would have it, Elisa had come early to town to get some supplies.

As she climbed from the wagon, she spied the big grey stallion. Her heart went wild, and she could scarcely breathe. Simultaneously, Cav stepped out of Bernice's boarding house, and Luke and Scarlett walked from Doc's place.

Elisa saw her one true love standing across the street with another woman. Luke barely noticed Elisa, but he recognized Cav as a wanted man despite his having ditched the black clothing and mustache. Scarlett beheld the very love of her life sneaking out to run away. Cav spied Scarlett but gave her not even a second thought, as though she was naught but another prostitute.

Naturally, Bernice and Agatha were taking this all in. Bernice sensed a strong dynamic at work but couldn't quite make it all out. She certainly was aware that emotions were running high. It was as though time had frozen for just a split second.

Then, the clock restarted.

Elisa ran back into the general store in tears. Scarlett began to cross the street toward Cav, who was on the move toward the stable. Luke was torn between trying to figure out what upset Elisa, whom he'd just noticed, and pursuing the fugitive. Fortunately, no guns had yet been drawn.

Luke tripped over Scarlett, enabling Cav to get to the livery stable, throw a saddle hurriedly on his horse, dash out the back door, jump a fence, and gallop away.

Scarlett strove to get out from under Luke. "What are you doing, you damned cowboy! My man is leaving!"

Luke got up and dusted himself off. He didn't have to be hit by a log up the side of his head to figure out most things. He quickly did the math for the love equation between Scarlett and Cav. But it seemed that Cav either didn't know or didn't care.

"Damn, Miss Scarlett! You in love with that killer?"

She gave Luke a damn-right look and mounted her horse, determined to follow Cav's dust.

Meanwhile, Luke had lost the advantage. He watched Scarlett ride off after Cav. Behind him, he heard a rough laugh. "Damn, son, that was the most incredible thing I've ever seen."

"What do you mean?" he demanded.

"You don't know, do you?" Doc would have shaken his head, but it would have made his headache worse. "That little girl in the general store has been waiting for you to return, and you show up with another woman. Are you that dense?"

Luke looked quizzically at Doc, then his eyes opened wider in recognition of what Doc said. He turned, crossed the street, and strode up the steps and into the general store. Cav and Scarlett would have to wait. They weren't going to be that hard to catch up with anyway.

Perez scanned Nuecestown from a distance. He and his *Caballeros Negros* stood clustered on a rise overlooking the town. He was close enough to have seen Cav and Scarlett leave. He'd caught sight of Luke but lost track of him. Wherever Luke had gone, he was hidden from Perez's view.

He wanted to catch the Ranger on the open trail, not in some flea-bit *Tejano* town. It was time to wait. Patience wasn't exactly his forte, but he didn't want to be foolhardy. All his prey were now within easy reach.

"*Vamos a acampar aquí esta noche, Caballeros.*" He was in high spirits as he ordered his *Caballeros Negros* to make camp for the night. They would be fresh in the morning and be able to think more clearly about the work at hand.

SIXTEEN

Trouble This Way Comes

For whatever reason, Luke recalled a piece of advice his father had given him back in Ireland: live the journey, for every destination offers a doorway to the next. As he passed through the general store doorway, he sensed that he was about to begin a new life journey.

"Elisa?" he called softly. "Elisa, it's not what you think."

She looked at him through tear-reddened eyes. The hurt was deep. "What do I think, you...you?"

"It was my job to give her protection. I just learned that she's running after that fugitive that just escaped." He moved toward her.

She pulled back.

Luke stood before her, all six-foot-three of handsome, well-muscled manhood within her reach.

She was only stubborn for a moment. She looked up at him, into the eyes filled with heartfelt caring. He was irresistible. "I've missed you." Catching him totally off guard, she buried herself in his arms.

Bernice had just entered through the back door of the store, drew up in surprise, and clapped with glee.

The blushing couple broke free.

"I've been thinking of you ever since I left Nuecestown, Elisa Corrigan." Luke paid Bernice no never-mind.

She laughed and her eyes brightened. No more tears. She had her man. "Do you believe in leprechauns?"

"Methinks not. They're supposed to be devious little mythical creatures."

"Come on, you two. I'll whip up some breakfast." Bernice, sporting an ear-to-ear grin, headed toward her boarding house.

Carlos Perez watched from afar as Luke walked Elisa to a house near the general store. He'd already decided not to rush his vengeance, as that could land him in trouble. Having lost one man to the drovers, he was inclined to be a bit more cautious.

The fire crackled and smoke billowed from the Comanche council fire. Three Toes, who had already shown his undying appreciation for his three wives by sharing himself with them soon after his return, had regaled the assembled Comanche with his exploits with Ghost-Who-Rides. Everyone was duly impressed. Three Toes was even awarded two feathers for his war bonnet. His stature as chief had risen. Long Feathers was also rewarded. There was much discussion of the Comanche future.

Three Toes shared his concerns about the future of the Penateka Comanche. The white settlers were expanding their territorial reach, and the U.S. Cavalry was beginning to win pitched battles with both Comanche and their erstwhile allies, the Kiowa. He knew that, soon enough, they might be joining Buffalo Hump at the government camp in the place called Oklahoma, though Camp Cooper up on the Brazos River was more likely. No longer was there talk of a sweeping offensive like Buffalo Hump had led years earlier. The days of the Penateka anywhere near the Nueces Strip were all but ended. He'd heard rumors that the government in Austin was going to organize the Texas Rangers again. He didn't want to have the Comanche experience what the Lipan Apache had endured.

Soon enough, they were all sharing a tribal pipe, and it wasn't long before the council broke the circle for the evening. As everyone headed off to their teepees, Three Toes stood alone looking out over the expanse of prairie in the dim moonlight. He wondered about his new-found friend, Captain Dunn, the Ghost-Who-Rides. Had he used his strong medicine once again to defeat another man of evil spirits? He smiled as he wondered whether Luke would return to the young woman on the farm. He sensed that Luke had feelings for her.

"Three Toes?" Long Feathers came beside his chief. "Are we to ride north to our ancestors' homes?"

Three Toes shook his head. "You will go before the full moon. You will lead our people north, Long Feathers."

"Are you not joining us?"

Three Toes found it hard to answer. "I will find you later. I feel drawn by strong spirits to find Ghost-Who-Rides." He hoped Long Feathers would understand. The Great Spirit was calling Three Toes on a quest.

"You will go alone?"

"That is what the Great Spirit tells me."

Long Feathers nodded knowingly and headed back to his teepee. Three Toes had just given him an important assignment.

Three Toes would tell his wives in the morning. For now, he was simply too tired to deal with them. Perhaps he'd impregnated one of them that afternoon, and he'd be father to a great Comanche warrior who would save their people.

Cav heard hoof beats galloping behind him. Was that fool Ranger following him? Or was it the girl? He pulled up at a live oak motte and looked back from whence he'd come. He pulled the rifle from its scabbard just in case.

"Cav!" the woman shouted.

"Dang," he thought. The last thing he needed was a woman to slow him down, especially some Laredo whore. "Over here." He yielded to the inevitable.

She rode to where he sat astride a pale buckskin horse. She half-smiled as she shook out her red curls. "Are you glad to see me?"

What was he supposed to say? Damn woman. "What would you like me to say?" Uh-oh, that was nasty.

A stunned expression swept across her freckled face. There was a sense that tears could flow at any moment.

"I'm sorry. Guess I can't believe you followed me." He dismounted and grabbed her horse's bridle. "Get down so I can get a better look at you." Their passionate dalliance in Laredo began to come back to him. She was no sooner dismounted than he pulled her close, joining in a tight, lustful embrace. He felt her body begin to yield, as sensual animal cravings invaded her inner core. She wrapped one leg around him, pulling him even closer. She could feel his rippling muscles beneath the rough cotton fabric of his shirt. This is what her chase from Laredo had been all about.

In seconds, he'd thrown up her skirt and began madly having his way with her. She locked herself around his hips. Finally finished, Cav broke free of her vice-like grip. He stood above her, looking down at his little Laredo whore as he refastened his trousers. "It's Scarlett, right?"

He saw the satisfaction on her face, no doubt delighted that he remembered her name. She smiled up at him, her long eyelashes fluttering down across her eyes. "Can I come with you to Corpus Christi?" she asked.

As he pondered that eventuality, he got to thinking that he'd be less likely to be discovered with her along. He reasoned that a couple would be less suspicious. "Yes, you can come with me to Corpus Christi, Scarlett." He said her name again as a sort of bonding sign.

She stood, straightened her skirt, and hugged him. The thought of the moment of passion they'd just shared lingered between them.

"We'd better get going," he said. "I don't want that Ranger to catch up."

She gave him a questioning glance, as if she wondered why he was concerned about Captain Dunn, but didn't say anything further.

Together, they turned toward their destination.

Luke noticed that Elisa couldn't stop talking through Bernice's breakfast. Finally, she stopped long enough to ask, "Do you have time to come out and see what I've done to the farm?"

He gave her offer some thought. He figured Cav and Scarlett wouldn't be getting so far off that he'd be unable to pick up their trail. That took care of one worry.

For the other, he was in a bit of a daze. This was a totally new experience, plus he had these new feelings to deal with. He'd certainly never had any lasses in Ireland make him feel this way, and there were many who tried. Perhaps it was something in the Texas air.

He nodded. "Sure. I'd be happy to come visit."

"Wonderful. Let's head out as soon as I get my supplies," she said, smiling at him with that charming way she had.

A scant hour later, they climbed aboard her wagon, Luke next to her on the seat and the big grey stallion tied behind as they headed out of Nuecestown.

"*Jefe, mira la ciuded.*" One of the *Caballeros Negros* alerted Perez, pointing in the direction of the road out of Nuecestown.

Perez watched as Luke and Elisa left in the wagon. He wondered where they were headed.

"*Hmmm. A dónde van?*" It was a rhetorical question. "*Vamos a seguir.*" He motioned them to follow him. They'd keep their distance to see what sort of opportunity presented itself.

About an hour later, Perez watched as Luke and Elisa climbed down from the wagon, unhitched the mules, and loaded a few supplies inside the house. A young boy joined them on the steps at the front of the cabin.

Perez was determined to remain patient. He didn't know if the woman or even the young boy could shoot, so was concerned at minimizing his risk. He watched as the woman gave what appeared to be a tour around the property. It looked as though the Ranger was holding her hand. This would make his revenge even sweeter. He determined to overcome Luke and rape the woman before the very eyes of the Ranger and the boy.

The sun was soon high overhead.

"Can I cook up a bit of lunch for you, Luke?" Elisa asked.

Luke smiled. "That sounds perfect, Elisa. I'll need to get back afterward, though. I do have my Ranger duties."

Elisa thought about the difference between Luke and Sheriff Whelan. In her admittedly biased judgment, her Texas Ranger was by far the better man.

She cooked up some beef she'd been saving for a special occasion. Unlike Bernice's pot roast, Elisa knew just how to bring the perfect flavor and juices from the meat. Soon enough, the three of them were seated at the little table in what served as a kitchen.

Elisa could tell that Luke was thoroughly enjoying her cooking. It confirmed what her mother had told her about good food being the way to a man's heart. They had just about finished when they heard a shout.

"*Senor Dunn, salga, por favor.*"

Luke had no idea who was calling. A quick look out the window revealed eight nasty-looking hombres. They were armed to the teeth.

"*Quién está aquí?*" Luke offered the inquiry in his halting Spanish laced with Texas twang and Irish brogue.

"*Mi nombre es Carlos Perez.*" Perez knew he was being watched.

"*He venido a materte. Me robaste el ojo.*" It was Perez at his boldest. Let your prey know you were there to kill him and why.

Luke quickly realized this was the rustler he'd chased off near Corpus Christi. He must have cost the man an eye, and now he sought revenge.

"*Rendirse y yo le perdomo a la mujer.*" Evidently, Perez figured he'd at least try to lure Luke into surrendering by promising not to harm the woman.

Luke was not falling for that old trick. He looked at Elisa. He'd go down fighting for her.

As Luke was deciding his next step, there was a faint whoosh, then another. Two of the *Caballeros Negros* fell from their horses with arrows in their backs. Perez's odds had suddenly been reduced. He wheeled his horse to face the new threat. He could see nothing. Another whoosh and another bandit fell from his saddle.

"*Vamonos!*" Perez yelled, and he and his remaining men turned and galloped away as fast as their horses could carry them.

"Elisa, stay here." Luke cautiously emerged from the cabin about the time Three Toes appeared.

Luke quickly recognized the chief. "My friend, you are a welcome sight." Luke stepped forward and hugged the Comanche war chief, who was caught off guard by Luke's expression of thanks.

Elisa joined them. "Luke, who is this?"

"This," he said proudly, "is Three Toes, a chief of the Penateka Comanche. We have become friends."

Elisa smiled at the chief, even though her only encounters with Comanche had not been positive experiences.

"Thank you." That was about all she could get out in her amazement.

"What brought you here, my friend?" Luke asked.

"I heard your call."

Luke wasn't going to doubt Three Toes.

"I see that you came back and buried your warriors." Luke had noticed the stones piled over the bodies of the warriors killed in the

141

attack on Elisa's farm. "I tried to respect your Comanche brothers."

Three Toes smiled appreciatively. "I told you, Ghost-Who-Rides. You are not like other white men. You have strong medicine." He took Elisa's hand. She reflexively wanted to pull back her hand as memories of the wild Comanche coming at her flashed through her mind, but she found herself allowing Three Toes to grasp it.

Three Toes looked deeply into her eyes. "This man will keep you ever safe. Be loyal to him, trust in him, and love him."

With that, he turned to Luke. "I must catch up with my people, my brother. I will see you in another place. We are leaving this land." He said the final sentence matter of factly. He mounted his pony and was soon gone. No tears. No sad good-byes.

Luke looked about the clearing in front of Elisa's cabin. "Seems that every time I visit, we have dead bodies to get rid of." It was a bit of sick humor. "I'm thinking we deliver these critters to Sheriff Whelan." He dragged the bodies over to the wagon and lifted them in one by one. It was a distasteful task and, while Luke was thankful to be done with it, he wasn't quite ready to leave. He moved the wagon away from the cabin a bit, as it wasn't an especially appetizing sight.

He walked over to where Elisa was standing in the doorway and looked down at her expectant expression. "Well, we've barely finished lunch. We'll take care of this later." The bodies of the *Caballeros Negros* in the wagon weren't going anywhere.

"Mike, would you please clean out the mule stalls?" Her brother dutifully headed toward the stable without question. "Captain Dunn and I have some matters to discuss," she called after him. "Oh, and be sure to clean your boots before you come back into the cabin." She knew that the boot cleaning would be a noisy affair and give fair warning of his return from the chore.

She looked at Luke. "What are you standing there for? We have lunch to finish." And she headed into the cabin with Luke close behind. They sat back at the table, only this time Elisa pulled her chair around next to Luke. She'd been talking to the ladies around Nuecestown and at a couple of neighbor spreads. She was cautioned to not be too forward. A woman didn't want to scare away a man by coming on too strong. Aggressive women did whoring; not sparking. She'd do well to follow their advice.

Luke shifted uncomfortably.

"What is Ireland like?" she asked.

The question hit Luke like a bolt from the sky. He started telling her his story, and found himself becoming more comfortable with her. He told the tales of his family and Ireland, of the clans and sects, and the heathers of County Kildare, of the Great Famine and the British, of the religious persecution, and why he immigrated to Texas. A few minutes quickly turned into an hour.

Soon, they heard Mike beating his boots with a stick near the front door. He'd be a bit hungry and thirsty after his chores in the stable.

Elisa realized they had only a few more minutes of privacy. She placed her hand over Luke's. "I want to learn more about you, Luke Dunn."

There was an awkward moment. Luke looked down at her next to him. Their faces were just inches apart. As if by some strange force, he found himself bringing his lips to hers. The sweetness was overwhelming.

Just then, Mike burst through the door. Elisa blushed. Luke pulled back and gasped.

Mike gave a knowing look inappropriate to his young years.

"I was telling Captain Dunn that we were worried that those bad men might return." Elisa gathered her wits. "Perhaps you can go with him this afternoon to take those men to Sheriff Whelan's office."

"Will you be safe, Sis?"

Luke stepped into the conversation. "You have a brave sister, Mike. She killed Comanche. I think those bandits are long gone. She should be safe with you and me gone for an hour or so."

They hitched the mules back up, Mike joined Luke on the seat, and off they went to Nuecestown.

They hadn't gone far before Mike started up his chatter. How did you catch Bad Bart? Who was that Comanche? Why did you become a Texas Ranger? Who are you going to capture next? What kind of gun do you use? Does your horse have a name? What did you do to your hand? Why do you squeeze that bandana? Where are you from? There seemed no end of questions, and Luke did his best to answer them in a way that a young boy could fully appreciate.

"Let me ask you a question, Mike."

"Sure…I mean, yes, sir, Captain Dunn."

"Have you given any thought to the three dead men in our wagon?" Luke asked him.

"They were bad men. They smell."

Luke forced a gentle, understanding smile. "Yes, they were bad men, and yes, they certainly do have an odor. But they were men, Mike. They were born, had mothers and fathers, grew up, perhaps had some trade or skill, but somewhere at some time they turned bad. Something went wrong in their lives, and they were not able to deal with it. Why might that happen, Mike?"

This tested young Mike's mettle. He strove for an answer, but could only offer an inquisitive expression of, "Why?"

"They lost hope, Mike. They lost the faith and trust in God that would have led them down a path to resist the bad things." He saw that Mike understood him. "I've never met a lawbreaker here or even in Ireland that had faith in the higher power of God."

Mike nodded. "I think I understand, Captain Dunn."

"So these aren't just the bodies of bad men we're hauling to Nuecestown, Mike. These are men who lost their way. It's sad. We can be forgiving, Mike, but it doesn't pardon the sinner from punishment. That's why men like me bring lawbreakers to justice."

Mike considered Luke's advice. His young mind turned, adjusting to the life reality Luke had just shared. Mike was having to grow up fast, and life lessons would often not be easy. He liked the idea of Luke being around.

Soon, they'd deposited the three dead *Caballeros Negros* behind the sheriff's office with a note to Whelan, and headed back to the farm. Mike was suddenly silent.

"Why so quiet, Mike?" Luke asked.

"Are you leaving us tonight?"

Luke understood. Here was a youngster who'd lost his parents and brother. The men in his life had abandoned him through no fault of his own. "I must leave, young man. It wouldn't do to have a man stay overnight in your cabin with your sister being unmarried. People would say some nasty things about her." He noticed Mike's crestfallen face. "But I'll be around. I'll always try to be around."

Mike was quiet for a while longer, then mustered up the courage for his most important question. "Do you love my sister?"

Luke stopped the wagon and gazed thoughtfully, first at the horizon and then at Mike. The thought of the kiss ran through his heart. "I reckon I might. Yes, it seems so." He chucked at the mules and urged them on.

The wagon lurched forward, and Mike sat with a satisfied smile on his sweet, still boyish face. "I like you, Captain Dunn."

They pulled up at the corral. "Can you unhitch these mules, Mike?"

"Yes, sir. I sure can, Captain Dunn."

Luke headed for the cabin. He smelled some good cooking going on as he drew closer. "Anybody home?"

The door opened. "You have an appetite?" She stood before him wearing the new blue dress she'd made special just for him.

"You sure are pretty, Miss Corrigan."

The meal was wonderful. Luke thought how he might grow used to this life. Why, Elisa as likely cooked better than his own mother.

"So you're headed back to Nuecestown this evening?" she asked him.

"You know I must, Elisa." His expression said he didn't want to but had to.

"Will you visit tomorrow?"

"I expect so, but then I must get on to Corpus Christi. I need to do my duties."

Elisa sighed. "Can we take a walk?"

By now, the nearly full moon lit the landscape, and there were stars as far as the eye could see. Elisa led him down the well-worn path toward the creek to a rocky outcrop. There they sat on a rock, listened to the gurgling creek below, and gazed up at the majestic prairie sky.

"We have beautiful skies in Ireland, Elisa. But nothing so grand as here in Texas. Here the horizon seems to never end. And the stars… they're like a million Irish fairies and pixies dancing and glittering across the night sky." It came easily to Luke. Out on the Strip alone at night where the only noise seemed to be the blinking of the stars, he'd learned to appreciate the magnificence of it all. He'd even studied them such that he was able to navigate by the heavens.

She was taken with the image Luke painted. The starry sky had become an image of their souls. She'd never imagined that this tough Texas Ranger, who'd just disposed of a much-feared desperado and fought Comanche, could have such a vulnerable side. None of the men in her life ever showed such feelings.

"I'm happy, Luke. I'm so happy you came back." She moved just a bit closer, so they were barely touching.

Luke put his arm around her shoulder. There was something in her closeness that aroused urges within him that he hadn't felt since leaving Ireland. The low sound of her breathing in the silent night caused his thoughts to drift to imagining how it might feel to pull her close, to hold her body against his, to love her as she ought to be loved. "I'll always be here, Elisa."

She wasn't sure quite how to interpret that. Was it a commitment? She snuggled closer under his arm. She could feel the strong yet tender muscles in the arm wrapped around her and his ever-quickening pulse. She began to feel urges she'd only dreamt of.

Luke lifted her chin with his fingers and gave her the deepest, longest kiss she'd ever imagined. She was enveloped in a deep warmth as her entire body seemed to catch on fire. He broke away and stood. "I must get back to Nuecestown."

"You won't stay?" Her mouth was still warm with the moisture of his lips. It was as though they were still kissing.

"Wouldn't be right." He couldn't miss her look of disappointment. He'd dashed cold water on their ardor. "Your brother asked me an interesting question today."

"What was it?"

"You'll have to ask him," Luke said mysteriously.

And they began to quietly walk back up the path to the corral. Soon enough, Luke had his horse saddled, gave Elisa a good-bye kiss, and was off to Nuecestown.

Perez's *Caballeros Negros* gang was now reduced to five. His mission of revenge was getting ever riskier. He was familiar with the territory southwest of Corpus Christi, so decided to head there. He needed to come up with a plan. Perhaps the Laredo whore and her lover would be easier targets…low-hanging fruit, so to speak. At least, some Indian wouldn't be guarding them.

They had ridden hard after escaping from whoever was firing those damnable arrows at them. After about a dozen miles, they pulled up in an arroyo.

A couple of men chortled silently and pointed to Perez's saddle.

"*Qué es?*" Perez literally gave them the evil eye. It was designed to silence anyone within sight. He looked behind himself at where they were pointing. A Comanche arrow was sticking in the cantle of the saddle. A couple of inches higher, and Carlos Perez could have been one of the dead men. It was no joking matter, despite appearances.

Perez dismounted and worked the arrow out of his saddle. He realized it was also fortunate that his horse had been spared. He looked at his men and relaxed the air with a toothless smile. "*Soy muy afortunado.*" Indeed, he had been very lucky.

The *Caballeros Negros* decided to spend the night there in the shelter of the arroyo. Perez needed to figure out his next steps. He certainly couldn't afford to lose more men. And, he needed food. The men would get increasingly unhappy if not well fed.

"*Mañana vamos a putear en Corpus Christi.*" A bit of good old-fashioned whoring would take their minds off any troubles.

They built a small fire and cooked up some frijoles and brewed coffee. It was filling if not nourishing. It made everyone drowsy, and before long they were all asleep.

Perez carelessly forgot to set a watch. Had he done so, he'd have noticed the gathering thunderheads to the west.

Long about two in the morning, the thunderstorm hit. The men were startled awake, but too late. The arroyo that had been so dry and sheltering was swept with a wall of water. The flash flood took saddles, bedrolls, and men a long way downstream from their camping spot. Shouts and curses were to no avail. When the storm finally subsided, it was nearly daylight. They spent most of the morning finding their belongings. Worse yet, one of the hobbled horses had tangled in the tie line, fallen, couldn't get back up, and drowned. They'd be traveling one horse short, at least for a time.

Finally, they dried out and began the brief trek to Corpus Christi. The heat and humidity were stifling, but they were all alive and the flood had given them an impromptu bath. The ladies of Corpus would be pleased with that.

Perez contemplated how he might find Scarlett and Cav. He needn't have worried.

SEVENTEEN

Crime Spree on the Strip

Scarlett luxuriated at awakening in a genuine four-poster bed with fluffy feather pillows, satin sheets, cushioned mattress and, of course, Cav. This was a huge improvement over Laredo. There were even sweet-smelling flowers and perfumes on the chest of drawers. The aromas of lavender and lilac filled the air. It was a living heaven for a woman whose dreams of a better life were dashed by her own attraction to ne'er-do-wells who stole her dreams. Wanted man or not, Cav fulfilled her visualization of a man.

The memories of the evening lingered with her. She'd bathed Cav, an experience of erotic sexuality he'd not soon forget. They'd had sex for all of ten minutes before Cav finished and promptly fell asleep. That was all. She hoped against hope for more in the morning. She wouldn't permit herself to think he was like those who'd gone before.

As the sun streamed in through the sheer curtains, Cav rolled on his side toward her and smiled. "Are you ready to see Corpus Christi?" There was no tenderness in this man that Scarlett had fallen in lust with. He'd done his duty the night before. In his eyes, she was still the whore from Laredo.

Undeterred, Scarlett stroked his chest. "Must we go?" She pursed her lips and kissed his hand, then his chest. It seemed almost as though her touch repulsed him. She wasn't ready to resign herself to the fate of simply being his whore. It might take some time.

Cav pushed her away. "It's late, and there's much to do." They dressed. Cav didn't even look her way as she momentarily stood fully naked before him. At last, he strapped on his holster and checked that his pistol was loaded.

"Why don't I meet you downstairs?" And, without waiting for her answer, he hustled out the door with nary another word.

Scarlett finished her hair and applied what little make-up she needed or had. She loved his attention last night, so far as it went. She gave a fleeting thought to how that Texas Ranger was treating the young girl he'd spoken of. She quickly put the thought from her mind. Scarlett wasn't his type of woman.

It got her to wondering what type of woman she really was. She needn't have wondered long, as her life had been crammed into a couple of all-too-short years. She thought back at how she'd run off with that soldier, the miscarriage, the riverboat gambler, and her eventual arrival in Laredo. She'd found herself a prostitute at the tender age of fifteen. With her long, fiery red hair, blue eyes, and a certain fragile facial beauty, she had been popular with drovers and soldiers from both sides of the Rio Grande. She'd been luckier than most in not getting pregnant or killed. She was only beaten a couple of times and nearly went to jail for shooting one of her customers who had insisted on whipping her. Now she found herself pursuing a man who turned out to have a price on his head. Was it another bad choice? Was there yet hope?

She headed down to the dining room, questions bouncing around in her head still.

Scarlett pulled up a chair on the opposite side of the table from Cav. "What have you ordered?"

"Not much choice. All they have is eggs, bacon, and biscuits," he said abruptly. He twitched nervously like he was in a hurry to get out of the place. "We have a lot to do, Scarlett. I want to find the so-called opportunities in this town."

"What do you have in mind, Cav?" she asked.

He thought about his sisters Belle and Cora. When he sent the note from Laredo, he'd optimistically left a return address of Corpus Christi. He was anxious to find the local post office. "I have some business to tend to. Why don't you stay here for now, and I'll be back this afternoon?"

What was Scarlett to say? She'd find something to do. Maybe she could make a few extra dollars here in Corpus, but she decided not to go down that road just yet. "I'll be here, Cav."

Cav left her sitting at the table. No kiss. No good-bye. He just up and left.

Scarlett absentmindedly ran her fork through the eggs. She had lost her appetite.

Cav headed to the post office. It had just opened up for the day, but there was a line of three folks waiting for service. He patiently waited his turn, scraping a bit of mud from his boots. It had rained just enough to turn the dusty streets to mud. When he finally got to the window, he noticed the wanted poster on the board next to it. There he was for all the world to see. He lowered the brim of his hat, turned, and left the place. He walked at a brisk pace back to the hotel. He decided to get Scarlett to retrieve any mail he might have.

He opened the door to their room. No knock, just walked in. Scarlett was lounging on the bed, repairing a tear in her satchel. "I need you to fetch my mail."

"Won't they give it to you?"

Hadn't she seen the posters? "You know the law is looking for me. Remember that fool Texas Ranger you traveled to Nuecestown with?

I just need you to ask for my mail at the post office."

"Can't you be nice to me, Dirk Cavendish? I don't need much, but nice would work real well."

Cav was taken aback. He'd only thought of her as a two-bit whore. It had never struck him that she could actually care for him. No one had cared for him since he was a little boy.

"I'm sorry, Scarlett. I'll try." Somehow, sincerity had been driven from Cav long ago. He had long since forgotten how to handle any feeling that resembled intimacy. "I do need you." Wrong word choice. "I mean, I want you with me." He was going to be a slow learner.

They strolled together from the boarding house. He waited across the street from the post office while she went in to inquire.

"Mr. Postmaster, I'm here to pick up a letter to personally take to my cousin in San Antonio," she told the man at the window. "He is unable to be here and asked for my help."

"What's the name, Miss?'

"Cavendish, sir. Dirk Cavendish."

"Let me look in the back room." The postmaster found a letter from Cora Cavendish and brought it out front. He'd already recognized the name from the poster. "You say your cousin is in San Antonio?" He started to hand over the letter. He was only supposed to hand mail to the addressee.

"Why, yes. That's indeed what I said, sir." She smiled sweetly at the man and gave him a peek at her cleavage.

"Do you know that your cousin is in a bit of trouble with the law?" Distracted by her sexuality, he looked over her shoulder into the street and right at Cav. "Apparently, they want him to account for a murder. I'd be careful, even if he is your cousin."

Scarlett took the letter from the postmaster's hand. "Thank you, sir, I'll be real careful."

She headed out the door and up the street a bit before crossing, annoyed that the hem of her dress dragged a bit in the muddy street. She joined Cav.

The postmaster locked the front door and left via the rear of the building. He didn't have to go far to reach Sheriff Whelan's office. He knocked, but there was no response save the sound of furniture being moved and an iron jail cell door being closed.

"Come on in."

"Sheriff Whelan?" The postmaster tried not to notice the half-clothed woman in the cell. "Sheriff, I think Dirk Cavendish may be in town."

That got Whelan's attention. "How can you be sure?"

"A woman claiming to be his cousin came into the post office to pick up a letter for him. She said he was in San Antonio, but I'd swear the man standing across the street met his description."

"Thanks, Harry. I'll look into it." Whelan shooed the postmaster out of the office. He had to finish his personal business before dealing with a lawbreaker. "Damn," he muttered, "Just what I don't need."

"Did you get the letter?" Cav pulled her close to him. He saw it in her hand and snatched it. He saw her hurt look. She'd not been appreciated for her effort. "I'm sorry, Scarlett. Thanks. I'm just anxious to hear from my sisters." He tore open the envelope and began reading the letter.

He was distraught, and thought for a moment that he might cry and embarrass himself. He inhaled deeply.

She stared at him. "What is it? Bad news?"

Cav handed her the letter. Cora had shared the news about Belle's murder and her own pregnancy. Apparently, whoring had taken them down a road to sad, undesirable ends.

"I'm so sorry, Cav," Scarlett said. She ever-so-gently placed her hand on his shoulder. "I can't imagine their pain, your pain."

For once, Cav accepted her offering of comfort. "They are all the family I have."

They walked down to the dock by the water's edge. Cav told her his story of abuse, and how he'd ended it with a pitchfork through his father's back. He described how he'd been on the run ever since, traveling from town to town, learning to gamble at cards, killing a man or two, and eventually wound up meeting her in Laredo on his way to Corpus Christi. He told how he'd hoped he'd be able to escape his past in Corpus, but that was apparently not to be. The postmaster had likely already told the sheriff of his suspicions.

"Where can we go?" she asked.

"I don't know," he said grimly, "but we can't stay here in Corpus."

"What about Mexico?"

"I don't think they like me after something I did in Nuevo Laredo. I'm wanted south of the Rio Grande."

"Could we head north?" He could see Scarlett's brain churning, trying to come up with ideas for escape. "Maybe Missouri or Kansas?"

Cav had begun to truly appreciate her caring about him. After all, she had the option of escaping before further trouble came.

"You don't have to stay with me, Scarlett," he told her. "There's likely to be danger for you." He was conflicted between her going or staying. She may have been a mere whore, but he cared enough to want to protect her. And now, she was his whore.

"I've come a long way to catch up with you, Cav. I don't plan on letting you out of my sight."

"Let's go back to that boarding house," he said. "In the morning, we can pack our things and get away from this town. I think heading north makes sense."

Sheriff Whelan finished his personal business and decided it was time to tend to the threat at hand. He shooed his friend out the back door, buttoned his trousers, pinned on his badge, strapped on his gun and holster, grabbed a rifle, and headed out the door. He'd start with the post office, and then try to track Cavendish from there.

Perez left their encampment, headed east, and soon happened upon a ranch on the outskirts of Corpus Christi. Before him was a corral with perhaps a dozen horses. They were fine mounts, too. Obviously breeding stock, to his practiced remaining eye. He and a couple of his men rode up to the corral and scanned for any sign of human life. There was a small cabin, but no one seemed to be stirring. One of Perez's *Caballeros* opened the gate and walked toward one of the horses. Of a sudden, the horse was attacking him. Its hooves cut through flesh and bone as the man tried desperately to escape.

A gunshot brought everything to a standstill. The crazed horse backed away from its attack. "What you boys lookin' for?" A man on horseback with a large-bore rifle was staring at Perez. "You're lucky that horse didn't kill your man. None of these broncs have been broken. If you were of a thieving mind, you'd have made a poor choice."

Perez backed away. In halting English, he offered apologies. "*Señor*, I am...I am sorry." As he spoke, he unholstered his pistol and shot the man clean through the throat. The cowboy gagged, grasped his throat, fell off his horse, and sprawled in a puddle of mud. He bled out in a matter of seconds.

Perez turned to his remaining man. "*Ayuda a Juan y toma el caballo muerto mans.*"

Perez's man helped the injured bandit to his feet, grabbed the dead cowboy's rifle and the halter of his horse, and headed back to their camp as quickly as possible. They'd need to find another route into Corpus Christi, but at least they'd replaced the mount lost in the flash flood.

Sheriff Whelan was about to head up the street to track down the wanted man and his accomplice. He'd only gone a couple of steps when a rider brought his steed to a skidding halt before him. "Sheriff, come quick. Seth Parks has been shot and killed. It's them Mexican bandits."

Whelan found himself confounded. In a town of less than two hundred people, there was suddenly a lot of action. It was as though the town had been hit with a crime wave. "Hang on, Pete. I'll get my horse." Cav and his whore would have to wait.

Cav watched Whelan and the cowboy who'd ridden in leave town. It created an opportunity. Perhaps he would find his fortune in Corpus Christi after all.

"Pack your things, Scarlett. We're going to give this town a time it won't soon forget." He checked his two Walker Colts to be sure they were fully loaded. He put one in his holster and the other in his waistband. "Scarlett, do you have a gun? Can you shoot?"

"Yes, sweetheart, I do and I can." He could see she was beginning to grasp what he had in mind. Across from the post office was the town's first and only bank of sorts. It was not exactly a bastion of security.

They walked briskly to the livery stable to fetch their horses. Once there, they saddled them and began to lead them from the corral.

"Pardon, sir…ma'am. That'll be two bits for stabling yer mounts fer the night."

Cav pulled the Colt, aimed, and said, "bang." He smiled. "If you care to live, boy, forget the two bits." Then, he and Scarlett turned and walked up the street toward the bank.

It was plain from the way Scarlett carried herself, head high and skirts swishing, that she was proud of Cav. He'd shown her he was certainly a man not to be trifled with. He hoped she had overlooked that he'd bluffed down a very young, unarmed stable boy. He picked up the pace, and she walked a bit faster to keep up with her man as they walked the horses to the bank.

As they approached the bank, a well-to-do-looking man in a fancy dark grey suit walked in ahead of them. Moments before, Cav had taken note of the man as he hit a young boy. Old memories of his abusive father welled up. Cav became so angry that he began to tense up and his hands literally shook. He fingered the handle of the knife at his waist.

"Cav, what is it?" Scarlett asked calmly.

"Just follow me." Her voice had settled him for the moment.

They hitched their horses to the post at the end of the dilapidated wooden walkway that ran along the front of the bank. They climbed the couple of stairs and entered through the heavy double door. The clapboard building, with shutters at the windows and those big green double doors, certainly wouldn't have passed for a bank in most towns of any significant size. But the fact that it kept folks' money made that a moot point. A bank was a bank regardless of appearance.

Cav stepped through the doorway with both guns drawn. He'd never robbed a bank before, but figured it couldn't be all that difficult. "Everybody, raise your hands!" he yelled. A bank manager in an alcove at the side of the bank foyer ran out but stopped short and raised his hands. The wealthy-looking man turned and appeared to go for a gun.

The shot rang out before Cav realized what Scarlett had done. The man lay on the floor, bleeding profusely. In mere moments, he stopped breathing.

"Unless the rest of you want what he got, put all your money in this bag." He motioned to Scarlett. "See what that bastard has that might be valuable."

He watched out of the corner of his eye as Scarlett turned the dead man over. The man was unarmed. He'd apparently been trying to hide his gold watch. She took the watch and some gold and silver coins. "Okay, we're ready."

By now, the teller and manager had filled the bag with gold coin to near bursting. It weighed a ton. "You men count to five hundred before you leave this bank. If you don't, you'll wind up like him." He pointed with the muzzle of his pistol at the dead man.

Once outside the bank, Cav hoisted the bag onto the saddle horn and climbed up. "Scarlett, we have one more thing to do."

She looked at him questioningly, but followed as he headed toward the post office. Once there, he dismounted and burst through the door.

"You sonofabitch," he shouted at the postmaster. "I ought to kill you for telling the sheriff about me." Instead, he handed the man a note. "You make sure this letter gets to Bozeman, Montana. You hear me?" He waved his knife at the postmaster. "If you don't, I'll come back and do worse to you than any Comanche."

The postmaster cowered in abject fear. "Yes…yes, sir. I hear you."

Cav ran from the post office and leapt into his saddle. "Let's get out of this town, Scarlett. Let's ride!"

Just at that moment, the bank teller came running out. "Stop them! Stop them! They robbed the bank!"

Cav fired twice. Both shots hit the teller.

Cav and Scarlett kicked their horses into a gallop, leaving the teller groveling in pain.

Within minutes, Sheriff Whelan came galloping back into town. He'd stopped on his way to the other crime scene when he heard the faint sound of gunshots from the direction of Corpus Christi. His law-abiding world seemed to be crumbling in the wake of a sudden crime spree. He pulled up his horse and dismounted in front of the bank.

The teller was badly wounded, but alive and likely to survive. The postmaster came running out with the letter that confirmed Cav's identity. "They headed west, Sheriff, toward Nuecestown."

Whelan went into action. While there was a lot of downtime to sheriff duties in a small town like Corpus, he needed to know how to do the right things when called upon. "Fred, get the doctor to look after the teller. Sam, put out the call for a posse. We need to be out of here and fast."

Cav rightly guessed the sheriff would have a hard time raising any posse quickly enough for pursuit. He and Scarlett stopped a few miles out of town to catch their breath. The horses were well-lathered and wouldn't mind a rest. Besides, the load of gold coin was a heavy added burden for a galloping horse. Cav drew a bottle of whiskey from his saddlebag. "I'm thinking we should celebrate, my sweet Scarlett."

"Shouldn't we get farther away?" she wondered aloud.

Cav looked around. They'd pulled up near a grove of live oaks. "Trust me. It'll be a couple of hours before they try to track us. We'll be long gone. We need to divide this gold to make it easier on us and the horses."

They spread a bedroll under the shade of a live oak and took a few swigs from the bottle. They were still caught up in the elixir of the bank robbery and gunfire. After a few drinks, Cav turned to Scarlett, tossed up her petticoat, and did his thing. There was a wildness about it, fitting the moment for both of them. He'd learned to abuse and she'd learned to enable abusers. They were now on the run together, and the thought of it was like an adrenalin rush.

Luke spent the night at Bernice's boarding house. He slept exceptionally well. He dreamed mostly of Elisa and that kiss, but it was tempered with thoughts of his duties that lay ahead. A bright sun broke through the skies that had brought heavy rains and flash floods only a few hours earlier.

He sat down to enjoy Bernice's offering of eggs, bacon, and biscuits for breakfast. He didn't expect her to sit down opposite him.

She looked sort of squinty-eyed at him, as though sizing him up. "So, Mr. Texas Ranger Captain, sir; is Miss Corrigan still an honest woman?" There was no holding back. Bernice was a woman that pulled no punches. She got right to the point, demanding to know Luke's intentions.

"Ma'am, I would never dishonor so lovely a lady. I would be untrue to my Irish heritage and my sense of morality as taught by my most honorable father and mother." He had a sense that what he said might actually have been fairly eloquent.

Bernice was a bit surprised, but his sincerity, if not his crediting his father and mother, convinced her. She knew how head over heels in love Elisa was, so admired Luke's apparent restraint. Still, she was curious. After all, she was the town gossip. For Agatha and her, it was like a career. "Did you kiss her?" she asked bluntly.

"Miss Bernice, I'm surprised." He feigned astonishment. "Why, even if I had, I'd never kiss an honorable woman and then boast of it."

Bernice smiled. She had her answer. They'd kissed. She could hardly wait to share the news with Agatha.

Luke was soon saddled up and heading up the trail toward Elisa's cabin. He found himself amused by Bernice's questioning. It would be great to spend one more day with Elisa before heading to Corpus Christi and certain trouble.

Sheriff Whelan was beside himself. He only had four volunteers to form up a posse, and they were a sorry sight to behold. He lamented that Corpus Christi hadn't seemed to progress growth-wise as far as he'd hoped since its day years ago as the Old Indian Trading Grounds. Colonel Kinney's dream had added the post office, bank, sheriff's office, a warehouse by the dock, a boarding house, a smithy, three saloons, and a couple of churches. Despite its unimpressive population, the town already needed far more than one man to enforce the law. Whelan was hardly more than a cover for Kinney's somewhat shady dealings. Now, with Kinney off playing at politics, Whelan had serious crime issues.

By late afternoon, Whelan had gathered his so-called posse in front of his office. A more rag-tag group he could never remember having seen. He duly deputized them. "We are heading up the road to Nuecestown in pursuit of a man named Dirk Cavendish and a red-haired whore that's riding with him. He's dangerous...wanted for murder, train robbery, and now bank robbery. They've run off with most of yours and your neighbor's gold."

That got the attention of the posse. Up until then, they'd been standing sort of lackadaisically.

"Y'all have horses, right?" That had been a requirement. The men nodded affirmatively. "Guns?" Another requirement. Whelan looked at the wide range of weaponry displayed before him. He hoped none of these men would get killed, but there was no guarantee.

About this time, the cowboy who'd come for Whelan earlier about the murder of Seth Parks showed up. "Sheriff! Where you been? Those Mexican murderers are getting away!"

Whelan couldn't have been more conflicted. He regretted not having hired a new deputy back when Luke Dunn joined Callahan's Texas Rangers. There really hadn't been any reason to do that up to now. Now, he was short-handed.

"Crap, Pete. I can't do two damned things at once!" Turned out he wouldn't have to.

"Sheriff, look! Look up the street!"

Just entering the main street not more than a couple of hundred yards away were Perez and what remained of his *Caballeros Negros*.

Pete was startled. "Sheriff, that's them. They're the ones that killed Seth!"

Seeing the sheriff and the posse, Perez halted to assess his position. He didn't have many options. He appeared to have ridden into a potential hornet's nest. He started to draw his pistol, then thought better of it. The odds were simply too even. He had no advantage. He turned to his men, *"Vamos a salir de aquí!"* He made the only viable choice and beat it out of town and away from the threat.

In a heartbeat, the *Caballeros Negros* had wheeled their mounts and headed northwest on the Nuecestown road.

"Men, get your horses! Pete, you're deputized! They're all headed for Nuecestown!"

A few minutes later, the posse was galloping out of town.

Cav and Scarlett had just finished their tryst when they heard the faint sound of hoof beats. "I don't like the sound of that," Cav yelled. "We'd better get out of here…and fast!"

Scarlett sighed. She craved more of that fabulous night cavorting in silk sheets in the big four-poster bed. Was this what life on the run was going to be like?

They mounted and headed toward Nuecestown as fast as their horses could take them. Cav wondered whether the sheriff had managed to assemble a posse. He had no idea, of course, that it was Carlos Perez and his *Caballeros Negros* that were right behind him. His fate with them could be far worse than that with the sheriff.

"Who's chasing us, Cav?" Scarlett shouted over the sounds of the horses.

That struck a chord. "There's some higher ground up ahead to the north. Let's go there and see whether we can make them out." Cav led them toward a low-lying bluff along an arroyo screened by some mesquite. They'd be able to scan the prairie behind them while having some semblance of cover.

They didn't have long to wait. Scarlett recognized Perez right away. "Oh, my God, Cav, it's that Mexican that came after me in Laredo. It's me he wants!"

Cav looked at her inquisitively.

"There were nine of them that came to Texas Jack's Saloon. They boasted that they were looking for the Texas Ranger. They got raging drunk, and the one with only one eye came after me. Thank God, he passed out before he could have his way with me. I escaped the next morning to join you." She paused to take a breath.

Cav was amazed at her bravery, but still didn't understand why she had chased after him, or even thought she loved him. Peering at the bandits, he said, "They must have run into some bad luck. There's only five now."

It wasn't the empathy Scarlett was seeking, but she wasn't surprised. "You heard me? I escaped to find *you*."

Suddenly, Cav got it, but he didn't know how to take it. Affection beyond sex wasn't in his constitution, wasn't part of him. He looked deeply into her pale blue eyes and smiled warmly. "You're crazy, but I'm glad you came."

He was getting used to the idea of having some company. He'd effectively been alone since his mother died. He leaned over and kissed her. Nothing passionate. Just a light kiss. Then he looked away at the horizon to see what progress the Mexicans had made. "Let's lay low and let them pass," he said.

Scarlett felt something between pleasure and consternation. Had she penetrated Cav's thick skin? Would it make a difference?

EIGHTEEN

The Prey

Luke arrived at the farm around mid-morning. As he hitched the big grey to the corral post, he saw Elisa out of the corner of his eye kneeling beside her family's graves under the live oak. She'd strewn purple and yellow flowers over them. Most likely, he thought, she had no idea what kind they were, but they were pretty and suited the moment.

Luke watched her for a moment. She was so focused on her flowers and family that she hadn't realized he was standing behind her. "Prickly pear flowers and winecups. Pretty."

At his voice, she leapt up wide-eyed and threw herself into his arms. They embraced tightly for a few moments. No words needed be said.

"You know flowers?" It hit her that he'd named the varieties of flowers she'd just scattered about. She had no idea what they were called.

Luke laughed. "Guess I know one or two. Of course, I'm partial to bluebonnets. They're like blue versions of our native Irish betony."

A Texas Ranger that knows flowers. Didn't that beat all? Elisa had been introduced to a perspective on Luke that she would never have imagined. She offered up a demure smile. "What other secrets am I going to learn about Luke Dunn?"

Luke laughed. "Time will tell…time will tell."

They stood for a few more moments at her family's graves. He recited an old Irish prayer, then they headed back to the cabin.

Mike was digging a hole for a hitching post. It was hard work for the little guy, but he was determined.

"Good morning, Captain," Mike said, looking up and catching sight of the lawman walking with Elisa.

Impressed at the boy's efforts, Luke pondered what Mike might call him familiarly yet respectfully. "Mike, how about just calling me Mr. Luke?" He gave the youngster a disarmingly friendly smile.

Mike put down the shovel and extended his hand to Luke. "Yes, sir, Captain, sir…Mr. Luke it is." His hand was lost in Luke's meaty paw. Mike looked up at him admiringly. "Mr. Luke, I hope I can grow up to be like you."

"Well, Mike, I hope you grow up to be like you."

"Are you hungry…er…Luke?" It was as though Elisa wanted to find something endearing to call him, but it wasn't the right time just yet. It was all so new.

Luke wasn't oblivious to her dilemma. "Why don't you call me by my given name, Lucas. No one uses it. It'll be special between us." He was as smitten with her as she with him, and it took all his will power to restrain his natural urges. There was a part of him that wanted to offer her more than life with a Texas Ranger, yet the lawman role was part of who he was. "Bernice fed me this morning," he told her, "but I sure could use a cup of coffee and one of your biscuits."

They soon found themselves sitting out front sipping coffee and watching Mike dig. "I've been thinking about the McGills' place up the way. I've heard they're selling and heading to California."

"Why would you want to buy their property?" Luke asked.

"I was thinking, mind you, just thinking, of raising some longhorns.

With their property added, we'd have enough land for close to twenty head. I could fatten them up and sell them in Corpus."

Luke was impressed at her thinking.

Their idyll was broken by the sound of a lone horse. Doc, drunk and barely hanging on to the saddle horn, came lurching in. He pulled up and all but fell from the nag.

"What brings you out here, Doc?" It wasn't lost on Luke that Doc was drunk before lunch. He helped steady the tottering doctor.

"There's bad medicine coming, Luke…er, Captain Dunn."

"Explain." The medical man had Luke's full attention.

"Dan had been on his way to Corpus when he heard about it." Doc leaned toward Luke conspiratorially, and the full strength of the alcohol smell came close to getting to him.

"About what?"

"Rumor has it, there's been a couple of murders this morning in Corpus and the bank's been robbed. Some desperado named Dirk Cavendish and his whore…" Doc glanced apologetically at Elisa. "And his lady friend are on the run and headed this way." He caught his breath. "But that's not all. Some Mexican gang that murdered a cowboy is headed this way, too. There's about five of them."

"Did the leader of the Mexicans have one eye?"

"Yes, yes, he did, Luke." Doc was starting to calm down. He craved another swig of whiskey but had left his bottle in Nuecestown. "Oh, and Sheriff Whelan put a posse together and is chasing the whole bunch of them."

"Doc, can you get back to town and get Bernice and Agatha out here?" Luke asked. "It'll be dangerous for them. Get that stable boy out here, too. We'll need every person who can shoot."

Elisa's head was swimming. Just when she thought her life had settled down and a bright future lay ahead, here was a new wrinkle to worry about. "Luke, can't we just head north from here to San Patricio?" She realized flight was not an option the moment the words left her mouth. She shook her head. "No, we must stop them."

166

Doc headed back to town. He hadn't a moment to lose. Luke and Elisa took inventory of their weapons. Luke had the two Walker Colts and the Colt rifle; Elisa had her Colt plus one of her father's two old rifles.

Mike had finished digging. "Can I help?"

"I'm afraid you're going to have to defend the farm, Mike," Luke told him. "It's an important job. If all else fails, you must protect your home."

Mike's chest puffed a bit. It made perfect sense to his nine-year-old thinking.

"Well, darling…Elisa, we'll have the advantage of surprise."

He'd lost her attention at the word "darling."

"Elisa?"

"Yes, surprise." She regathered her thoughts. "Surprise for sure, Lucas."

Their tentative steps at familiarity weren't lost on either of them.

"Mike, go get the ammo and your father's other rifle," Luke ordered.

As the boy went inside, Luke swept Elisa up and kissed her—a deep kiss.

"Lucas?" She was trembling, but in a good way.

In his subconscious, Luke wanted her to remember his kiss in the event anything bad…like being killed…should happen to him.

Mike reappeared with the rifle and ammunition.

After what seemed like an eternity given the situation, Doc and the stable boy finally arrived in a buckboard with Bernice and Agatha.

Luke gathered everyone together. Doc had already passed out on the doorstep. Luke could do naught but shake his head resignedly at that. "These killers are headed to Nuecestown. The Perez gang is going to be extra angry if they see the bodies of their gang stacked behind the sheriff's office. Perez wants to kill me, plus he's seeking vengeance against the outlaw Cavendish and his lady friend."

He looked at the women and boys standing before him. The odds weren't exactly in his favor. The stable boy was an unknown quantity, and only Elisa had any skill with a gun.

"Bernice and Agatha, I want you to stay here with Mike," Luke said. "He'll protect you." He prayed the youngster could use the rifle.

Bernice looked apprehensively at Mike. "He's just a boy, Captain."

Elisa stepped up. "Bernice, he knows how to shoot. And, besides that, he's all you've got." She looked up at Luke. "Lucas and I, along with Dan, need to go to Nuecestown and head off trouble if we can. I think Lucas is of a mind to set a trap."

"She's right, ladies," Luke agreed. "We don't want to be the prey. We have to take aggressive action. I wish we had time to reach some of our neighbors. There's going to be a lot happening."

Bernice nudged Agatha knowingly and whispered aside, "Lucas… she said, Lucas. Did you hear that, Aggie?" She nudged her sister again. "They're in love."

She smiled, then dropped the smile, as Luke urged them to stay in the protection of the cabin. "Elisa's not really going with you to Nuecestown, is she?"

Luke ignored her question. They had their horses ready. Doc finally snored himself awake. "Doc, why don't you stay here with Mike and the ladies?" He didn't want Doc spoiling any defense of Nuecestown. In his drunken state, he was simply too unpredictable.

They headed into town, with Doc still half dozed-off on the front step of the cabin.

Perez realized that he and his *Caballeros Negros* had passed their quarry when the fresh hoof tracks disappeared. He now was about a mile outside Nuecestown. By his reckoning, the whore and her lover couldn't be very far behind him. He knew that the sheriff and his posse was chasing all of them. He didn't have any idea how big the posse was but, in his experience, towns the size of Corpus Christi had trouble pulling together ordinary citizens willing to risk their lives chasing hardened outlaws. There were likely no more than five or six, including the sheriff.

Perez also knew that the damnable Texas Ranger was out there ahead of them somewhere. And he had no idea where the Indian chief was. He hoped the Comanche was long gone. So he was outnumbered by roughly two to one, depending on whom was hunting who. In any case, it wasn't an enviable quandary to be in.

Perez rode to within a half mile of the town. *"Establezcamos el campamento aquí. Necesitamos descansar."* The bandit decided his group would set up a temporary camp with a defensive perimeter and rest at this spot. He himself wanted to reconnoiter. He dared not ride blindly into Nuecestown.

The bandits would rest tonight and be fresh to pursue their prey in the morning. They'd keep an eye out for the posse while they waited for sunset. Perez would steal into town under cover of darkness to check things out. He couldn't afford any more surprises. He didn't want to lose his quest for revenge by attrition.

Cav and Scarlett decided to lie low near the mesquite from where they'd spotted Perez. Before they got too drunk, Cav watched where Perez stopped to bed down. A bit before sunrise and nursing just a bit of a hangover, he snuck away from Scarlett.

There was just enough light from the stars and nearly full moon to enable him to see where he was going. He got close enough to Perez's camp to inch up to within around fifty feet of the lone sentry. The sentry never heard the thrown knife. The knife sank deep in his throat, severing the carotid artery before he could react.

Cav wasn't going to go after any more *Caballeros Negros*. He didn't want to push his luck. He'd just improved his odds, and that would be a help.

Scarlett was looking for him when he returned to the mesquite trees. "Where you been?" she whispered.

"Improving our chances, Scarlett, just giving us a better chance."

She saw the blood on his shirt sleeve and the knife and sensed what he'd done.

Cav pulled the bottle out of the saddlebag again, and they finished it off. Soon, they fell into a drunken stupor and sleep took over.

Sheriff Whelan brought the posse to a slow walk. He was getting closer to Nuecestown and didn't want to ride into a trap. He wanted to be the hunter, not the hunted. Only Pete, the cowboy from the ranch, was likely worth his salt as a fighter. The others might get lucky.

He noted the sun sinking in the late afternoon sky and decided to wait until morning. He very much preferred being able to see what he was hunting. With the tall prairie grass that came up as high as a horse's withers and the deep arroyos, anything could be lurking out ahead of him.

Luke, Elisa, and the stable boy cautiously walked the horses the five miles to town. Only the ferryman and a couple of townspeople were still around. Luke quietly and efficiently went to each of them to warn them of the impending mayhem.

Following Luke's instructions, Dan led the horses to the stable and hitched them inside so as not to be readily visible to anyone coming into the town. He stored the tack away out of sight, then picked up his rifle and reported back to Luke.

"Dan…I can call you Dan, right?" Luke stood in front of the boy and placed his hands on his shoulders to be sure he had his full attention. "I don't want you to fire that rifle until you hear me shooting. Is that clear?" Dan nodded. "Now, I want you to position yourself on the roof of the general store."

Luke looked off thoughtfully in the direction of Corpus Christi. He knew that, if these killers were smart, they'd circle around and come in from the west end of Nuecestown. But he knew they were not so smart, and he felt confident that wouldn't happen.

"Lisa, how about going to Doc's place? It would give us a crossfire between you and Dan."

Elisa noticed he'd called her Lisa, and assumed that was some sort of an affectionate thing. "Yes, Lucas, that sounds good." She smiled. "Pray we don't get hurt."

"Indeed, and we better pray that Whelan gets here with his posse." He took her hand, smiled at her, and turned away to take his position at the boarding house. He prayed deep inside that she'd not get hurt.

Carlos Perez awakened with the sunrise. He noticed almost immediately that no sentry was in sight. "*Maldita sea! Qué ha pasado?*" He was none too pleased

"*José está muerto!*"

Of a sudden, the *Caballeros Negros* were down to four men. The realization that, at some time during the night he'd been attacked, was startling, if not unnerving. He was used to doing the hunting, not being the hunted. The role of prey wasn't one he was the least bit comfortable with. Someone had killed Jose. Who? The sheriff? The outlaw with the whore? The Texas Ranger?

Perez ordered his gang to break camp. He decided they would become the hunters, and that would start with riding closer to Nuecestown.

Sheriff Whelan gathered his posse, motley crew that it was, and told them his plan. "We're going into Nuecestown, men." It was simple, likely too simple. Whelan had no idea as to what might be lying in wait in the town or even its outskirts.

As the posse headed up the trail, they came to a rise that gave them a panoramic view of the prairie before them. It was similar to the position Cav had taken. Whelan pulled up. "Pete," he whispered. "Pete, look ahead." About a half-mile off were four horsemen headed toward the town. At a half mile, Pete squinted and announced, "I think one of them is the man who murdered Seth."

Whelan was relieved. At least they'd stayed on the trail of some of the lawbreakers. He didn't want to have the town shot up, as innocent folks could get hurt. It wouldn't be the sort of legacy he'd want to be remembered for. "They're moving slow-like. Maybe we can overtake them before they reach Nuecestown."

The men in the posse looked at him as though he were crazy. "We could get killed, Sheriff!"

Whelan tried to contain his anger. "Damn bunch of cowards! You are deputy sheriffs. We have innocent citizens of Texas to save. Any of you can't stand the heat, get out of the fire. Go! I don't want to ride with any lily-livered cowards." He spurred his horse into a gallop, hoping he'd be followed.

A shot rang out from just behind them, to the north and east, not far from the Nueces River. A bullet knocked one of Whelan's deputies from the saddle. He was wounded, but not badly.

"Damn! Where the hell did that come from?" Whelan ducked low and spurred his horse again. "Come on, men. It's an ambush!"

Cav slid his rifle back in the scabbard. He and Scarlett rode off to the northwest along the river, figuring to skirt around Nuecestown proper. They hoped to commandeer the ferry that would take them across the river to possible freedom. He had no idea why he'd risked the shot at the posse. He hoped to further better the odds should he have to confront Perez as well as the sheriff. It had all become a huge gamble in a game he never imagined he'd be playing.

He and Scarlett reined in their mounts at the ferry, dismounted, and walked the horses the few feet to the landing. The ferry stood ready to cross the river.

The ferry master stood before them with arms crossed. "Halt! What's your hurry?" He couldn't duck fast enough to totally avoid Cav's knife. It was enough to knock him down.

Cav barely glanced at the ferry master as they ran by with horses in tow. Suddenly the bags of gold didn't seem so heavy. The fugitives boarded the ferry and began getting it ready to push off from the landing. Freedom was on the opposite bank of the Nueces River.

Whelan lost two members of his posse, one wounded and the other caring for him, but actually avoided any gunplay. Now, it was just the four of them. He rode hard, whooping and hollering to get Perez's attention. He was desperate to catch up with the Mexican bandit before they reached the town. As he closed to within a hundred yards, he'd finally made enough noise.

Perez turned, drew his pistol, and began firing in Whelan's direction. He realized they needed to get to the town where they'd find some cover. "*Rápido! Vamonos!*" They rode at breakneck speed for the town with Whelan closing on their heels. In moments, Perez's *Caballeros Negros* were thundering into Nuecestown.

From his vantage point in Bernice's boarding house, Luke was first to see them coming. He opened fire, and Elisa and Dan followed suit.

Greeted by a hail of bullets from Luke's modest but effective ambush, two of Perez's men were killed instantly. One, his foot trapped in a stirrup, was dragged down the dirt main street.

Whelan's posse galloped in behind. Perez made the decision of his life, ducking low along the side of his horse and riding as fast as he could right on out of town. The last of his *Caballeros Negros* dismounted and put up a valiant but brief fight before falling from a well-placed shot from Elisa.

When the dust cleared, Sheriff Whelan and his posse had come to a halt just inside the edge of town and were able to survey the scene of carnage. They'd missed most of the action, but had the pleasure of having incited it.

Luke walked out from the boarding house. "Where you been, Sheriff?"

Elisa emerged from Doc's place and sidled up beside Luke while the stable boy climbed down from the general store roof. They looked around at the dead. Luke's and Whelan's eyes met. "Where the hell is Carlos Perez?"

"Nuts!"

Just then, there was a loud noise coming from the direction of the ferry landing. It sounded like the desperate cries of the ferry master. Whelan spurred his horse forward. "Come on, men, this ain't over just yet!"

As they rode down the gentle slope leading to the ferry, they came upon the ferry master lying wounded with a knife wound from Dirk Cavendish. Cav, meanwhile, was struggling to pole the ferry across the Nueces River.

"Get back here, Cavendish!" Whelan shouted to no avail. Cav kept poling. Scarlett fired a shot aimed above the posse. It was intended to keep them at bay while she and Cav escaped.

Neither Cav nor Scarlett saw the figure in the grove of trees lining the river's edge. The rifle was aimed and trigger squeezed. The shot rang out, echoing across the river. Cav slumped to the deck of the ferry.

Scarlett gasped, dropped her rifle, and fell protectively over his body. "No! No!" she screamed.

Luke emerged from the trees, rifle in hand. He was cool as cool could be. He casually walked over to Whelan. "You can give the bounty to Elisa, Sheriff. She's fixin' to buy some more land around here." His words were delivered so calmly they caught Whelan off guard.

Luke Dunn had stopped another lawbreaker, delivering frontier justice on the Nueces Strip.

One of the men in Whelan's posse started hauling in the ferry mooring line, while another saw to the ferry master. Scarlett looked up to find herself slowly being dragged to shore. Her dream, ill-conceived as it might have been, had been shattered. Her lover was dead, and she didn't yet know that Perez was still on the loose.

At last, the ferry was drawn into the landing, and Sheriff Whelan stood before her on the dock. "Miss Scarlett Rose," he said, "you are under arrest." He took her into custody and marched her up the road to the sheriff's office.

Luke followed along with Elisa. As Whelan entered the office, he was overwhelmed with an obnoxious odor.

"What's going on here?"he gasped, holding his bandana up to his nose.

The three dead *Caballeros Negros* had been forgotten. Their decomposing bodies behind the sheriff's office had begun to leave a tell-tale stench that permeated the surrounding area. Whelan went around back and saw the outlaws stacked against the wall, arrows still protruding from them.

"Comanche arrows?" Whelan was dumfounded.

"Sorry, George. I thought you'd get back here sooner. They are compliments of a Comanche friend of ours." Luke smiled. "And you might want this." He handed the gold to the sheriff. "You have a safe or strong box here?"

Whelan nodded that he did. He scowled at Luke as he held his nose and pushed Scarlett into a cell.

"Sheriff, you can't leave me here. The smell is awful." She held her dress over her nose.

"Get over it," he told her as he slammed the cell door shut.

Between the posse and the stable boy, Luke and the sheriff managed to get the three bodies buried, along with the rest of Perez's gang and Cavendish. They'd had enough heart to bring Scarlett out of her cell in chains to grieve at Cav's burial. The Nuecestown Cemetery was becoming just about full up.

The foul odor ultimately dissipated enough such that the office became habitable. Whelan left the office door open for a while to help air the place out. It struck him that the first criminal occupant of the Nuecestown jail was a woman. She'd be charged with bank robbery and the killing of Mr. Johnson.

"Lisa, let's head back to your spread and let them know all is well for now." Luke's judgment was that Perez had kept on riding. Besides, he wanted a couple of more folks to know that Whelan was guarding the gold from the bank robbery. He trusted the sheriff...up to a point.

They saddled the horses and headed back to Elisa's farm. Doc, Bernice, and Agatha would be happy to see them safe and sound.

Perez rode as hard as he could as long as he could. It wouldn't do to run his horse into the ground. With all the bullets flying around, he was lucky to escape unscathed. He'd ridden a couple of miles before his terror turned back to anger at having lost the immediate advantage in his quest for revenge. His anger was exacerbated by having ridden into an ambush. How could he have been so careless? Perhaps he'd let his passionate drive for vengeance overcome his better senses. He'd have to carefully consider his next moves.

NINETEEN

Escape

Sheriff Whelan sat at the small but serviceable desk. Scarlett curled up on the bed in a corner of the cell, crying her eyes out. Between sobs, she tried to get Whelan to promise to let Cav's sister in Bozeman know what had happened.

Whelan had had just about enough of her sniveling. "Look, lady. I'll take care of it. Will you please stop crying?"

He wanted to tell her to get over it. The guy simply wasn't worth her tears.

She fell asleep at last.

The sheriff had already noticed that she was a right pretty young lady.

He sensed that something was going on between Luke and that young Corrigan girl. She'd certainly made it clear that she wasn't interested in a more mature lawman. She sure was a pretty little filly and had filled out right handsomely. He regretted that he'd approached her in such an uncouth manner, at least by her reckoning.

A knock at the door interrupted his musings about could-have-beens. "Come on in. It's open."

"Sheriff, how are you holding up, my old friend?"

Captain Luke Dunn walked through the door. Whelan sort of resented that he was about six inches shorter than the Ranger. It was intimidating.

"Any news about that Perez fella?" Luke glanced over at the cell where Scarlett was sleeping peacefully and then sat down next to the desk. "I expect I'm gonna have to chase him down. He sure got lucky today."

"I thought you'd be with your lady friend."

Luke wasn't sure of the implication. "George, where I grew up, a gentleman didn't go staying with an honorable single woman. It wouldn't do." He let that sink in. "Like I said, I figure to head out tomorrow and catch up with Perez. I brought Doc and the ladies back to town with me."

"How did it go with that Strong fella that injured your hand?"

Luke was a bit surprised. "You didn't hear? Damnedest thing, George. We flushed him from his ambush and had him dead to rights. He was about to try to shoot his way out when a rattlesnake struck him from a ledge and caught him clean in the neck. He was dead in minutes."

Whelan frowned. "Terrible. Not a pleasant way to die. You had help?"

"A fellow Texas Ranger Clyde Jones helped a bit, but Strong ambushed him before we flushed him out." Luke thought about how to phrase this story and decided to keep it simple. "I had made friends with the Comanche Chief Three Toes. You might recall, it was his braves who raided the Corrigan place. Anyway, he saw me as having some sort of big medicine and insisted on coming with us. He helped me find Strong. I rewarded him with Strong's horse and scalp."

Whelan winced. "You let him scalp Strong?"

"Didn't matter to Strong. He was getting all discolored from the snakebite, too. Anyway, Three Toes decided to visit the scene of the Corrigan attack a couple of days ago and happened upon Perez fixing to attack us. The chief shot a few arrows. That's how those three dead Mexicans wound up with Comanche arrows in them."

"Is Three Toes still around?"

"No. He said he just wanted to say good-bye. The Comanche call me Ghost-Who-Rides. Catchy, huh? Anyway, he headed out to join his people. I think they might have been headed to the reservation fort up north." Luke got up to leave. "Oh, George, please do be sure that Miss Corrigan gets that reward money. I'll be back after I catch up with Perez."

Whelan caught an implication that Luke didn't trust him to get the money to Elisa. "Not to worry, Luke. I'll be sure she gets it." He escorted Luke to the door. "I'll be sure to get the gold back to the bank, too. Good luck with Perez."

As Luke closed the door behind him, Whelan saw Scarlett stir in the cell. He unlocked the cell door and undid his trousers. After all, he thought, she was nothing but a common whore.

Perez had ridden hard. He'd endured a hornet's nest and come out unscathed. At last, he reached San Patricio, where he hoped he could hide out and gather his wits. He had a lot of unfinished business to take care of, and he was running out of patience. Revenge should have been easier than this. It had cost him eight men and, but for the errant aim of a Comanche arrow, he and his gang might have been wiped out entirely.

He knew the sheriff would give up the chase since he was now so far from Corpus Christi. The Texas Ranger was another matter. He would certainly be coming after him. Once again, Carlos Perez had become the hunted, the prey. Escape turned out to be an illusion.

He rightly guessed that the lawmen would be tied up cleaning the aftermath of the gun battle. Had he known about the gold, he might have decided to double back. Gold has a way of affecting men, and Perez was no exception. However, he didn't know…yet.

Perez camped near a live oak motte just outside San Patricio. He'd head into town in the morning. Perhaps he could learn something about what was going on in Nuecestown. The only downside he could see was that he was a Mexican. He was a bit far north and many Texans still didn't take kindly to his countrymen, often treating them as subhuman. Justice under the law for Mexicans in Texas was an aberration. It simply didn't exist. Nevertheless, he was still far enough south that there should be some of his kind around. He'd find out what he needed to know.

Scarlett laid unmoving as Whelan had his way with her. She really didn't care. He even came back after having dinner at the boarding house and raped her again. She seemed to have lost her will to live.

After he'd finished, the sheriff turned absentmindedly and gave her some food that Bernice had sent over. "Here." He shoved the plate at her. "Eat this."

"What happened to the Mexican?" she asked dully.

"Perez? He escaped. The Texas Ranger is going after him in the morning."

In a way, Scarlett felt lucky she'd been arrested. With Perez on the loose, he might yet seek his revenge. "What are you going to do with me? Where will you take me?" She already knew what the sheriff would do with her; the second question was the one that mattered.

"We're going to Corpus tomorrow, where you'll answer for your crimes. You'll likely avoid the hangman, Miss Scarlett, but you'll surely see the inside of a prison."

She had to find a way to escape. She'd have to wait until the sheriff was most vulnerable, and then make her move. She pushed her empty food dish out beneath the cell door and lay back to catch some more sleep...and wait for Whelan.

Luke saddled the big grey. He'd said his good-byes to Elisa and was preparing mentally to pursue Perez. He headed toward Nuecestown. The man had only one advantage, Luke figured, a sort of underworld of Mexicans in the Nueces Strip. They might hide him and help him escape to Mexico. His hope was that Perez's desire for revenge was stronger than his desire to escape. He hitched his horse outside the sheriff's office and strode up the steps, entering without knocking. First thing that caught his eye was Sheriff Whelan in the cell hog-tied by his pants. Scarlett was gone.

She'd done Whelan the indignity of tying him up naked from the waist down. "Damn, George. What the…?" Luke didn't have to ask how. The man's pants were at his ankles and he was doubled over in obvious pain.

"She pulled a fast one on me, Luke."

Luke proceeded to unlock the cell and cut Whelan loose. "Where's the gold?"

They looked over at the strong box. It was open. The gold, or at least much of it, was gone. The whole cache was simply too heavy for her.

"I messed up, Luke," Sheriff George Whelan said forlornly in a tone of understatement.

Scarlett feared for her life, such as it was. She'd used her wiles to persuade the stable boy to "sell" her a horse. It hadn't taken all that much, as young Dan was thrilled with a simple flash of breasts, combined with a gold coin. From the time she'd escaped the cell to having climbed aboard the horse and headed out of Nuecestown, it had taken not more than ten minutes.

She had no idea where Perez had headed but, in her way of thinking, he was Mexican and logic would have him heading south. She rode north. Besides, it was the direction she and Cav had been going. She thought she might start life anew in Austin.

As with Perez, Scarlett's escape was more illusion than reality. They were both slaves to their passions.

TWENTY

Revenge a Sparse Meal

Luke was now doubly incentivized and doubly aggravated. He had to pursue, and capture or kill Perez before the man could assemble another gang of cutthroats, plus he had to find the prostitute who'd run off with the bank's gold before Perez found her. While he felt confident that he could handle the tasks on his own, he missed having capable company like Three Toes and Clyde Jones. He wished the folks in Austin would fund another company of Texas Rangers. He could only hope that popular opinion would ultimately prevail. There seemed to be an ever-growing number of Texans regretting the decision to join the Union. The settlers on the Nueces Strip felt especially vulnerable.

During the gun battle in Nuecestown, Luke had seen what turned out to be Perez riding away hard on the road toward San Patricio. The killer likely stayed on that road, as the town was only about fifteen miles to the northwest. His quarry likely would have arrived on the outskirts before sunset. Luke believed his search should begin there among the Mexican community. He knew Perez was a creature of habit and would inevitably return to Mexico. Luke's gamble was that Perez would leave tell-tale clues in San Patricio that would be easy to track. The man was not very subtle, yet he was not to be taken lightly. He lacked the strategic finesse to double back and trap Luke.

Luke's other worry was Scarlett. If she was headed for San Patricio, she could encounter Perez. The Mexican bandit and the red-haired Laredo whore apparently had a less-than-friendly relationship. Scarlett needed to pay for her crimes, but not her bad life choices.

Sheriff Whelan headed back to Corpus Christi. He had been deeply embarrassed and appreciated Luke's discretion at not telling anyone in Nuecestown about the condition in which he'd been found. He was bringing back what was left of the gold, though roughly two-thirds had been stolen by the red-haired whore. He was of a mind to resign as sheriff, but felt he could trust Luke to keep their secret.

Other than lawman and philanderer, he really had no other skill sets. At least they'd stopped Cavendish and killed off most of the Perez gang. He consoled himself in having helped solve both the murder and horse thievery on the ranch near Corpus, as well as the bank robbery. He'd lick his wounds in Corpus, maybe get lost in some drinking and carousing.

Pete, the cowboy who had alerted Whelan to the murder of his partner by Perez and then joined the posse, had already returned to Corpus Christi. He didn't even know that the Laredo whore had escaped with some of the bank's gold. Thankfully for Whelan, he wouldn't know how she escaped. The last Pete had seen of Scarlett, she was locked in the cell.

Pete stopped at the bank and told them of the success in Nuecestown and that the gold was on its way back.

Whelan arrived late in the morning. He stopped at his office first, took his horse to the livery, and then took the satchel with the remaining gold coins over to the bank. As he walked into the bank, he noticed there were still blood stains on the floor.

"Sheriff, we're glad to see you," the teller Cav had wounded greeted Whelan.

Whelan silently handed the satchel to the bank manager.

"Er…Sheriff, this seems very light." The bank manager was almost apologetic. "I thought the gold had been fully recovered."

Whelan finally found his courage. "The woman found a way to escape while I was indisposed. She took all the gold she could carry. Captain Dunn is pursuing her."

The bank manager wondered what indisposed was supposed to mean, but decided not to ask about the circumstances. "I'm sure Captain Dunn will be successful, George. He's built quite a reputation since he served as your deputy."

"Yes, yes, he has. We're fortunate to have him on the Nueces Strip. With the soldiers pulled out of Texas and no Texas Ranger companies authorized, he's important to protecting our homes and businesses."

"And banks." The bank manager shook his head. "A lot of folks are depending on Luke Dunn, Sheriff."

Whelan couldn't get out of the bank fast enough. His next stop was the saloon up the street. A couple of drinks and a local whore would prop up his spirits.

In the morning, Perez rode into San Patricio. It didn't take long to find the local barrio. He dismounted in front of the house of the nominal mayor of this part of the town. The Mexicans tended to stay off by themselves in these barrios or neighborhoods. Only the very wealthy *patrones* lived among the Anglos.

"*Buenas dias.*" He greeted the mayor warmly. "*Me llamo Carlos. Viajé desde Corpus Christi.*"

The mayor invited Perez into his house, and they sat in the garden to talk and drink coffee. "*Qualiquier noticia de Corpus Christi?*"

Perez was non-committal as to goings-on in Corpus. "*No mucho.*"

The mayor scratched his stubble beard as he tried to figure out this one-eyed man. He sensed that Perez was not a law-abiding person. He shared what little he knew of goings-on in Corpus Christi. "*Un *forajido fue asesinado, pero un mujere escapó con oro."*

Perez smiled deviously as he took in this information. The man the Laredo whore had been chasing was dead, shot by the Texas Ranger. She was on the run with stolen gold. *"Hay más?"*

"Un guardabosques de Texas la está siguiendo."

Perez was almost beside himself with a perverse joy. He could still have his revenge on the Ranger as well as the whore. Revenge might yet be sweet. *"Muchas gracias, alcalde."* He bid the mayor good-bye and found his way to the nearest saloon in the barrio.

As he nursed a glass of whiskey at a table in the saloon, he wagered that the whore would not return to Corpus Christi, but would escape toward San Patricio. If she was carrying a satchel of gold, it would slow her down both by its weight and her need to protect it. It was also obvious to Perez that she would not come to the barrio, but would head for some more genteel part of the town.

A dark-haired, ruby-lipped woman at the bar smiled his way. Perez motioned her to join him.

As she sat in the chair beside him, she lifted her skirt to reveal ample leg and more.

"Te gustaría ganar dinero?" Perez didn't waste time getting to his purpose. Of course, she was interested in making money. What did he want her to do to him? But it turned out to be for him, not to him.

Perez shared a plan by which she'd lure the red-haired whore to his room above the saloon. He didn't share with this San Patricio whore that he aimed to first prove his manhood, then kill the red-head and take her gold. In fact, he was careful not to mention gold.

Perez took the whore's hand and led her to his room. He was of a mind to get in a bit of hands-on practice for what he hoped would be sweet revenge. Afterward, he could figure how to trap the Texas Ranger.

Scarlett was dead tired by the time she reached San Patricio. As a woman traveling alone, she'd be under some suspicion. She easily distinguished the barrio from the rest of the town and skirted wide of it. She finally found a boarding house.

She persuaded a young boy to take her horse to the livery. She used the same technique she'd found useful in Nuecestown. Upon entering the boarding house with her heavy satchel, she secured a room. The housekeeper was surprised at being paid in gold. "I'm paying in advance. Is there somewhere I can get a bath and some new clothes?"

"Come around to the back room in an hour, ma'am, and I can have a hot tub for you. The general store is still open, so I'd be pleased to find a dress for you."

"Thank you. Is there a stage coach from here to Austin?"

The housekeeper thought a moment. "I'll check, but I think one leaves the day after tomorrow in the morning." She looked down at the obviously heavy satchel. "I'll get that bath ready for you."

Scarlett prayed her satchel would be safe in the room while she took her bath. She regretted not hiding it before her arrival in town. She decided on a bit of deception. Once in the room, she emptied the contents under the mattress. She snuck out and gathered enough rocks to fill the satchel, and then left it on the chair near the bed.

She enjoyed the hot bath and appreciated the housekeeper's good taste in clothes. The dress would be serviceable for stage coach travel. She was in much better spirits, even stopping to have a bit of dinner before she returned to her room.

Her first clue was that the door was unlocked. Inside, the room had been ransacked. The satchel had even been turned inside out, and the rocks strewn across the floor.

She took a deep breath and raised the mattress. The thieves had overlooked what was probably the most obvious place to hide valuables. She put the gold back in the satchel and slipped it under her pillow. She'd be sleeping on top of her glittering horde that night.

At breakfast, a pretty black-haired woman was eating. She

appeared to be crying. Scarlett had a soft spot for women who might be struggling. "Are you all right?"

The woman shook her head and continued to cry.

Scarlett went over, sat beside her, and put her arm over her shoulder to console the woman. "Can I help?"

After Three Toes said his good-byes to Luke, he slowly made his way northwest to join Long Feathers and his people. His wives were none too happy that he'd chosen to make the visit to Ghost-Who-Rides. The Comanche were at least a day ahead, but Three Toes was in no hurry to catch up.

He pondered what had become of his people, the once-proud Comanche. How had they come to this inauspicious end? Why were they heading to a place where they'd be under the control of the Anglos? It was a bitter outcome. He hadn't heard any encouraging words about Camp Cooper and his Penateka brethren.

The first night after leaving Luke, he built a small campfire and meditated under the stars. He heard great peals of thunder and saw flashes of lightning far to the south. He prayed to the Great Spirit for direction. Now in his early forties, he had much life ahead and intended to guide his Penateka Comanche through possible tough times ahead. Is that what the Great Spirit would have him do?

He prayed, looking up at the expanse of heaven above him. He had heard of the lamentations of the Sioux to the far north of him. He'd seen his brother Comanche tribes surrender one by one as they succumbed to the incursions of the white man, increased killing of the buffalo, rampant starvation, and dreaded white man's diseases.

Three Toes felt pulled from his people by some strong invisible force. It was frightening. He'd begun to fear being alone in what was now ever-more-hostile country. What indeed was the Great Spirit telling him to do?

For the next two nights, he meditated and prayed. He was torn by what he believed he was hearing. On the third day, he came within sight of his people. He could delay no longer. He had to come to a decision. Once he entered the Penateka Comanche camp, he'd be committed to a future that the Great Spirit seemed to be pulling him away from. In the distance, he could barely make out Long Feathers and see his three wives pulling the travois. He wondered if one or more might be pregnant. Perhaps one day he would know, he thought, as he turned south and rode from his people.

Three Toes would follow the commands of the Great Spirit, going wherever he felt led.

Luke rode into the barrio section of San Patricio and stopped at the mayor's house. As a big man on a big horse, he was noticed. The word would travel quickly. He knocked on the mayor's door. *"Senor Garcia! Hola!"* Luke's Irish Texas Spanish wasn't half-bad.

The mayor opened the door and furtively motioned Luke inside. *"Como estas?"*

"Muy bien, alcalde. Gracias." Luke was running to the limit of his knowledge of Spanish, but was trying.

"What brings you here, my friend? You have *un enemigo aquí.* He's here in the barrio."

"Entiendo, amigo. And I need your help."

Luke explained in greater detail what had happened in Corpus Christi and Nuecestown, especially focused on Perez, but also inquiring about the woman with the gold. Garcia had met Luke back when he was deputy sheriff in Corpus and had come north to find out about some rustler. Garcia had been helpful, and they had established a bit of a friendship. Garcia brokered livestock, so was very appreciative of Luke's efforts to stop rustling. Men like Perez, who only wanted the cattle hides, were highly undesirable. They were called hiders.

"Do you know where Perez is staying?"

Garcia actually had learned to speak English just enough to be one of the most popular men of Mexican descent in the barrio. The mayor, or *alcalde,* title was more an honorific. He was respected in the Anglo portions of San Patricio. Very little went on that he was not aware of. "He's staying on the outskirts of the barrio. I hear he's setting a trap for that red-haired woman you spoke of." The mayor stroked his chin thoughtfully. "I have also heard that she hopes to take the stage coach day after tomorrow to Austin."

"Does Perez have any friends with him?"

"No. He is alone." Garcia gave Luke directions to the place where Perez was staying. "*Buena suerte, amigo.*"

Luke thanked him, and agreed that he might need some luck.

Perez kept watch from the second-floor window. He dared not venture onto the balcony, as his face was becoming too well known. He had a good view of the street below. He wouldn't miss Scarlett's arrival if the black-haired whore had done her job. He'd rented an adjoining room so as to make her less suspicious of trouble.

Soon enough, there they were walking up the street together. Scarlett carried what appeared to be a heavy satchel. Perez slicked back his hair and adjusted the eye patch. At last, he heard noises in the room next to his. The time was near.

The black-haired whore knocked softly on his door and whispered, "*Senor, ella esta aquí.*"

He opened the door and slipped her some coins. "*Muchas gracias.*"

Perez's trap was set. He was ready to show Scarlett how much of a man he was before killing her and taking the gold. He slipped quietly from his room and journeyed the several steps to the door of the room Scarlett was in. He was full of great anticipation.

He swung the door open. No knocking. He simply swept in. "*Hola rojo.*"

Scarlett was dumbfounded. She'd been trapped! Perez, the swarthy Mexican bandit with one eye and hardly any teeth, began to move toward her. He unbuckled his belt and started to drop his pants. He pointed to himself to show how ready he was.

In the next moment, Perez's world fell apart. The explosion in that small space was almost ear-shattering. Perez doubled over in excruciating pain. Scarlett had blown his testicles clean away. She grabbed her satchel, stepped over the groveling Perez, and headed out the door. She walked headlong into none other than Luke.

"Going somewhere, Scarlett?" Luke looked at her and then beyond into the room where Perez lay in a pool of blood, writhing in agony. "Damn, Scarlett. You done him in."

He grasped her arm and pulled her back into the room. He bent down to disarm Perez.

That's when Scarlett clobbered him with the heavy satchel of gold coins. Luke fell on top of Perez, causing him to scream with pain, while Scarlett freed herself from Luke and ran out the door as fast as she could.

Luke got up. His head throbbed.

Perez was out cold. Luke staggered after Scarlett but it was too late.

Meanwhile, Perez was bleeding all over the floor and was unconscious. Luke half-picked him up and dragged him downstairs and out the front door. Perez's horse was out front, so Luke threw him over the saddle like a sack of potatoes. The jail was just up the road. He'd take care of Perez and then look for Scarlett. She seemed to be having some regular success with escaping.

Luke carried Perez into the jail, past the sheriff, and deposited him in the first of two adjoining cells. "This man has a price on his head, Sheriff. He's wanted in Corpus for murder." That's when he got a better look at the man seated at the sheriff's desk.

The man had a shotgun pointed at Luke. "Mr. Texas Ranger, the cell over there is for you." He waved the muzzle of the shotgun at the cell. "You can leave my friend Carlos where he is."

Luke obeyed the man. It seemed that the barrio mayor might not have been such a friend as Luke had hoped. The cell door clanked behind him and was locked. By this time, Perez was starting to come around. He'd lost a lot of blood and was quite woozy in addition to the pain.

There was no way Perez was going to sit in a saddle. A wagon was brought around, and the man with the shotgun laid him in the back. They headed out of San Patricio as fast as the horses could pull the rickety old wagon.

About three hours later, the *alcalde* entered the jail. He looked around. "*Donde esta el sheriff?*" He acted as though he were oblivious to Perez's escape. Slowly, he walked over and unlocked the cell.

Luke wasn't sure how to act with the mayor. He didn't want to judge. "Which way did Perez go?"

The mayor pointed north. That was the giveaway. Luke knew they went south toward Mexico. He gave serious thought to putting the mayor in one of the cells, but he might need him one day. He'd give him a pass today. At least Luke knew how far he could trust the man.

Now he had a dilemma. Both his quarries had escaped. The whore was headed north and the killer south. Which to pursue first? Luke gauged that Perez being wounded would slow him down. He didn't have a big head start, and Luke could likely catch up within a day. Scarlett could be found easily enough, though getting the gold back was a major concern. She had a few folks' life savings in that satchel.

He headed to the stage coach station. He entered and quickly saw her trying to blend in with one of the benches. She was anxiously waiting for the stage. Luke came up behind her and stuck the muzzle of one of his Colts at the back of her head. "Don't move a muscle, Miss Scarlett. You're under arrest."

At that moment, the stage came barreling in to the station. It diverted Luke's attention for a split second. Scarlett turned and swept Luke's pistol aside and made a dash for the stage. She left the satchel behind. Escape was more important to her.

Luke regained his footing and peered into the satchel. It was filled with gold coins.

The stage didn't stop long. It was behind schedule.

Luke grabbed the heavy satchel and headed for the door. He was in time to see the stage pull away with Scarlett waving good-bye. She had a few gold coins in her hand.

A voice inside his head told Luke to let her go. In her profession, she wasn't likely to survive long. She'd murdered that man in the bank, but they could pin that on Cavendish. Now Luke was free to drop the gold at the bank in Corpus Christi on his way to chasing after Perez.

Luke waved back at the departing stage. He knew where to find her, and she knew it. He decided it likely as not gave Scarlett a safe feeling that someone cared, regardless of the reason why.

Luke couldn't know it, but Scarlett at last breathed a sigh of relief as he faded into the distance. She'd set her hopes on Austin. She was still young and pretty, and she had enough gold to get a fresh start. Maybe she did have a chance for a new life.

Luke went back to his other problem. He knew Perez had been badly wounded. Riding in a wagon was going to make for slow travel and obvious trail sign. It seemed most likely the man would head for Mexico and take his chances with the law south of the Rio Grande.

He hung the satchel of gold from the saddle horn. The added weight didn't bother the big grey a bit.

Luke was tempted to stop at Elisa's place, which was along the way to Corpus. He was sorting out his feelings about her, and she was very much on his mind. But no, he decided, it was his responsibility to get the gold delivered first. It would take extra time, but he was in no hurry to get back on Perez's trail. He'd be moving twice as fast as the outlaw.

Luke rode all day. He bypassed Nuecestown proper as he didn't want to delay his travel there talking with Bernice or Doc.

Whelan was despondent. He'd failed big time. His vice had been costly. Citizens of Corpus Christi had trusted the bank with their savings. It wasn't Whelan's job to protect against robbery, but he was entrusted with the responsibility to recover the stolen gold. He wished he could have stopped the robbery before it happened. Fate had conspired to burden one man with the occurrence of simultaneous crimes.

He considered resigning. Only Luke knew the truth of what happened in Nuecestown, and he was not going to tell anyone. But that wasn't enough. Whelan's shame was lodged deep in his gut. He knew, and that was what mattered.

He also knew Colonel Kinney was heading back from Austin. Whelan could resign then. Except for his peccadillos, his indiscretions with the ladies, he was an upright, fully reliable lawman. He'd been sheriff for better than five years, the longest he'd held a job. Kinney might very well refuse his resignation. What then?

Instead of his usual evening ritual of walking up the street to the saloon and finding companionship, he sacked out by himself on one of the cell cots. He didn't even tap the unopened whiskey bottle. He yearned to escape from his misery. He thought about Elisa. He'd started that out all wrong. Maybe she'd let bygones be bygones and give him another chance. Shoot, he might even give up his whoring for a woman like her.

He resolved to ride out in the morning and see how she was doing. Maybe he'd bring her some flowers to pretty up the place. On second thought, he figured the flowers might be taken the wrong way. Nope, he'd just drop by friendly-like. He began to get drowsy and soon fell asleep. Emotion had the effect of wearing some folks out.

TWENTY-ONE

Road to Purgatory

The bank manager was overjoyed to see Luke walk into the bank with the satchel. "Captain Dunn, I am so glad to see you. Have you recovered the gold?"

"We got most of it." Luke handed the satchel to the manager. "The girl made off with a few coins and likely spent a couple on niceties." He glanced through the window at the sheriff's office. "I expect that Sheriff Whelan brought some of it to you."

"Yes, he did, Captain Dunn. But this appears to be most of the rest. We'll have to count it to be sure."

"Is the sheriff in town?"

"I didn't notice him leave his office. He may still be there."

The manager took the bag to his office. "Oh, Captain, I believe Sheriff Whelan notified the folks in Austin about the reward for that Cavendish fella. I heard that you wanted to give that money to Miss Corrigan."

"That's true."

"Well, folks think that was a right nice thing to do, Captain, what with losing her parents and brother. She is certainly a sweet but determined young lady."

195

"Thanks. It'll be good to see her be successful with her farm."

"Can I ask something personal, Captain?" the man paused.

"Don't ask, if you have to ask to ask." Luke smiled as he said it. He knew the question. Why were there gossips seemingly everywhere?

Luke strolled across the street and knocked on the sheriff's door. He opened the door and peeked inside. He could hear snoring and figured there was no point in waking Whelan.

The wagon offered a rough ride, but was far preferable to the saddle. It'd be a bit before Perez would be fit to ride. He'd gotten intimately acquainted the night before with the man who'd helped him escape. The guy cleaned and bandaged Perez's wounds. It wasn't a pretty sight. Relieving himself had already proven to be pure hell. It wouldn't just be horse riding that he'd miss. Now whores would be safe from Carlos Perez.

"*Como se llamo?*" He realized he didn't know his savior's name.

"*Me llamo Jorge. Jorge Valdez.*"

The name sounded familiar to Perez, but he couldn't quite place it.

"*Por qué me salvaste?*"

Valdez explained it was a long story that he'd tell Perez during their journey.

"*A donde vamos?*"

"Carrizo, *señor.*" Carrizo was a little village on the Texas side of the Rio Grande where the river was shallow enough to cross on horses or in a wagon. The downside was that it was nearly a hundred fifty miles from San Patricio. They'd be making roughly fifteen miles a day. Perez's condition would likely worsen. If infection could be avoided, he might have a chance to survive.

There was still something about Valdez that was familiar to Perez. He couldn't quite place the man. In any case, he was in so much pain that he decided he'd worry about it later. He thought about his foiled plans to get the Texas Ranger and how he'd underestimated Scarlett.

Vengeance was still on his mind. He wasn't exactly feasting on the fruits of his revenge. Thus far, it has been a very sparse meal.

They stopped to rest for the night. The trip through the prairie was especially tiring on the horses. The wagon alone was a heavy load, pulling through heavy grass and in and out of arroyos. They kept an eye out for the weather. Perez didn't feature being the victim of a storm again with its flooded creek beds.

Valdez helped him from the wagon.

Perez's pain was excruciating. If his wounds got infected, he'd be in far deeper trouble. "*Es un doctor en* Carrizo?"

"*No, pero hay uns mujer que puede ayudar.*"

Just what Perez needed: a woman.

"*Ella es Apache medicina mujer.*"

The thought of some witch doctor playing with his very tender privates raced through Perez's mind. But what choice did he have? He hoped that he'd make it to Carrizo with what he had left intact. He sensed that Valdez was almost taking some pleasure in this.

As he'd promised soon after rescuing Perez, Valdez had shared with the bandit how his uncle was one of Perez's *Caballeros Negros*. He'd been visiting in San Patricio when he heard of Perez's plight and felt inspired to rescue him.

Perez once again suffered the indignity of Valdez changing the dressing. It wasn't looking good. The wounds hadn't gotten infected just yet, but they looked ugly just the same. Perez desperately needed help. He felt as though he were on a road to hell, to certain purgatory. Perhaps, this was punishment, his very own purgatory. The punishment Scarlett delivered had certainly fit the crime.

Three Toes decided he was called by the Great Spirit to track down his friend, Captain Dunn. He followed the Atascosa River that eventually spilled into the Nueces. He took his time. He'd actually lost track of how far he'd traveled since the encounter with Perez near Elisa's ranch.

He spent part of each evening meditating, giving his prayers for guidance to the Great Spirit. Three Toes had been seeking and was finding his vision quest, a supernatural mission assigned from the Great Spirit to strong Comanche warriors. He sensed that Luke would once again need his help.

Elisa awoke early. It was a warm sunny day, and she thought she might seize the opportunity to bathe in the creek. The rains had formed deep pools of clear water. It would be a luxury.

Mike was still asleep. He had a habit of sleeping late. So far as Elisa was concerned, that was a good habit for this day. She walked on down to the place where she washed clothes and turned a few yards upstream to the waiting pool. Stripping off her clothes, she laid them neatly on the rocks, placing the Colt carefully under the folds of her skirt. She tested the water with her toes. It was just cool enough to be refreshing. She immersed herself, lying back in the cool water. She once heard her mother refer to these pools as cups for God's tears.

She rolled over, then stood and washed her hair. She hummed a tune, then realized it was an Irish lullaby her mother had sung. When her hair was clean, she sank back in the depths of the pool to rinse it.

Elisa felt a chill. She had a sense that something or someone was out there. Could someone be watching?

Whelan had regretted it the moment he spied her from upriver. He couldn't help himself. He had to sneak closer to get a better view.

"My God," he thought, "she's gorgeous." Her wet reddish blonde hair spread over her ivory skin made for a beauty beyond his wildest imaginings.

His horse took a drink and snorted. Whelan moved closer into his hiding place. Had he been discovered?

Elisa cocked her head and looked around. What was that noise? What was its source? She made her way over to where her clothes lay and lifted the Colt from under her skirt. She was still wet as she slipped her shirt and skirt on with one hand. Her clothes clung seductively to her wet body. They didn't offer much improvement over being stark naked.

"Who's there?" she called out.

Whelan had been made. What to do? His lusts had gotten him into a jam again. "It's me…Sheriff Whelan." His voice drifted down from upstream. It was far away but not far away enough. He'd seen too much.

"Get the hell out of here! Get out!" The vision of the Comanche warrior coursed through her. She'd always remember the look on the warrior's face when he realized her bullet had torn out his heart and he was a dead man. "Come no closer."

Whelan took a couple of steps closer until he was perhaps thirty feet from her. "I'm terribly sorry, Miss Corrigan. I meant no offense. I was just traveling through and heard your humming." His face wore a pleading expression, but his soul held dark intentions. What did he have to lose? He'd bungled his job as sheriff. He even liked that she was resisting.

"You shouldn't be here, Sheriff. Now leave." She tried to sound strong, yet she felt fully vulnerable.

He took a step or two nearer before he realized the Colt was aimed at him. She couldn't miss at the distance, but would she shoot? Whelan dropped the horse's reins and lifted his hands above his shoulders. "I…I'm sorry, Miss Corrigan." This wasn't how it was supposed to be.

He took another step toward her.

"You have a hearing problem, George?"

Whelan knew that voice.

"You heard what the lady said."

Whelan backed away, tripping on a rock and landing in a pool of water. Now dripping wet, he got his soggy self up, slapped his wet hat on his thigh, mounted his horse, and started on his way. He knew his days as sheriff in Corpus Christi were likely finished. It was time to move on. He didn't look back.

Elisa turned to see Luke standing above her on the path that led down to where she was. "Lucas? Thank God you're here." She waded out of the water and started to run up the path.

Luke was embarrassed. Even fully clothed, nothing about her was left to the imagination.

Before he could move, she was on him with a bear hug. He lost his balance, and the two of them fell back into a grassy area. Their world came to a stop as they savored the moment of reunion.

Luke felt her body against his. It was wonderful, but he knew it wasn't right, at least not yet. He extricated himself, stood up, and pulled her up to him. He kissed her. "Lisa…"

She placed her fingers over his mouth. "I know, Lucas." She smiled mischievously. "But I'm not sorry."

Luke couldn't help but smile. "Let's see if Mike is awake."

They walked arm in arm up to the cabin. Mike came running out headlong into Luke. "Mr. Luke! You're back!"

Luke swept the youngster off his feet, tossed him high in the air, and then set him down. "Say, I see you finished that hitching post. Great job, Mike."

Mike flushed with pride at Luke having noticed. "Yes, sir, Mr. Luke. Ain't it a dandy?"

"Isn't, young man. Isn't it a dandy?" Elisa corrected his slang.

Luke turned his attention back to Elisa. "Got any coffee for a thirsty Ranger?"

"Of course, Lucas, there's always coffee brewing. Are you able to stay for a while?"

"I must still chase down that Mexican, Lisa. He's wounded right nasty and can't ride a horse, but I need to get him before he escapes to Mexico."

"Won't that be dangerous?"

"Depends as to whether he got some help. Somebody helped him escape up in San Patricio."

Elisa didn't press any more questions about his Rangering duties, though she was curious about Scarlett. She handed him a cup of steaming hot coffee and sat beside him.

"I heard at the general store that the reward money for Cavendish had been placed in an account for me at the bank in Corpus Christi. You are a sweet man to do that, Lucas." She half-wondered if his generosity was a hint that he was serious about courting her. It was a pretty crazy set of lines to try to connect. He sure seemed very interested in her.

"Have you spoken with the McGills?"

"Yes," she said. "They want about seventy-five dollars for their spread. They were trying to get a hundred, but I persuaded them that the land hadn't been sufficiently improved and I was paying them in cash."

"Sounds like you did right well, Lisa." He grinned at her, proud of her business acumen. "Now we'll have to buy a few longhorns. I have a cousin with a spread west of here, and he might part with a half-dozen cattle at a reasonable price. He's an experienced speculator, but he'd give family a good deal."

"Lucas, I'm Irish, but not a Dunn," she retorted.

Luke gently blew away the steam rising from the coffee and thoughtfully took a long, slow sip. "Not yet. Not yet, Lisa."

She didn't know quite what to make of that. What was Luke saying? Did she hear what she thought she heard?

"Lucas," she said softly. "What did you just say?"

He just grinned.

Whelan headed north toward San Patricio. He was deeply despondent. He thought he might salvage some of his life if he could get the Mexican or the Laredo whore. He figured he'd need to do something more spectacular than that Texas Ranger's exploits. Captain Dunn was building an outsize reputation, and Whelan had to admit it was impressive. Just a couple of years earlier, Dunn had been an Irish immigrant looking for work.

Whelan hadn't been to San Patricio in quite a while. He wondered how the town was faring and whether there were lots of ladies that might interest him. He removed his sheriff's badge and stuck it in his vest pocket. It wouldn't do to misrepresent himself.

At least he was drying out. That scene with the Corrigan woman had been embarrassing. He was perversely grateful that he hadn't been shot. She would have put a bullet in him if it hadn't been for Luke. Whelan recalled hearing that she'd killed a Comanche with a single shot.

Whelan went a few miles before dismounting and cleaning his gun. The warm sun and a slight breeze hastened the drying process. His gun cleaning done, it wasn't long before he rode into San Patricio. He didn't especially care for the barrio, as he despised Mexicans in general. Like many Texans at the time, he saw them as subhuman. Morally, it wasn't right, but it wasn't about morals to the likes of Whelan. If it were up to him, they'd all be chased south of the Rio Grande.

He took a deep breath and turned down the dirt street toward the barrio mayor's house. He looked around. Other than some young children playing and a woman carrying a large basket to market, it was quiet. He knocked on Mr. Garcia's door.

"*Buenas dias.*"

The mayor saw right away that this was an Anglo. "Can I help you?"

Relieved that the mayor spoke English, Whelan tried to be friendly. "I'm looking for a red-haired woman that came through San Patricio a couple of days ago."

"*Quién es?*" The mayor reverted to Spanish. This was not good.

Whelan held up a silver coin. "I'm just trying to find out where she headed."

"Austin. *Entrenador de etapa a Austin.*"

Whelan let that ruminate through his brain. If she took the stage coach to Austin, she'd be a couple of days ahead of him. Still, he didn't exactly have many options.

"*Muchas gracias.*" He handed the silver coin to the mayor.

"*Una mas?*"

The mayor nodded and held out his hand.

"*Donde está Perez, el Mexicano?*"

The mayor smiled broadly and held up two fingers.

Whelan produced two silver coins.

"*Perez,*" laughed the mayor. "*Yendo a Mexico, pero con no cajones.*" He burst out laughing. "*La pelirroja le disparó.*" He made a gun signal with his hand and pointed at Whelan's crotch, telling the sheriff Scarlett had shot the bandit in the privates.

"Holy smoke," Whelan said in awe. She'd done Perez far worse than she'd done to him. Whelan knew first-hand how effective Scarlett could be in disabling men. He pretended to laugh, but it was just a bit too real for him.

The mayor laughed again as though sharing the joke, "*Él no puede montar a caballo.*" It was hilarious to Garcia that Perez couldn't ride a horse.

Whelan thanked Garcia, climbed back on his horse, and turned north. He winced as he thought of Perez trying to ride a horse. In any case, he was anxious to put some distance between himself and the barrio.

He wasn't excited about going to Austin, but the whore was likely going to be easier to capture than Perez. The Mexican was probably going to be able to attract a couple of *compadres* despite his condition. Besides, he owed Scarlett for the embarrassment she'd caused him in Nuecestown. He headed toward Austin.

TWENTY-TWO

Strong Medicine

The *alcalde* in the San Patricio barrio had told Luke that Perez was headed to Carrizo, where his wagon could cross into Mexico more easily. It was a long ride, but Luke would be moving at least twice as fast as Perez's wagon, plus could put in a longer travel day. Elisa had helped him pack plenty of rations.

He thought on her. More than that, he simply couldn't get her out of his mind. He wasn't getting any younger and needed to settle down. They'd have to make some decisions on his future, whether ranching versus Texas Ranger. He'd heard rumors that Rip Ford was going to assemble a couple of new Ranger companies once funding had been approved in Austin. Likely as not, it'd be next year.

She had truly grabbed his heart, and it was obviously mutual. He figured Ford would exert a lot of pressure on him to remain a Ranger. He'd deal with it all after he dealt with the Perez matter.

The weather was bone dry. He passed plenty of grazing cattle and even buffalo and wild horses now and then. He hoped those drovers he'd passed a week or so back had delivered their cattle safely. Their way of life wouldn't be going on forever. The range was wide open, though he knew in his heart it likely wouldn't remain that way. Folks that owned land had a tendency to possess and protect. In Texas, land was king. The Texas government even preferred to pay law enforcement and militia with land rather than cash.

For three days, Luke saw no one. He looked out across an empty prairie vista. He sang his favorite Irish tunes to while away the time and kept squeezing the bandana to keep strengthening his hand. He calculated that he was no more than a day behind Perez. Whether their paths would cross was in question. In fact, it was highly unlikely. There were no direct roads that might increase the likelihood of an intercept.

Luke figured he was better off simply heading straight to Carrizo. It wasn't much of a town and was peopled mostly by Mexicans. With his size, he'd be quite a contrast to the shorter, darker-skinned Mexicans. Perhaps that could be used to his advantage in bringing Perez to him. At least he wasn't worried about Perez turning the tables on him and lying in ambush somewhere. Luke much preferred being the hunter rather than the hunted.

Perez was still in agony. His anger was building hour by hour. He was heading in the wrong direction if he hoped to waylay the Texas Ranger or the Laredo whore. But he couldn't even ride a horse. Frustration and anger were the twin fates he was enduring. He'd even accommodated Jorge cleaning his wound each evening.

By Jorge's reckoning, they were about halfway to Carrizo. There were no towns or villages along their route. The Nueces Strip was still mostly undeveloped raw frontier. That was likely good news, given their vulnerability with the wagon. They were a perfect target for Apache, rival Mexican gangs, and any other outlaw that chose to make a life of waylaying underdefended targets of opportunity. Jorge had the common sense to have acquired a pistol and a couple of rifles before they left San Patricio. The rifles were old breech-loaders, and Perez was unimpressed. Nevertheless, they were better than nothing.

They'd have a fighting chance defending against attackers, though couldn't mount much of an offense.

Perez wasn't a particularly religious man. He grew up in a family of Catholics, but his faith was more a perfunctory exercise. That having been said, he found himself praying. He worried about his wound as well as his safety. What if infection set in? What was that woman in Carrizo going to be able to do for him? It made him even more angry at the red-haired whore. As soon as he healed, he'd head back north and take care of that little tramp. His patience was wearing thin.

In a perfect world, they'd simply take the wagon across the Rio Grande and into Mexico. What could possibly go wrong?

Scarlett checked in to the Bullock House Hotel upon her arrival in Austin. The ride from San Patricio had taken five days, including a stopover in San Antonio. The Bullock House was fancy, but she had enough gold coin to afford it until she could get established. Austin was thriving, and she hoped to find opportunity other than her chosen profession. More important, she had put plenty of distance between herself and Corpus Christi.

She enjoyed a warm bath. Shopping would be next in her plans, as she sought an appropriately stylish wardrobe. After all, she needed to look prim and proper to have hope of finding a respectable position in the Texas capital.

Scarlett knew no one, so needed to find someone who could get her oriented to the city. Ideally, that person would be a respectable citizen of Austin. She figured that the hotel restaurant might be a good place to start.

Scarlett enjoyed a wonderful day of shopping and had done well for herself. As she entered the Bullock House Hotel restaurant at dinner hour, she scanned the dining area for possible contacts. Only two folks were sitting unaccompanied. Both were men, well-dressed and apparently middle-aged.

Scarlett had already created a cover for herself. She'd let it be known that she was visiting from Richmond, Virginia and seeking opportunity in the great state of Texas. At least, she remembered enough about the place to carry on a credible conversation.

As she ordered dinner, the younger of two men nodded to her. Before he could come over and make her acquaintance, a gentleman from an adjoining table stepped forward and invited her to join him and his wife.

"Young lady, my name is Colonel Rucker. My wife and I would have you do us the pleasure of joining us. We don't hold with young women having to eat alone."

Scarlett saw the colonel and his wife as the lesser of evils by far. She had a habit of getting into trouble with lone men. She did take note of the colonel's impressively tailored uniform with gold sash and fringed epaulets. He appeared every bit the military officer.

"What is your name, young lady, and where are you from?" Mrs. Rucker seemed nice enough. Scarlett smiled as genuinely as she could.

"Scarlett," she said with the hint of a Southern accent. "Scarlett Rose, ma'am. I hail from Richmond." Despite Scarlett's youth, there was still a hint of the used woman across her face. Too many men in too many places were already taking their toll.

"Oh, why, we've visited Richmond. What part of the city did you grow up in?" Mrs. Rucker asked.

"Actually, Mrs. Rucker, my parents were killed in an accident when I was young, so I was raised by my grandparents on the outskirts of the city. I'm afraid they are quite elderly, and I was a burden. I left to seek my fortune. I was told that Texas offered great opportunity."

Colonel Rucker acted intrigued, but strove to not be overly ingratiating. His wife tended to be the jealous type. "What sort of opportunity are you seeking?" he asked.

Scarlett had an intuitive feeling that she wasn't a total stranger to Colonel Rucker, though she was certain he'd never been one of her customers. It was as though meeting the Ruckers was not by chance.

Mrs. Rucker had already noticed the way the colonel was giving Scarlett the once-over. "Yes, dear. What sort of opportunity would interest you?"

"To be honest, ma'am, my skills are limited to what a young lady in Richmond might be expected to learn. I do have some education, but my skills are mostly what one might expect for housekeeping. I can sew and cook."

Colonel Rucker glanced at his wife. She gave a reluctant nod of approval. "We are looking for a housekeeper. How are you with children?"

Deep inside, Scarlett rolled her eyes. Taking care of children was not something she found desirable. "How old are they?"

"Fifteen and sixteen."

They were nearly as old as Scarlett. "I expect it would work."

Mrs. Rucker spoke up. "We had an elderly housekeeper, but she wasn't able to deal with our children. We travel a bit, so it's important that our housekeeper be able to understand our children's needs." She looked over at her husband and then back at Scarlett. "Are you up to it?"

"Yes, ma'am." Scarlett smiled again, but inside she was not as confident as she appeared.

Three Toes rode into the clearing in front of Elisa's cabin. He was naturally reluctant to enter Nuecestown, given the general attitude toward Comanche and Indians in general. Mike saw him first.

"Sis! There's a Comanche in front of our cabin!"

Elisa grabbed the Colt, slowly cracked open the door, and peered out.

Three Toes smiled and raised his hand as greeting. "I am looking for Ghost-Who-Rides."

Elisa stepped out of the cabin, with Mike cautiously behind. "Welcome, Three Toes. Would you care for some coffee?"

He slipped down from his pony. "Captain Dunn is a lucky man to have you as a friend."

Elisa smiled. "I think we'll soon be more than friends." She extended her hand to the chief. "Mike, fetch some coffee for our friend."

Three Toes took Elisa's proffered hand and shook it in the Anglo way. "I am pleased you are well, Miss Elisa."

"Lucas is headed back toward the southwest to capture Carlos Perez, the Mexican killer that threatened us. I remember how you saved us with your arrows." Elisa smiled at her recollection. "Perez is apparently wounded and has no *Caballeros Negros* left."

Mike appeared with two cups of hot coffee and handed one to Three Toes, the other to Elisa.

The chief took a sip of the steaming liquid. "I think I will try to catch up with my friend."

"Chief, what brings you here?" she asked him. "Why are you not with your people?"

"Among the Comanche, we have vision quest. The Great Spirit sets us upon such a quest. After much meditation, I have been drawn to the strong medicine of Ghost-Who-Rides. My people will do well with Long Feathers as their leader."

Elisa nodded her understanding. The ways of Indians such as the Comanche really weren't all that complicated. Despite losing her father and brother to the Comanche attack, she lamented that their simple ways would spell their doom.

The Comanche were both enemy and friend. They lived from the land, befriended it wherever they traveled, yet were the enemy of anyone they deemed a threat to their way of life. She sipped from her own cup. "I think I understand what you are saying."

Soon enough, Three Toes was ready to resume his quest. He reached into his quiver and pulled out an arrow. "Mike, this is my gift to you. The arrow flies straight and true. Always be straight and true with your life."

Mike was totally thrilled with the gift. His face wore a thousand thanks.

Three Toes dug deep into his wampum bag. Elisa sensed he was searching for something special. At last, he drew out a beaded amulet on a necklace. "Never forget your friend Three Toes, Miss Elisa. I pray for you and Ghost-Who-Rides. May your lives be ever fruitful." He reached out and placed it around her neck.

She reflexively placed her hand over the amulet, feeling the beads. She pondered whether there might be a power within the colorful beadwork. If so, it was illusive for the moment. "Thank you, Three Toes."

"Stay safe, Miss Elisa. I am going to find Ghost-Who-Rides. I feel his strong medicine."

Elisa and Mike watched longingly as Three Toes mounted, turned his pony, and headed out to find Luke. For her own sake, she wished she could go with him. If only she didn't have a farm to purchase and a young boy to watch after. If only…

The rickety old wagon jounced along through the tall grasses of the Texas prairie. Ruts and arroyos from mostly dried-up streams and occasional gully-washer rains tended to slow them down, but they were making progress.

Every time the wagon lurched, Perez moaned from the pain in his groin. He feared infection, as it still oozed blood. He was anxious, even desperate to get to Carrizo. To make matters more challenging, they were getting low on water.

By Jorge's reckoning, they were about half-way through their journey. Then the unthinkable happened. As the horses pulled hard to haul the wagon up from a dry creek bed, the rear axle snapped at the wheel. Perez nearly slid out of the wagon as its rear end dropped suddenly into the sandy soil. There was no way they could go on.

There they sat, two men in a broken wagon with water running low and two nags that could, only loosely, be called horses. Perez remained totally unfit to ride, especially without a saddle.

"*Qué pena, amigo.*" Jorge was distraught over the circumstance. "*Qué hacer?*" What indeed would they do?

Perez tried to gather his thoughts as he writhed in pain from the jolt he'd just suffered. They clearly weren't going to unhitch the horses and ride off to Carrizo. Perez hurt at the mere thought of it. He so wanted to get his revenge on that red-haired whore for putting him through this agony. The anger alone would likely keep him alive.

Jorge was looking for a solution. "*Qué tal un travois?*" The travois was a way the Indians moved their villages. The contraption was pulled behind a horse. The elderly and young could ride the travois behind horses, along with teepees and other family belongings.

A look of panic swept across Perez's face. How could Jorge even think of that? He could barely endure his pain from the jostling of the wagon, and it had wheels. "*No travois.*"

They considered the possibility of Jorge riding for help. If he was able to find any help out on the expanses of grassland, could he find his way back to the broken wagon and would whatever he found have a spare axle and perhaps extra water? Their quandary was exacerbated by the knowledge that, if they did nothing, they would surely die.

As if on cue, the fates intervened. Off in the distance, Jorge saw a couple of wagons. Depending on whose wagons they were, there could be a chance for help.

He leaped at the opportunity. "*Iré a los carros y obtendré ayuda.*" He swiftly unhitched one of the horses and swung himself up. He was off at something resembling a gallop to intercept the distant wagons.

Perez was left in the wagon to ponder his fate. He could only hope that Jorge would succeed. However, he was a man of caution. What if the people Jorge was riding out to turned out to not want to help? What if they were bandits like himself? Perhaps a rival? He loaded the rifles.

It took about an hour before Perez heard the sound of voices and wagons. The man holding the reins of the lead wagon appeared to be an Anglo. By his clothing, he wasn't a native *Tejano.*

"*Puedes ayudarnos?*" Perez called out.

"I don't speak your language, but I think I can help." The man had an unfamiliar accent.

Perez had heard Germans talk in Mexico, and it sounded German. A woman was driving the second wagon. From the look of their loads, they were moving a large household. Apparently, she didn't want to leave anything behind, so two wagons were required. The horses were fine specimens. Perez surveyed the situation. It was just the man and the woman. There were no children.

The man climbed down to look at the broken wagon. "I have an extra axel that should fix this." The man was generous as well as naïve. Offering help to strangers on the Nueces Strip could be troublesome, to say the least.

Perez nodded furtively at Jorge and by hand signal made like a pistol shooting. He picked up the rifle. The man had been bent over examining the broken axel. As he raised himself, Perez's bullet caught him in the chest. Jorge was about to shoot the woman when Perez stopped him. "*Violarlo primero.*" He advised Jorge to rape her first. "*En frente de mí.*" And Perez wanted to watch.

The woman was so horrified at what she'd just seen that she was momentarily frozen in her seat. She was fragile-looking and might have been considered by some to be pretty. She had blonde hair and wore a calico dress. Surprisingly, she was unarmed. After those couple of seconds of frozen hesitation, she realized where she was and what had just happened. She nearly dove from the wagon to get to her dying husband's side.

Jorge yanked her away. In one swift motion, the calico dress ripped and was lifted over her head. Perez kept the second rifle aimed at her.

"No! No! Please kill me! I cannot…" Her words were stifled by Jorge's dirty sweaty hand planted hard across her mouth. His odor nearly caused her to pass out.

He'd already opened his trousers and forced her to the ground, pinning her under him. He pressed his lips hard against hers. He did as Perez had ordered. It didn't take long.

Perez found that he regretted ordering Jorge to rape the woman. It got him excited and caused excruciating pain. Again, his anger at the red-haired whore flooded his thinking. He wished he could be on the woman instead of Jorge. "*Violarlo primero, de nuevo.*"

Jorge smiled. If he must rape her again, so be it. Who was he to argue?

By now, the woman was all but passed out. Jorge's heavy sweaty body on top of her was nearly suffocating. Jorge smiled. "*Aquí vengo mujer.*" He spit the words in her face. He would rape her again. Just as he sought to enjoy violating her even more, he felt a sharp pain in his side. He'd forgotten to remove the knife from his belt.

She plunged it in a second time. Deep between his ribs went the razor-sharp blade.

At the third stabbing, it was all Jorge could do to push himself away. He looked down at his side. Blood seemed to be everywhere. The woman was covered with his blood and now she was half-crying and half-laughing in her intense, panic-laden fear. Jorge stood, fell, stood again, and keeled over dead.

She stood over him, nearly naked save for a sunbonnet on her head, the shredded calico dress barely covering her. Anger swept over her. Bloodied, she started to come at Perez with the knife held high. She was at the back of his broken wagon and trying to pull herself into it to get at him. He pulled the trigger. Nothing. The gun had misfired. He wacked the woman across the side of her head as she went to plunge the knife into his leg. She missed Perez and fell over unconscious.

Perez was still very much in pain, but he was alive. He took stock of his situation. With great effort, he managed to crawl out of the wagon and stand. He was shaky, but at least he was standing. He took a tentative step while steadying himself on the wagon.

Looking down, it was clear that Jorge Valdez was dead. Perez actually felt sorry for him. He'd tried to help him and as yet had asked for nothing in return. He smiled. The circumstances of what Jorge was doing when he died had at least been pleasurable to him. He almost laughed, but it caused too much pain.

Perez looked at the woman, as she lay half-naked and out cold. He tore some strips from her calico dress and bound her wrists behind her. He figured to take one of the wagons, so with great effort managed to get her up into the lead wagon just behind the seat. He bound her ankles. She'd not be running away and might eventually prove useful. Nearly naked, she'd have tough going on foot on the Texas prairie.

The horses were too good to leave behind, so he spent another hour in pain unhitching the team from the second wagon and tying them behind the first. He placed the two rifles and Jorge's pistol in the wagon, and then slowly and painfully hauled himself up into the seat. He'd placed a blanket under him, but the pain was still just shy of unbearable.

He took a final look at the scene around him. Some buzzards were already circling overhead. Once he was gone, they'd swoop in.

He had a general idea as to the direction to Carrizo and headed out.

Luke was drawing ever closer to Carrizo. He'd seen no sign of Perez. The only life he'd encountered in his travels thus far, other than the indigenous longhorns and an occasional varmint, had been a couple of folks moving their household goods in two wagons. He'd advised them to be cautious. He moved on, as they were traveling far too slowly for his purposes.

As Carrizo came into sight, he decided to find a place to camp. There was enough high ground that he could get a fairly good panoramic view of the area east of the village. The landscape wasn't unlike what he'd encountered weeks earlier when he was hunting Bad Bart Strong. With any luck, he'd spot Perez and his wagon long before the outlaw could discover him. The Ranger felt it wise to avoid the local residents, as there was still enough resentment from Callahan's adventures of the previous year that they just might give him away to Perez.

Luke got to thinking on some of the questions Elisa's little brother Mike had asked. One of them especially confounded him a bit and that was trying to define what a Texan was. He didn't find it easy, as the folks he'd encountered were drawn from multiple cultures, though Texas could hardly be called a melting pot.

It began with the indigenous tribes, from the cannibalistic Karankawas along the coast to the thieving Apache and marauding Comanche and Kiowa of the prairies. The Spanish came in and tried, mostly unsuccessfully, to establish a string of missions, one of the most famous having been the Alamo in San Antonio. Moses Austin cut a deal with the Spanish powers-that-be to settle in central Texas. Moses died and his son Stephen brought frontier-tested transplants from Pennsylvania, Kentucky, and Tennessee to settle central Texas.

To their south, the population was heavily Mexican. At this stage of Texas history, a cultural mix of mostly Catholic and Protestant religions had evolved combined with French, Irish, and German cultures. Soon enough, they'd be joined by wealthy plantation owners from the southeastern United States. They formed a loose coalition to settle the land while fending off frontier threats.

Luke concluded that a Texan was a sort of amalgamation. The common thread that seemed to be the Texans' strength was a sense of loyalty to Texas whether as state or nation, combined with an inner resolve and abiding commitment to family and faith. Yes, loyalty, family, and faith. Texans were a tough bunch that you'd want on your side in any fight, but it all comprised what Texans were about. Thinking on family brought Luke back around to thinking of Elisa. He'd long since given up on ever returning to Ireland, as his commitment, his loyalty, was to Texas. He smiled knowingly as if he'd just enlightened himself of some grand truth.

TWENTY-THREE

Laredo Surprise

Sheriff Whelan made it through San Antonio without incident. He avoided the saloons. He needed to stay focused on the Laredo whore, and steeled himself against any distraction.

He continued to deal with his guilt over Scarlett's escape. He realized the irony in her using the very wiles he found unable to resist. Perhaps there'd be some redemption if he brought her back to Corpus Christi.

One night, he found a place to rest along the banks of the Guadalupe River. He made a fire and cooked up a coyote he'd managed to shoot a bit earlier in the day. He was about to pour some coffee when he was interrupted.

"George? That you?"

The voice from the darkness sounded familiar. "Sam? Sam Smith?"

Smith approached, walking his horse behind him. "Haven't seen you in a long time, my friend. Where you been?"

"You hungry, pilgrim?" Whelan motioned the man to join him.

Smith pulled a cup from his saddlebag and sat opposite Whelan. He grabbed the coffee pot and filled his cup. "Where you headed, George?"

"Austin. You?"

"Actually, I'm headed to Victoria. Have a bit of livestock buying to do," Sam told him.

"You're welcome to bed here and share my fire, Sam."

"Thanks, George, but I need to just about ride all night to get there on time." He paused. "What's in Austin?"

"Chasin' down a whore who escaped from jail in Nuecestown. She's wanted for murder in Corpus Christi."

Smith shook his head with concern. "I don't figure you heard about the shooting in San Patricio?"

"Shooting? No."

"Might be the same bitch you're chasin'."

"You know more?"

Smith laughed. "It was a sort of fitting circumstance, George. As I heard it, she shot the *cajones* off some Mexican bandit who was out to get her. Sort of turned the tables on the sonofabitch. Now, he's headed to Mexico in a wagon, and that Ranger, Captain Dunn, is on his tail."

Whelan tried to fully absorb what he was hearing. He felt confident that Scarlett Rose was the woman in question. "Sounds like something she'd do, Sam. Damn!"

"You'd best be careful, my friend. She ain't no one to mess with." Smith tipped his hat to Whelan and put his cup back in his saddlebag. "I best be goin', George. Thanks for the coffee. Best of luck. You be careful, you hear?"

"Thanks for the warning, Sam. You ride careful now." Whelan had a feeling that his old friend wasn't dealing in a legitimate livestock deal. It wasn't in the man's bones to be an honest broker. In any case, he'd sure given him something to think about. He'd need to be extra cautious in Austin, as this might not be as easy as he thought it might be. He also rather envied Luke on his hunt for Perez. Getting Perez while he was vulnerable was a good strategy.

Once he had a good idea where Ghost-Who-Rides was headed, Three Toes made good time. He found some wagon ruts that the Nueces Strip weather hadn't yet destroyed. It looked like two wagons with heavy loads. There were no outriders or trailing horses, so it would be easy to stay on the track.

He rode through the night, being especially wary. He had too many potential foes on the prairie, ranging from rival tribes to Mexicans to Anglo settlers to soldiers. He looked forward to catching up with Luke. He sensed that Ghost-Who-Rides was conjuring up more strong medicine. Three Toes felt it in his bones.

His thoughts occasionally strayed to his people. He wondered how his wives were and whether any were now pregnant. He was confident in Long Feathers leading the Penateka to join the rest of the Comanche up on the Brazos in the Texas panhandle. The weather would be turning cold soon, and he hoped there'd be no problems.

Carlos Perez was making good time. This stolen wagon was in far better condition, with well-greased wheel hubs and a sturdier frame. He calculated that he was about a day out of Carrizo.

The woman finally came to. She quickly became aware of her dire circumstance. She felt vulnerable in her near-nakedness, and was helpless to defend herself, much less cover herself with the torn calico dress. Modesty wasn't an option. She remembered the swarthy Mexican who'd raped her and paid with his life. If she got the chance, the ugly man up on the wagon seat would meet the same fate.

She didn't know a lick of Spanish. She wanted to know where they were going and what he was going to do with her.

Finally, Perez looked back to see how she was doing. It pained him to turn in the seat. She noticed by his facial expression that he was injured; likely seriously.

"Are you okay? *Bueno*?" That was one of the few Spanish words she knew. Perhaps she could ingratiate herself with him.

"*Cállate!*"

She had no idea that translated into her shutting up. Its firm delivery gave her a vague idea of his intent. She looked pleadingly up at him.

Perez spit in her face and turned back to driving the team.

The pain was getting worse. Sitting up had been a bad idea, even with several blankets under him. Combined with the extraordinary effort it had taken to unhitch horses, get the woman in the wagon, and climb up himself, he was exhausted. He actually began to feel faint, an undesirable outcome.

As he focused on staying awake, a thunderhead rolled up to the west. The lightning from such a storm was a great worry. The grasses were widely known to be highly flammable. Prairie fires were an all-too-common occurrence on the Nueces Strip, especially up toward Laredo and San Ygnacio. Being in a slow-moving wagon in a prairie wildfire was highly detrimental, to put it mildly.

The woman was able to poke her head up above the seat level. She could see the fast-growing thunderheads as easily as Perez. She knew enough to be worried, even to the verge of panic. Wildlife running from any fire could be nearly as dangerous as the fire itself. Rattlesnakes, longhorns, javelina, fox, deer, coyote, and all manner of varmints would flee the flames.

A bolt of lightning shot from the sky, then another. The storm was moving fast toward Perez and his captive. Soon enough, he spotted the tell-tale smoke. He was headed toward a prairie wildfire. It was spreading quickly. Wildfires were natural to the Nueces Strip, but Perez was convinced that a higher being had it in for him. "*Dios, te odio!*" He screamed out his hatred for God. His Catholic upbringing was far behind him.

Perez pulled up the wagon. He needed to decide which direction to go. He spotted what appeared to be some sort of break in the grasses a few hundred yards to the south. Could he reach it in time? Would it be adequate?

His woman captive was now in total panic. Her eyes bugged and she began to scream. Perez reached behind him and hit her twice across the face. Once again, his pain was excruciating. *"Como se llamo?"*

Why did he care what her name was? If she got a chance, he'd be a dead man.

Perez glanced back with his good eye.

"Gretchen. *Me llamo* Gretchen." It wasn't great Spanish, but she was trying.

Perez smiled. She might be worth keeping alive for when he was healed. After all, she wasn't a bad-looking woman. He'd frequently thought of having an Anglo as his personal whore...an Anglo other than Scarlett.

Along with the storm and fire came wind. The fire was being blown at considerable speed. Perez whipped the horses, hoping to reach the break in the grasses. Sure enough, he soon found himself in a large area of bare ground. It was likely caused by some earlier wildfire, as the ground was dark.

He sat in the wagon seat watching the wildfire sweep by. He heard a tapping on the seat. Gretchen was pleading to be freed. "I need to pee, whatever your name is." She nodded toward her crotch. "Pee? Agua?"

Perez didn't at first comprehend. Then it dawned on him. He nodded and tried to stand. The pain was bad. He reached over, steadying himself on the back of the seat, and grabbed her under one arm. Slowly he got her standing. He pointed to the fire and hot soil. There was nowhere for her to run. There was no escape. He untied her ankles and tied a rope to her hands to serve as a leash. Every motion hurt.

She noticed his intense pain and then saw the dark brown blood stain at his crotch. She stored that in her memory for future reference. She slowly let herself down from the wagon, went around the back, and relieved herself. She had the presence of mind to grab a blanket from the back of the wagon. She felt incredibly vulnerable in her nakedness, but became keenly aware that her captor was helpless to do anything to her sexually. She threw the blanket up onto the seat and climbed onboard. She wrapped it around her, but not before standing and stretching to torment him. She felt she'd yet have her revenge on this animal who had murdered her husband and commanded her rape.

Three Toes had noticed the wildfire, too. The Comanche had long used the wildfire as a tool in hunts. All manner of animals would flee the flames and fall victim to Comanche arrows. He guessed that Luke was long past the fire.

He decided to investigate, as the tracks he followed headed in the direction he was going. He was soon at the scene of two wagons in flames. At least two partially scavenged bodies were nearby. The buzzards hadn't quite undone the evidence of their deaths. One had been shot and the other stabbed several times. The varmints couldn't enjoy the fresh kills with a wildfire bearing down on them.

Three Toes noticed that two horses had died in the flames. One of the wagons had apparently broken down. The second was full of white man's house furnishings, but the horses were missing. In the burned-out soil, Three Toes saw wagon tracks and evidence of at least four horses, two pulling and two trailing. Whoever had been here was still headed toward Carrizo. As he climbed on his pony, he noted one more thing. A torn calico dress lay under the darker of the men. There was no female body around, so there must be a woman with them. Three Toes guessed she was a captive.

The wagon tracks were a clue that was almost too obvious. A wiser prey would have attempted to cover the trail. Then again, it was conceivable that the quarry wanted to be followed. Three Toes followed the wagon tracks. The ruts continued in the direction of Carrizo. Since the fire had passed and most of the grass had burned off, the wagon tracks were especially easy to follow. If they continued toward the border town, he surmised that Ghost-Who-Rides would likely be waiting for whoever was in the wagon.

Scarlett accepted the Ruckers' offer. The colonel and his wife seemed nice enough.

After dinner, she gathered her belongings in a new satchel and met the colonel in the hotel lobby. He greeted her warmly, perhaps too warmly, but Scarlett thought nothing of it. Men were men, and women seemed destined to have to suffer their indiscretions. Of course, she had no model in her life of a functional family.

The ride in the Ruckers' carriage only took about an hour on a fairly well-maintained road. It seemed that civilization was catching up with Austin. Thankfully, Mrs. Rucker had joined them. She peppered Scarlett with all sorts of questions on the ride to their ranch. She even wanted to know whether Scarlett stood with free states or slave states. Not having paid any attention to these issues, Scarlett demurred, "I'm sorry, Mrs. Rucker, but these sorts of things were not discussed by my grandparents." She almost slipped and revealed her dallying in Laredo and travel to Corpus Christi. She was determined to keep that hidden.

Ever the southern gentleman, Colonel Rucker helped Scarlett and Mrs. Rucker from the carriage. Two teenage boys appeared as if from nowhere. "Rex, Stephen, help with the bags." It was an order, delivered as an officer rather than father. "Oh, Miss Scarlett Rose, I'm pleased to introduce our sons, Rex and Stephen." The boys nodded impatiently, picked up the bags, and carried them inside the house.

The house was a two-story affair with white siding and black window shutters. There were four white columns that supported a porch across the front. The walkway leading to the front steps was laid out with red brick. The landscaping was exquisite, as there was obviously someone around who truly understood flowers and bushes. The inside was well appointed. Mrs. Rucker showed Scarlett to her room and gave her a bit of time to unpack and settle in. "We'll have dinner in about an hour, dear. You can more formally meet our sons at that time."

Scarlett thanked her and turned to unpacking. She thought about the boys. They were certainly handsome lads. She rather suspected that their father would expect them to follow him into the military. She had already learned that the colonel was a graduate of some military school in New York. From the way it was presented, she assumed it was prestigious.

At dinner, Rex and Stephen mostly sat rigidly at attention. They didn't act as she understood boys to behave. Colonel Rucker spoke, and the boys only spoke when an answer was required. Mrs. Rucker looked prim, proper, and awkwardly uncomfortable with the conduct at the dinner table. She'd apparently been enduring the colonel's rules their entire married life. Scarlett quickly recognized her as an abused woman, not physically, mind you, but abused nonetheless.

With dinner over, the colonel sent the boys off to curry and feed their horses. "Remember, boys, the horse in battle is an extension of your body. Care for them and they will serve you well."

Scarlett decided he should apply the same advice to his family.

Mrs. Rucker excused herself. "Scarlett, we'll go over your duties at breakfast. Sleep well, my dear." She exited the room rather swiftly, as though escaping more than simply leaving.

"Miss Scarlett, would you care to join me in the study?" It seemed more like a command by its tone than an invitation. He escorted her from the dining room.

Scarlett found herself comparing the house to those she'd envied in Richmond. It was a shade smaller, but still quite impressive. She took the colonel's arm and walked with him to the study.

The colonel picked a cigar from a wooden thermidor on a large ornate desk. The walls were surrounded with shelves filled with books and a couple of framed paintings. Scarlett guessed that the portraits were the colonel's ancestors.

Colonel Rucker lit the cigar, drew on it. and blew a few smoke rings. The gesture seemed surprisingly frivolous to Scarlett.

"How long have you actually been in Texas, Miss Scarlett?"

She wondered why he would ask this. "I only just arrived, Colonel Rucker."

"The house you described in Richmond burned down a year ago. Your grandparents died in the fire. Where have you been since then?"

Scarlett needn't have answered. She knew that he knew. She didn't understand how he knew, but that was beside the point. He now held power over her, and he could wield it as he so chose.

The colonel moved close and blew cigar smoke in her face. She coughed. He pulled her to him. "This can be a safe place for you, or a dangerous place. The choice is yours." He furrowed his brows and looked leeringly into her eyes to be sure what he said had sunk in. He was so near to her that she could almost feel his mustache against her face.

He decided she wasn't ready quite yet to learn about the general.

She looked down in acquiescence. She'd been trapped by a man once again. She'd have to figure how to use this new situation to her advantage.

The colonel pulled her more tightly to him and put down his cigar. He made certain she knew who was in control. He released her. "Go, we're finished here."

Once back in her room, she tried to gather her wits. It hadn't taken the Colonel long to figure her out. How had he known? That in itself was scary.

Luke had seen the wildfires miles off in the distance. In big sky country like the Nueces Strip, objects that were many miles away could seem close enough to reach out and touch. He guessed the wildfires at twenty or more miles away, a good day's ride, likely two in a wagon.

He still had enough food to be comfortable. He caught enough sleep that he remained reasonably alert. He thought a lot about Elisa. It was different to have someone he'd be going home to. He assumed she understood his commitment to her, to them. Upon his return, he'd be likely making a choice between rancher or Ranger.

"Ghost-Who-Rides." A whisper from the other side of the live oak motte.

"Three Toes?"

The chief led his pony into the camp circle, emerging with a broad smile.

"Welcome, my friend."

Three Toes hobbled his pony and sat cross-legged at Luke's campfire.

"What brings you here?" Luke tore a piece of meat from the shank on the spit and handed it to Three Toes.

The chief smiled. "You still eating dog, my friend?" He'd quickly identified the meat as coyote. He was thinking about how best to explain why he'd traveled so far. Actually, it was simple. "The Great Spirit called me." That about said it all.

Luke acknowledged Three Toes' reason with a head nod. "You have traveled far."

"My people, the Penateka Comanche, are headed north to the white man's fort." He was measuring his words toward eventually sharing what he'd found on his journey. "Miss Elisa sends greetings. I shared coffee with her and her brother. They told me where to find you." He took a bite of coyote and chewed thoughtfully. "You are a man with strong medicine, Ghost-Who-Rides."

Luke nodded again and sipped some coffee. "Have your travels been easy?"

"You saw the wildfire. The Great Spirit threw his bolts of fire and set the grasses on fire. Fire cleans the soul. It reveals much." Three Toes leaned forward. "A wagon is headed this way. There is a wounded man with a captive white woman. They have four horses. They left two dead men with other wagons two days ride from here."

Luke thought back to the wagons he'd passed a couple of days earlier. If it was the homesteaders, it seemed especially sad. They'd been foolish to travel with such heavy loads and insufficient protection.

You couldn't afford to be careless on the Nueces Strip.

"Do you think the wounded man is Perez?" Luke asked.

"I followed their track and scouted their camp at night. The wounded man has one eye. The woman is bound."

Luke pondered that. So Perez was close. "Did you see the nature of his wounds?"

Three Toes offered an ironic sort of smile. "He keeps the woman naked, but he is unable to mount her. He is in great pain." He shook his head.

Luke winced. What he'd heard was true, then. The Laredo whore, Miss Scarlett, apparently had unerring aim. Now, Perez had a hostage and was keeping her vulnerable. "I think we will meet them tomorrow."

"We must separate the woman from Perez." Three Toes was already thinking of how to get the Mexican outlaw while protecting the woman. "I think we should approach them on foot, hiding in the tall grasses."

"Perez will be on his guard as he approaches Carrizo. Both are human with human needs." Luke's implication was to catch them at their most vulnerable, most likely when they had to answer nature's call.

Smiling in agreement, Three Toes suggested they get some rest to be at full strength for the adventure of the next day.

Perez figured they must be very close to Carrizo. He turned to the woman. "*Necesitras orinar?*" He didn't want to have to stop again for nature's call.

Gretchen didn't understand.

"*Orinar!*" He made a hand motion from his own crotch.

"Oh, that. Yes."

Perez untied her hands and ankles. She stood to climb down from the wagon. He grabbed the blanket from her. He didn't feel she'd be likely to run away if she had no cover. She stepped onto the ground and moved to the back of the wagon to relieve herself.

"*Levanta tus manos!*" A commanding voice in halting Irish-Spanish came out of the tall grass close to the wagon. Luke stepped forward with his rifle aimed at Perez.

The Mexican was incredulous. How could this be? Before him not ten yards away was the man he'd sworn to kill, not just kill but to do it as brutally as possible. But he was frozen in place. His anger was not enough to overcome his physical pain. He had no choice and complied with Luke's command.

Gretchen reappeared from behind the wagon. She saw Luke and was determined to hide her near-nakedness. She reached up to grab the blanket from the wagon seat. As she did, it placed her between Perez and Luke's line of sight.

It was the split second the bandit needed. He reached for the rifle next to the seat. As he did, there was the tell-tale whoosh as an arrow found its mark. Perez dropped the rifle, looking down at the arrow head sticking from the right side of his chest. At close range, Three Toes' arrow had nearly gone clean through him. He slumped in the seat, gasping for breath.

Luke turned to Gretchen. "You okay, ma'am?"

She fainted.

Perez passed out. He was barely alive, so far as Luke could tell. With Three Toes' help, they made room to lay Perez in the back of the wagon bed. His hands were tied behind him. They made no attempt to pull out the arrow. They searched a trunk, found some clothes for the woman, clothed her as best they could, and sat her behind the wagon seat.

They drove the wagon to Luke's encampment, tied the extra horses to the back of the wagon, and turned north toward Laredo. Three Toes served as outrider with two of the horses tethered on leads behind him. They looked like a traveling circus. Now and then, Three Toes peeked inside the wagon to see whether Perez was still breathing. The Mexican bandit's black hair made the Indian covet Perez's scalp.

Gretchen finally came to. Luke had the good sense to fully cover Perez's body, as it was close quarters in the wagon. She noticed that she was clothed. They hadn't done a great job of dressing her, but at least she had her modesty back, and her hands weren't bound. She stood, navigated the swaying wagon, and crawled onto the seat next to Luke. To her left was an Indian on horseback and driving the rig was a stranger.

"Who are you? Where are we going?" Her English was with a heavy German accent, but Luke understood.

"Howdy, ma'am. I'm Texas Ranger Captain Luke Dunn. My friend here is Three Toes, a chief of the Penateka Comanche. We're headed toward Laredo to deposit Carlos Perez." He smiled reassuringly. "We're pleased to offer you safe passage."

"How did you find me?"

"We've been tracking him from up near Corpus Christi. He left a clear trail, thanks to the broken wagon you found. What were you doing out on the Nueces Strip? I think I passed you a couple of days back."

"We were looking to homestead." She looked down sadly. "He murdered my husband. I killed the beast's companion. He raped me." Tears welled up in her eyes. She was finally able to release the pent-up emotions of her brush with death. For the moment, she could feel safe.

Scarlett awoke to banging outside. Something was being hammered. She looked out the window and could just about make out Rex and Stephen fixing the corral gate. She asked herself why on earth they had to make so much noise so early?

Mrs. Rucker was in the kitchen with a servant when Scarlett arrived for breakfast. "It's about time you woke up, Scarlett. We begin our days early." She flashed a smile tinged with annoyance.

"I'm sorry. I didn't know. I'll try to remember that." She sat at the table, and a plate of eggs and ham were placed before her. She picked up her fork.

"We usually say a blessing around here."

Scarlett dropped her chin, closed her eyes for a moment, and pretended to pray. Soon enough, she was eating ravenously.

"The Colonel and I are going away for a couple of days. It will give you a chance to get acquainted with the boys."

Scarlett chewed on that. She wondered what fantasy world this woman was living in. Her "boys" were full-grown men physically, and her husband was a philanderer-to-be up to no good as concerned their new housekeeper. "I think I can handle them, Mrs. Rucker."

"They need to do their book learning. They generally do that in the library. The Colonel also likes them to practice their horsemanship. He's of a mind that they follow his lead, going to West Point. He's convinced that the Army will soon be adding cavalry officers." Mrs. Rucker leaned forward and softened her voice to a near whisper. "Be sure they don't bring any women here to the ranch. They're getting to that age." She smiled patronizingly. She was clearly oblivious to Scarlett's past. Scarlett wondered whether she knew what the colonel knew. She realized that Austin may not be far enough north; not far enough away from her past.

Whelan finally arrived in Austin. To his knowledge, the only hotel was the Bullock House and that was far too pricey for his now meager pocketbook. To his way of figuring, he'd need to check out the Bullock as a woman with some gold coin might have spent a night or two at the place. Being unfamiliar with the Texas capital, he thought his best option was to find a saloon to get his bearings and possibly find a room. To his mind, a brothel would do.

After a bit of exploring and asking passersby, he found a livery stable and directions to the best saloon in the city. He sauntered on down Congress Avenue and walked through a pair of swinging doors into the saloon. The place was alive with mostly men playing cards and drinking. The bar was the longest he'd ever seen.

From the look of the clientele, ranging from itinerant cowboys to businessmen in suits, he determined he'd made the right choice in keeping his sheriff's badge in his pocket. He sidled up to the bar and ordered a whiskey.

The barkeep seemed a friendly sort and returned shortly with Whelan's drink. He was an outsized man in height and girth. Whelan caught his attention. "Pardon, but where could a tired traveler find a room in this town?"

The barkeep looked him over. Whelan wasn't Bullock material. "There's a boarding house just up Congress Avenue that should suit you, pilgrim. Tell them Big Max sent you."

Whelan thanked him and surveyed the saloon and its clientele once again. Might the Laredo whore come in here? He caught the eyes of one of the women working the tables, and she walked over to him. "Can I help you, cowboy?"

He kept his voice low. "It depends." He strove to look secretive to heighten the importance of what he was going to ask. "I'm looking for a red-haired woman, 'bout as tall as you, and very pretty. Likely would have arrived a couple of days ago and has some gold in her purse."

"You a lawman?"

"Do you need me to be?"

"I haven't seen anyone matching that description. Have you tried Rhett's Place or the Bullock?"

"I'll check them out." Whelan returned to form. "You have an exciting evening planned?"

"Maybe."

"How'd you like to learn first-hand about the recent exciting goings-on in Corpus Christi?"

"Your place or mine?"

"Yours."

"Cost you extra." She led Whelan up a staircase at the rear of the place. "You can call me Misty."

They were finished soon enough. Whelan got himself together, paid up, and headed toward the door. "If you see that red-haired woman, I'd sure like to know." Seems Whelan never did get around to telling Misty about the exciting life in Corpus Christi.

Misty was curious about the red-haired woman Whelan was pursuing. "What is she to you, mister?"

"She's a whore from Laredo who thought to do business in Corpus Christi. She got involved with a no-account outlaw and wound up robbing a bank and killing a patron."

"You a bounty hunter?"

"You could say that." He gave her a tip. "If you see her, I'd sure like to know about it." He headed to the boarding house.

Next morning, he was at the Bullock House Hotel first thing. He found the manager straightaway. Now was the time to be sheriff again, so he'd affixed the badge on his vest. "Good morning. I would be obliged if you could help me. I'm the sheriff in Corpus Christi. I'm trying to locate someone."

The manager looked at the badge. He was most pleased to help. "Was it someone who stayed with us, Sheriff?"

"Could be. She was a pretty red-haired woman a bit shorter than you. Likely paid with gold coin."

"Why, yes, there was a young lady of that description here a couple of days ago. She spent one night and then left with Colonel Rucker and his wife." The manager looked pleased with himself and acted as though he expected some sort of reward.

"Where might I find the Ruckers?"

"Their ranch is east of here. Did she break the law? Is there a reward?"

Whelan looked hard at him. Seemed that everyone had their hand out. "Bank robbery and murder. She's also a prostitute." He turned to leave. "If I find her and get the reward, I'll be sure to remember you." Whelan walked out the door and headed to the livery to fetch his horse.

★

Perez finally came out of his stupor on the second day of the trip to Laredo. Leaving the arrow embedded through his shoulder had probably kept him from bleeding out. Other than the continued pain from his wounds and his seriously damaged ego, his only discomfort was fouling himself. He called out weakly from under the canvas wagon cover. "*A dondé vamos?*"

Luke smiled. "*Vamos a Laredo, amigo.*" He enjoyed the touch of irony in calling Perez a friend.

They allowed Perez to sit in his own stench, giving him a small amount of water. They'd do him no favors. His type was giving Texas' southern neighbors a bad name.

The trip to Laredo took three days. Luke's little traveling caravan rolled into town tired but in good spirits. Three Toes once again wisely remained with the horses on the outskirts lest he run afoul of some citizenry with grudges against Indians. Luke pulled the rig up in front of the sheriff's office.

"Sheriff Stills! Sheriff Stills! We have a gift for you." Luke climbed down and knocked heavily on the door.

"I'm coming. Hang on." Stills opened the door and looked out groggily at Luke. "Sorry, I was taking a nap. What do you have that's so all-fired important?" He now recalled Luke from when he delivered Strong's bloated body. "You again."

"You have an interest in Carlos Perez?"

"The hider from Mexico? Yeah. There's a reward on the murdering thief."

"Well, we have him in the back of the wagon. He murdered this woman's husband and stole their wagon and horses." They walked around to the back of the wagon and pulled Perez out. He groaned as his body hit the dirt. "Sorry about the stench. If you throw a bucket of water on him, it might help."

"Is that an arrow sticking out of his chest?" Stills smiled. "Have you started using bow and arrow, Ranger?"

"Long story, Sheriff. Seems a Comanche chief has decided to adopt me as his friend. He believes that I possess some sort of strong medicine. He shot Perez when he went for his rifle to get me."

"We don't pay rewards to no Comanche, Ranger."

Luke frowned. He found himself dismayed at how humans acted at times. Some lives apparently held more value than others. "Money means nothing to the chief. I've already paid him with horses. This woman should receive the reward. She's lost her husband and much of her belongings."

Stills pondered Luke's suggestion. "I think we can work that out, Captain Dunn."

"Great, Sheriff. I'll leave Perez in your capable hands." Luke judged from Perez's condition that the prisoner was unlikely to live but another day or so. They'd likely get someone in the town, maybe the butcher, to remove the arrow. Luke wasn't sure what they'd do about the man's nether region. It gave Luke a creepy feeling to imagine what Perez had endured. That Laredo whore had made quite a statement.

Gretchen had been standing beside the horses taking this all in. She deeply appreciated what Luke was doing. Finally, Stills went back in his office to make arrangements to clean Perez and deposit him in a cell. She walked over to Luke to thank him in her thick German accent. "Captain Dunn, I am very grateful for your saving me and for your kindness and generosity. I am forever in your debt."

"It's my pleasure, ma'am. What do you figure to do?" Luke noted that she was young enough to start again, if she could put Perez's horror behind her.

"I'll try to get back to my people." She'd try to start life anew. "What of you, Captain Dunn?"

"I've got someone waiting back in Nuecestown." He escorted her to the boarding house, said his goodbyes, tipped his hat, and left her. As he mounted the big grey stallion and ambled out of town, he took it all in. He could only wonder at whether he'd ever return.

He caught up with Three Toes on the edge of town. "My friend, you have been a great help to me. You talk of my medicine, yet have saved my life twice. Have you not fulfilled your vision quest?"

Three Toes thought for a moment about Luke's suggestion that he'd fulfilled his quest. "I will have to talk with the Great Spirit about that."

"It would be fitting to return to your people. You have more stories to share at the campfire. Your children must know of the power of their chief and father."

Three Toes nodded. Luke was making sense. He'd sleep on it.

When Luke awoke, Three Toes was gone. He left behind a ceremonial pipe as a gift. It was a token of peace.

TWENTY-FOUR

Justice on the Nueces Strip

Rex and Stephen Rucker dutifully entered the library where Scarlett stood in front of their father's desk. "I understand you know what your father intends that you study. I'm here to be certain you do as he says." She turned to leave the room.

Rex nudged Stephen and smiled mischievously. "Miss Scarlett, we could use your help."

She turned back to face them. "What sort of help? I'm a housekeeper, not a teacher."

"That's not what we heard."

Not them, too, she thought.

"We want to study anatomy."

"That's a big word, boys. Where did you learn that?" She edged herself out of the library and into the hallway. "Perhaps we should get permission from your father."

"We think he'd approve, Miss Scarlett." They moved toward her. It had clearly become a threatening situation.

About three steps separated them from Scarlett. She regretted leaving her pistol upstairs. "Don't do something you'll regret later."

They were about to take another step, when they were stopped cold. "You boys have a problem?" It was a deep male voice.

Scarlett was relieved yet concerned to find Sheriff George Whelan standing behind her with his gun pointed at Rex and Stephen.

"You boys want to take another step?"

The Rucker boys froze. "Who…who are you?"

"My name is George Whelan. I'm the sheriff of Corpus Christi, and I'm here to arrest this whore for bank robbery and murder. You boys were about to make the dumbest move of your lives."

The boys' jaws dropped.

"Let's go, Miss Scarlett. We have some long travel ahead." He escorted her upstairs to gather her things, leaving the boys gaping in the library.

Once in the room, Whelan closed the door behind them, then hauled off and punched her in the stomach. She nearly threw up breakfast. "That's for what you did to me in Nuecestown."

"You deserved it, you sonofabitch." She glanced at her clothes spread on the bed.

Whelan saw the pistol grip in the folds of her dress and grabbed the gun before she could move for it. "You won't do to me what you did to Perez, you murderous whore."

He manacled her arms behind her. "Let's get you a horse and be gone from here." He grabbed her satchel and pushed her out the door.

Rex and Stephen were waiting at the bottom of the staircase. Now, they were armed. Two young boys with 1851 Navy Colts in their hands. The pistols likely belonged to their father.

"You boys should reconsider." Whelan hadn't expected this. He'd underestimated these spoiled children. He was taking away their sex toy, and this was their childish tantrum. Problem was that bullets had a nasty habit of killing.

Scarlett wasn't sure what to do. She was in the field of fire if any shooting started.

"I expect you boys understand that death is sort of final. When your mother and father return to find you boys lying dead in pools of blood at the bottom of the stairs, they'll be very sad."

Rex and Stephen looked at each other. "We just wanted our fun with her, sir."

"Put the guns on the floor and back away."

They obeyed.

Whelan picked up the guns and pushed Scarlett toward the front door. As they reached the door, he turned her to face the boys. "I wouldn't want it to be a total loss for you boys." He smiled and tore open Scarlett's bodice, exposing her breasts. "That's all you get."

He pulled her out the door, looking back over his shoulder. "You boys stay where you are until we've ridden away. If not, I'll make your folks very unhappy." He pulled Scarlett along. "And the folks in Corpus will pay for the horse."

Whelan dragged her to the stable, and soon enough they were mounted and headed south. He kept her shackled. She wouldn't be pulling any more of her tricks.

Whelan rode due south. His plan was to skirt far to the east around San Antonio. There was no sense pushing his luck with Scarlett in tow.

The first night turned into a challenge. Rather than free Scarlett from the shackles, he fed her. But then came a moment of truth, when nature called. He tied one manacle securely to a live oak, leaving her other hand free to take care of her needs. When she was finished, he forced her free arm back into the iron cuff. She had to sleep sitting up, tied securely to the tree. In the morning, Whelan fed her again. He broke camp, untied her from the tree, and boosted her up onto the horse. It was an uncomfortable routine, but he was determined to get her back to Corpus Christi to face justice.

By the third day, they had already crossed the San Marcos River.

Colonel Horace Rucker was beside himself. "You let a two-bit, small-town sheriff come in here and take away the housekeeper we found to watch over you boys and this house? What the hell am I raising here?"

Mrs. Rucker was rather relieved, but the colonel would be a long time cooling off. "I spent damned good money on that detective to find out about that whore, and I'm not about to lose her." In the back of his roiling brain the real concern was disappointing his commanding officer.

"Pack us some food." He didn't often give his wife a direct order. "Boys, saddle three horses and get the pack mule ready. Grab the Sharps rifles and each of you boys grab a Colt and a Bowie knife. We're going after that sonofabitch sheriff."

About an hour later, the colonel said good-bye to his wife, and he and the boys started down the trail headed toward Corpus Christi. He rightly figured they could make up the two-day differential by riding through the night as far as possible. He also figured that the sheriff would be delayed by having to deal with the personal needs of the very woman he was chasing. At the risk of having to answer questions from his commanding officer, General Truax, he stopped by the fort to give notice that he was taking emergency leave over a family problem. Fortunately, Truax was in Austin, so Rucker lucked out. He didn't fully understand Truax's obsession with the Laredo whore, though he sensed the general was getting orders from someone powerful.

Rex and Stephen weren't sure what to make of this adventure. They'd never ridden with their father on any mission of consequence other than some game hunting.

Luke was more than pleased to be headed back to Nuecestown. He was all too aware that he had a long ride ahead and, given the rough nature of the country and the animal and human denizens that lurked there, uncertainty was assured. He decided to take Three Toes' advice and not make so much noise. His hand had healed and squeezing that bandana seemed to have helped it almost fully regain its strength. The road Colonel Kinney had built from Corpus Christi to Laredo was a far easier ride than directly overland.

He felt comfortable with his pace as he stayed ever-vigilant. He was confident in what Three Toes had told him about the Comanche headed north, though no one could be sure how permanent that arrangement might turn out.

He passed occasional longhorns and varmints like coyote and javelina, as well as deer. He was ever on the lookout for rattlesnakes, especially having witnessed Bart Strong's demise. Every now and then, he'd dismount and walk the big grey. There were very few treed mottes to afford shade. Given little or no relief from the sun, he simply kept a steady pace. He had the good sense to have stocked up on water, as most of the creeks and pools he'd counted on for water had dried up. He looked forward to seeing Elisa.

Whelan was frustrated but determined. Scarlett was a very unpleasant traveling companion. She had names for him that he'd never heard a man utter, much less a woman. While he remained tempted to avail himself of her, he'd lost any attraction he had for her. The jail cell incident still weighed heavily on his psyche.

They were traveling south at a good pace. By the tenth day, they arrived at the San Antonio River. It seemed about time that he and Scarlett got cleaned up as best they could. He kept her manacled, and made her strip down to wash in the river. He had her on a long tether as a precaution.

As they saddled up after their bathing, Whelan began to sense they were being followed. He couldn't be certain, but he just felt intuitively that they might have company. He decided to circle back and see, so he made a wide circle east and then traced north before arcing back to the south. The entire exercise took about two hours. He hoped that if anyone were following, he'd be able to position himself and Scarlett behind them.

Whelan calculated that once his diversionary track had been found, Rucker would double-back and come after them. He considered the risk it involved and found it acceptable. He'd be outnumbered three to one, even though two were young boys. Whelan figured he had hooked the colonel like a fish on a line. He'd see how well he could evade the pursuit. He headed east again before heading due south. Once he crossed the Nueces River, he'd be in territory he knew well and would have a distinct advantage. He'd need to pick up his travel pace, and Scarlett seemed more than amenable to that.

It was fortunate for Whelan that the colonel was not a very good tracker. It was said around Austin that, when he took his sons hunting, they'd often come back empty-handed because of the colonel's less-than-stellar tracking ability. Had Whelan known, he'd likely have worried a bit less. However, sometimes ignorance can be bliss in the sense that Whelan kept his guard up. The colonel had likely relied too much on hired Army scouts, when he should have learned a bit of the craft himself.

As for Scarlett, she was ever looking for an opportunity to escape. If she could just get her hands on one of Whelan's Walker Colts, she might yet escape and head north out of Texas. She was well past shame or any sort of embarrassment around Whelan. They'd been about as intimate as anyone could get, if rape could be perverted as intimacy. Scarlett also noticed she'd missed her cycle…twice. It was possible she was pregnant. Whose was it? Whelan's? Cavendish's? In any case, she wasn't about to mention it to Whelan just yet.

She had mixed feelings. She expected that her chances for escape were far better with Whelan than with the colonel. She decided, out of fear of the Ruckers, to be more help than hindrance to the sheriff. She wished he would trust her with a gun, but could hardly blame him for not giving her one. She didn't exactly inspire trust.

Scarlett felt that every step toward Corpus Christi reduced her chances for escape. Whelan was a curse and a blessing. On the one hand she was his prisoner and, on the other, he was protecting her from Colonel Rucker and his sons. Now, the possibility that she was pregnant added a new dimension to her plight. That she had no idea whose child she might be carrying increased her mental burden. Soon enough, her burden would become more physically evident.

Colonel Rucker and his sons were now the hunted. By the time they reached the San Antonio River, they knew they'd lost the track. The colonel sent the boys west while he went east to try to find it.

He was seething at the possibility of having been tricked by a no-account, hick-city sheriff. These searches were costly. At last, he found where Whelan had turned northward. It confirmed his fear that the sheriff was now behind them. Sonofabitch wasn't a no-account after all.

Colonel Rucker was beside himself. Whelan had doubled back a second time. Rex and Stephen were losing patience with their father, as his incompetence as a tracker was becoming increasingly unbearable. They couldn't understand how he'd fallen for the sheriff's tactic a second time.

"Father, shouldn't we move faster?"

"We'll move at the pace I feel is best." He was noticeably irritated. He took no truck with his boys disrespecting or challenging him.

"Father, I expect we outnumber and outgun the man."

The colonel was exasperated. "If we fall into a trap, he can seriously reduce our numerical advantage." He was trying to explain as he might have at West Point or in Vera Cruz in the Mexican-American War. The colonel felt, and probably rightly so that, if Whelan was smart enough to double back, he might be smart enough to ambush them. "Keep your eyes and ears open. I sense they're not that far away."

In reality, Whelan had gained distance and was at least a half-day ahead of the Ruckers. After they crossed the San Antonio River, the countryside became more familiar to him. He began to give thought to the ambush that the colonel feared, yet remained committed to reaching the relative sanctuary of Corpus Christi. Taking time for an ambush with uncertain outcome was simply too risky. With three against one, he couldn't afford to miss, even once. If he shot Rucker, the sons became unknown quantities. Likely as not, they'd turn and run, but Whelan couldn't count on that.

He also began to sense a change in Scarlett. When they stopped to rest and she relieved herself, he noticed she seemed to have gained just a bit of a belly. They hadn't been eating all that much, so he was at a loss for how she might be gaining weight.

His perspective had begun to change as well. He was beginning to make the effort to understand her plight. He was seeing her more as victim and less as the Laredo whore. But Whelan was Whelan, and he kept shaking these images from his mind lest he go soft on her. After all, she was a robber and murderer.

Elisa had closed the purchase of the McGill place. She looked forward to Luke's return so he could help her begin to populate the land with longhorns. In addition to tilling a small section of her farm, she had to take on the typical chores that went along with day-to-day life such as cooking, sewing, washing clothes, churning butter, drying and smoking meats, and general repairs that Mike wasn't old enough to handle. She'd also begun to think about what other adjoining properties might become available. Her determination had begun to be noticed in Nuecestown, as she made more frequent trips for supplies. Each time, she asked for any word about Luke.

She shared Luke's apparent commitment to her with Bernice

and Agatha. They were excited, but tempered with the reality of a lawman's life. Still, thoughts of a wedding were swirling around in their fertile minds.

Doc and the general store manager assured Elisa that they'd alert her if and when they heard any news about Luke.

Normally, her brother Mike joined her on her trips into Nuecestown. On one particular day, Mike begged off. He was working on a project in the stable and wanted to complete it before sunset. He'd noticed that the hinges on the gate to the mule stall were breaking down, and he had an idea on how to repair them. He was growing up fast owing to the responsibilities thrust upon him to help Elisa.

Mike was focused on supporting the heavy wooden gate so he could better get at the hinges. He heard Elisa driving the mules toward the stable, as she'd just returned from town.

He lowered the gate so he could run out to help unload the wagon. As he did, he heard the buzz of a rattlesnake's tail. The fool snake struck him before he could react. He'd been squatting, and it bit him in the thigh. He clubbed it to death with a nearby shovel before staggering from the stable. "Elisa! Elisa! Help!"

His desperate shout brought her running. "What, what is it?"

"Rattler got me. Sis, it hurts!"

"Where?" She saw the twin punctures through his trousers. "Oh, my, Mike. Let's get to Doc fast!"

She lifted him into the back of the wagon, jumped into the seat, and headed the wagon to town as fast as the mules could pull them. She pulled the rig up in front of Doc's house. Mike was already having a tough time breathing.

"Doc!" Elisa hammered on his door. "Doc!"

Bernice heard Elisa's shouts. "What's happening, sweetie?"

"It's Mike. He's been snakebit."

Bernice and Agatha ran over to Doc's house and forced the door open. Doc was inside half-passed out from his boozing. "Doc, wake up. We've got an emergency!"

Elisa had already half-dragged Mike into Doc's examination room. She cut and tore his pant leg apart, revealing the nasty wound and major swelling and discoloration. It had been more than an hour, and the venom was already working on Mike's circulatory system. He was sweating profusely. He'd taken a full load, and his prognosis wasn't great under even the very best of circumstances.

The ladies got Doc awake enough to be reasonably coherent. "What's wrong?" he rasped. He gazed at Mike lying on the table.

Tears began to well up in Elisa's eyes. "He's been bit by a rattler, Doc." Tears traced rivulets of mud down her dust-covered cheeks.

Doc whipped out a knife and cut at the puncture wounds. He wrapped a belt around Mike's keg above the wound to stem the blood flow from the leg. "Get me that damned whiskey bottle." Bernice handed it to him, and he took a hard swig and spit it out. He began to suck the wound, trying to draw the venom from it.

Elisa and the ladies stood by helplessly as Doc continued to suck from the wounds. It became obvious that Doc wasn't winning the battle against the venom. If the wound hadn't been so high on the thigh near the boy's butt, Doc might even have considered cutting off the leg to save the child. Mike was having an increasingly difficult time breathing. As his breathing became more labored, the color left his face and arms. He began to have a seizure. Doc knew that signaled the beginning of the end.

Elisa pushed Doc aside and began trying to suck out the venom. She was in tears and the ladies were sobbing. Doc had never felt so helpless and utterly defeated. If Mike had been a grown man, they might save him, but the boy was fading ever faster.

Finally, Mike appeared to breathe his last. Doc closed the child's eyes and wrapped an arm around Elisa to comfort her. "There's just nothing we could do, Elisa. I'm so very sorry."

Suddenly, Mike coughed. He wasn't finished fighting. He looked terrible, but his little body was fighting the onslaught of the rattler's venom.

Elisa collapsed on the chair next to the table. She was inconsolable for a few moments then suddenly stopped. She wiped away her tears.

"Can we stay here, Doc?" She said it almost desperately. She would be strong. There was a determination in her. It was as though she'd decided at that moment she was going to take on whatever the frontier threw at her and defeat it. She'd see Mike through this, whatever that entailed.

Doc nodded. "Of course, you can. You can stay as long as you need to." He gave her a hug of reassurance. "We can't be sure of what he may be like after the bite heals, but we're here for you."

"Can we get you anything, Elisa?" Bernice and Agatha were ready to help.

Colonel Rucker sensed that his sons were losing faith in him. Why were they chasing this whore, anyway? He dared not tell them.

Rex and Stephen lagged a few yards back so they could carry on their own conversation as teens often do.

The colonel stopped and turned to face them. "You boys have some sort of problem? You have something to say? I know it's been a long journey, but we aim to get back what is ours." He made it sound as though they owned Scarlett. In a manner of speaking, they did.

Rex and Stephen were seeing a side of their father they were unfamiliar with. They couldn't know that it was this sort of obsessive behavior that had kept him from making general officer rank. "Yes, father. We understand."

As the colonel turned his mount back to the trail, he saw a flash and heard a shot. A bullet tore through his left arm. He sagged. He'd led them into an ambush. A second shot rang out, and a bullet whizzed past Rex's head. The boys turned and rode hell-bent for leather in the opposite direction of the gunshots. The colonel didn't waste any time joining their escape. It appeared that Whelan had decided to set an ambush after all.

After about a mile, they pulled up. The colonel dismounted and pulled off his jacket. The bullet had gone clean through, no broken bone. "Come on, boys, help out here. Wrap my arm to stop the bleeding." The boys did as he directed.

The colonel felt clumsy for having ridden into an ambush. The sheriff had darn near ended the hunt. It was mid-afternoon. "Let's rest here for the night. We can find their trail in the morning." He gritted through the pain in his arm and unsaddled his horse. "Rex, build a fire. Stephen, see to the horses."

He'd have to give this situation some further thought. In an unmilitary fashion, he had extended his front well beyond his supply lines. He had become vulnerable to an enemy he couldn't even see.

Stephen boiled up a pot of coffee that didn't taste half bad, while Rex began to cook up some beef. They didn't have much food left, as the colonel had misjudged the time it would take to catch Whelan and the whore. If they were going to do anything, they needed to do it soon. He knew they were close enough to San Antonio that they could resupply before heading home with Scarlett as captive.

Luke turned a tad south before reaching Nuecestown, as he was anxious to see Elisa. He rode the big grey slowly into the clearing in front of her cabin. As he dismounted and hitched the reins, he visually took in all that was around him. She had been doing a great job of keeping the place up. He walked over and knocked on the door. Silence. He knocked again.

The door cracked open. Elisa literally fell into Luke's arms. She released great sobs of relief. He was home safe. Her world was set right. Her man was home. Not a word was yet spoken.

"What is it? What's happened?" he asked.

She held him close a few moments more. "Rattlesnake nearly killed Mike." She pulled partially free. "Happened just a couple of days ago. He's at Doc's place. He's real sick."

Luke embraced her. He instinctively felt her need for him. After a few moments, he bent down, lifted her chin, and kissed her. "I'm here, Lisa, I'm home."

"Oh, Lucas, why is the world this way?"

Luke looked thoughtfully at her. "As I understand it, the Lord giveth and the Lord taketh away. It's the way it is."

It registered in her thinking that Luke had just said something about being home. "Did I hear you say you were home?"

"If you'll have me?"

They kissed a long deep kiss.

Reality set in. It was midday. "Come in. I'll rustle up something. You must be starving for a home-cooked meal, my love."

Luke paused. "I suppose that was a yes?"

She kissed him lightly, nodded, and went into the cabin. "You go wash off that trail dust, Lucas Dunn."

They enjoyed her cooking and spent time catching up on her experiences and Luke's adventures. "We'd best head back into Nuecestown, Lucas. I need to check on Mike."

They hitched the wagon. Luke tied the big grey to the back, and they headed to town.

"So, that Perez outlaw is dead?" she asked.

"He wasn't when I left, but I don't expect he held on to life much longer," Luke told her. "If he does live, he'll be hung right quick. Either way, he's finished."

"I love you, Lucas. And I'm so proud of you."

"Well, Lisa, do we have a town official that can wed us?"

The question caught Elisa off guard. Everything for the past couple of days had focused on Mike. She had been thinking about getting hitched, but Luke's forthrightness surprised her. "I think the Doc has some sort of license. I'll bet he could do a ceremony. And Bernice and Agatha would be excited to help."

Elisa appreciated Luke's respect for her honor, though her entire body ached to be with him. The anticipation was almost unbearable.

After tending to Mike, they spent the afternoon discussing going to Luke's cousin to purchase a few longhorns and other concerns in getting the ranch up and running. She shared her plan to try to buy up other adjacent properties. If need be, they'd move away from Nuecestown.

The colonel's arm throbbed all night. At least, they didn't have to pull a bullet out of it. That might have tested the limits of one or both of his sons. At the break of dawn, they prepared to press their numbers advantage on the sheriff and the whore. They mounted up and checked their weapons. Rex and Stephen were especially excited to see their first combat.

Colonel Rucker led them out at a brisk pace. They hoped to catch up with Whelan rather quickly, and catch him by surprise. Unfortunately, they sounded as though an entire army was moving forward.

Whelan figured they were a half-mile away when he first heard their commotion. He and Scarlett were about a half-day ride north of the Nueces River. There were plenty of vantage points to make a stand; it was simply a matter of choosing.

Finally, he found a live oak motte that afforded excellent cover for them and their horses. He hitched the horses and tied Scarlett to a tree trunk. He had his Walker Colt and a Sharps breech-loader rifle at the ready. He figured his first shot would be with the Sharps, as the pistol was best at closer range. Ideally, he'd stop the colonel, and the sons would turn and run. He didn't feature killing misguided young boys.

It took less than half an hour riding through the rough landscape for Colonel Rucker and his boys to come within visual contact. Whelan aimed the Sharps. As he prepared to squeeze the trigger, the colonel spotted him and Scarlett.

Rucker turned his horse just enough that it took the bullet intended for him, and he was tossed over the head of the dying animal. Rex and Stephen pulled up alongside their father. He'd not just fallen in dirt, grass, and leaves, but in several cowpies left by grazing longhorns.

Rex lifted his father up behind him on his horse. They hadn't gone but a couple of steps when the colonel pushed his son out of the saddle and turned back toward Whelan.

Whelan was incredulous that the colonel was so determined. He really didn't want to kill the man, but was being left no choice. The colonel charged with a saber in hand. The sheriff fired his pistol twice, ripping the soldier from his saddle for the second time. His right arm and shoulder had been hit, and he writhed in pain.

Rex ran forward and Stephen dismounted to come to their father's aid. "We surrender! Please don't shoot!"

"Drop your weapons and back away," Whelan shouted as he moved toward them from his cover, keeping the Colt aimed at the colonel. The boys did as they were directed.

"Get your father on a horse, and get the hell out of here," Whelan ordered. "Go home. Don't ever think of coming anywhere near Corpus Christi."

The sheriff couldn't have cared less about the colonel's wounds. They weren't that bad. He could have been killed had Whelan's aim been better. As it was, Rucker was lucky the slug from the Sharps had missed him. The .44 caliber bullets from the Colt were sufficient to make for a nasty wound. What was left of the man's pride had been seriously damaged, but he would live.

The boys did as Whelan had told them. The colonel sputtered and cursed, but didn't resist.

Whelan watched the Ruckers ride off and then gathered their weapons before returning to make sure Scarlett was safe.

The damned whore was gone. He sighed audibly. She'd cut through the tether but was still manacled. Moreover, she was on foot. How far did she expect to get? This was highly inconvenient. He mounted up and quickly picked up her track.

He caught up within a few minutes. "Where do you think you're going?"

She said not a word. She was crying.

Crying women usually presented a challenge for men, but this was an especially great challenge for Sheriff Whelan. Women were objects of gratification for him. He simply did not emote with women. It wasn't that he didn't care; it was just that most of the women he'd ever interacted with flirted with the wrong side of the law. His caring stopped at a prisoner's cell door or a whore's room door.

Whelan dismounted and approached her. "What's the problem?"

"I...I wanted to see if you'd chase after me."

"Of course I would," he said, "you're my prisoner."

Whatever else was swimming in her head, Scarlett wanted to be wanted. It didn't matter that she was Whelan's prisoner. She knew he could never understand. It was the way it was with men, especially rough men on the Texas frontier. Men had always used her and then run from her.

"I may be carrying your child," she told him softly.

"What?" Whelan wasn't sure he heard her. "What did you say?"

"I'm pregnant," she repeated. "It may be yours."

"Damn!" Was it his, Cavendish's, or someone else's?

A curse was not exactly what Scarlett was looking for. She began to cry again. "What do I do?" she whimpered.

Whelan slapped the side of his face as if to jolt his brain. "I've got to think this out, Scarlett," he replied.

What if it was his child? Could he take the mother to jail? The internal conflict he was dealing with was hurting his brain. He couldn't show up in Corpus Christi with Scarlett Rose as a free woman. Yet, if he didn't bring her in as his prisoner, he couldn't save face over his earlier embarrassment over her escape from the cell in Nuecestown. If there was to be justice on the Nueces Strip, he had to bring her in.

"Could the child be Cavendish's?"

It was a rough question for her given the emotions she was dealing with. "I don't know. It's either yours or his. No one else."

He had no choice. "I'm sorry. We'll deal with this in Corpus Christi." He pulled her over to the horse and forced her up into the saddle. He remounted, and they were on their way.

She remained tearful. "Will we stop in Nuecestown?"

"Probably." He knew the circumstances would be quite different this time. He headed them south. In a few hours, they'd cross the Nueces River, well west of the ferry so as to avoid attention.

Colonel Rucker was beside himself. He swore that as soon as he got his wounds cared for he'd head for Corpus Christi. He didn't give a tinker's damn what the optics might be. He wasn't going back to Austin without the red-haired whore. He'd invested too much in her to let her go. Besides, he had a bigger reason to capture her.

Rex and Stephen did not understand their father's obsession. It all seemed like far too much trouble. Their father had already taken three bullets chasing this whore. It did not make sense. There had to be something they didn't know. For now, though, they remained totally oblivious. It reflected a combination of youth and naiveté, exacerbated by the colonel's secrecy.

TWENTY-FIVE

Live to Fight Another Day

Three Toes maintained a steady pace northward through what had become known as the Comancheria. It was a wide swath of Texas and a bit of New Mexico that encompassed virtually everything west of the 98th Meridian, running from north to south through Austin and San Antonio. The Comancheria was a no-man's land for all but the hardiest and bravest souls. Comanche and Kiowa ran free across the region, and even desperadoes thought twice about risking their scalps.

He hoped to join his fellow Penateka Comanche at Camp Cooper up on the Clear Fork of the Brazos River west of Fort Worth. He assumed that Long Feathers had already arrived and joined up with the Penatekas under Chief Ketumse. He had heard that, in accordance with a new treaty, they were to be taught farming. On the upside, there was plenty of water and supposedly good hunting.

Three Toes was conflicted about the reservation. He was inclined to support many of his band that left Fort Cooper periodically to join hunting expeditions or to savage the frontier as marauding bands. He'd also heard that unprincipled traders were selling firewater to the Comanche. Heavy drinking of the white man's whiskey invariably led to poor outcomes. The 2nd U.S. Cavalry had been sent in to keep order. Upon his arrival, Three Toes would seek word of a rival of Ketumse, Chief Sanaco, who was leading many Penateka away from Camp Cooper.

He had been traveling for several days, passing Fort Mason near San Antonio. Just north of Fort Mason, as he was negotiating the beautiful hills of central Texas on the eastern portion of the Comancheria, Three Toes was surprised by a patrol of six blue coats. They were mounted U.S. Army troops under command of a wet-behind-the-ears second lieutenant fresh out of West Point. Three Toes had ridden up out of a valley and had been outside the line of sight of both he and the soldiers. All of a sudden, he was faced with a half dozen rifles aimed at him.

The lieutenant was just a bit flustered. "Halt!"

The patrol sergeant looked down and covered his mouth to avoid laughing.

"Who goes there?"

Three Toes had never before encountered this sort of situation. He raised one hand as a sign of peace. "Me Three Toes, chief of Penateka Comanche. I go to Camp Cooper."

The lieutenant had not been fully briefed on Camp Cooper, which was a few days' ride to the north. "Surrender. You are my prisoner."

The sergeant couldn't contain himself any longer. He'd been on several campaigns fighting Comanche, Kiowa, and Kickapoos. He knew of Camp Cooper. "If I may have permission to speak, lieutenant?"

"What is it, sergeant?"

"Sir, this redskin is likely telling the truth. The Penateka band has been on the reservation at Camp Cooper for more than a year. I expect the chief is telling the truth."

The lieutenant had observed the aftermath of an Indian raid about a week earlier. The vision of the tortured victims was deeply embedded in his mind. "How do we know he's not a spy?"

The sergeant shook his head. "That's not how they work, lieutenant.

If he was leading a raiding party, he wouldn't be out here alone, much less falling into a chance meeting with a U.S. Army patrol. I respectfully suggest that you let him pass."

Three Toes waited patiently. He tried to appear as unthreatening as he could, though it was difficult, given that he had a quiver full of arrows, bow, and lance featuring several scalps. He certainly was not looking for a fight, especially considering the rifles aimed at him. He hoped that his string of three ponies would be a hint that he was traveling in peace.

The lieutenant had no idea how he should treat the situation. On the one hand, he'd been told that the only good Indian was a dead Indian and, on the other, he was favored with such an overwhelming advantage that to kill the chief would be tantamount to murder. He knew that charges could be brought against him, though they weren't likely to stick. Finally, after what seemed like ages, he gave his order. "Men! At ease! Let the Comanche pass."

Three Toes continued on his way. As he rode past the lieutenant, he stared at the soldier's face as though to memorize it. Three Toes liked to remember these sorts of things, as they could be useful at some future time.

The lieutenant for his part would not forget the close encounter with a Comanche chief. It was an education for him. At some later time, he would surely learn of Three Toes' impressive exploits.

Next morning, following his arrival in San Antonio, Colonel Horace Rucker penned a note to his wife to let her know where he was and that he was extending his stay. He didn't mention his wounds, as that would surely drive her to near apoplexy. He decided to let Rex and Stephen ride north to deliver the note, with a promise not to reveal his condition. He'd given them just a little exposure to the nature of armed conflict that would benefit them at West Point. He saw the delivery as a chance for his sons to have a mission of sorts.

Most important, it helped preserve his secret. He suspected they were wondering about what drove him to undertake what seemed like a foolhardy pursuit.

The boys departed after purchasing a good horse for their father. They were in a light-hearted mood, owing to being out from beneath their father's iron fist, and looked forward to the trip home.

The colonel rejected the advice of the doctor to get some rest and made preparations to ride to Corpus Christi. His right arm was necessarily placed in a sling, making mounting and dismounting a challenge. His biggest concern would be bleeding if he reopened the sutures. Three bullets had passed through him. None threatened vital organs. It could be said that the colonel was leading a charmed life.

His sons had chosen a mature, well-trained steed for him. The horse was even sensitive to pressure from the colonel's knees. It had apparently been a cutting horse at some point used by cowboys to cut cattle from the herd. In any case, the colonel was comfortable in the saddle and he took the road south at a pace that was fairly easy on horse and rider.

Luke and Elisa said their vows before Doc that morning. Bernice, Agatha, and Dan, the stable boy, served as witnesses. The closest priest was several days ride away, so Doc had to suffice. They'd get the priest to stop by, if and when he made one of his rare visits.

The wedding was about as memorable an affair as could be created on short notice in a little place like Nuecestown. Happiness was far too rare a commodity on the Nueces Strip to let any of it go to waste. In addition to a bridal bouquet of bluebonnets, Bernice and Agatha had enthusiastically decorated the wagon with flowers for the occasion. Even the mules were decked out with flowers.

The newlyweds headed back to the farm in the rig drawn by that pair of trusty old mules. Luke resisted the temptation to identify the flowers the ladies had used for decoration.

Elisa, for her part, simply sat as close to her new husband as she could. She stroked the amulet that Three Toes had gifted her with. Perhaps it did contain some sort of power, as her life had suddenly seemed to have turned magical.

Upon arrival at the cabin, Luke jumped down and then helped Elisa alight. He grabbed the reins to lead the mules to the stable but stopped short, as though incredulous at himself for what he was about to do. He wrapped the leads around the hitching post, turned to a momentarily bewildered Elisa, and drew her to him. She tilted her face upward and found her lips melting into his. He swept her into his arms and carried her across the threshold.

Elisa had made new bedding, and the blissful couple was quickly absorbed into the folds of blankets and linens. She responded eagerly to his caresses. She'd never been so touched by a man before, yet natural urges came surging from her inner core. His kisses lifted her into paroxysms of ecstasy.

Luke's hands explored her, caressing her sweetness as he'd imagined only in his dreams. His lips sought every inch of her lithe, yielding body.

"Lucas...Lucas, I want you so..." she whispered. She thought she'd explode if he didn't take her virginity...now. She opened herself to her man and took him completely to her.

"My God, but I love you, Lisa..." His words trailed off in a deep kiss and a heightened urgency as he pushed ever deeper.

Exquisite sensations coursed through their bodies. Explosions, spasms, more gentle caresses, parting, and laying back as though in some dreamscape. It was as though they had been transported to some heavenly realm. No words were spoken. They didn't need to be. It had been all they'd ever hoped for, all they'd ever yearned for. Elisa had her real man, and Luke had his loving woman. It was a Godly match.

Luke emerged a couple of hours later to unhitch and stable the mules, then quickly returned to the cabin and Elisa's passionate kisses and loving arms. Luke had done right by her. He could easily have pressed his advantage and had his way with her before they married, but his Irish upbringing and God-driven morals wouldn't allow it. It was about as idyllic as could be imagined there on the edge of the Texas frontier.

Calling it the edge might be debatable, as the frontier at that time was ill-defined. It wasn't a straight line of demarcation whereby you simply crossed from one side to the other: frontier on one side, civilization on the other. Slowly, inexorably, it would move westward. Luke and Elisa aimed to be part of moving the frontier westward.

Next morning after breakfast, Luke revealed a wedding gift. He blindfolded her and led her out to the corral alongside the stable. There stood a beautiful chestnut mare, saddled and ready to ride.

"For me?" She was giddy with joy as she walked over and hugged the steed's muzzle.

"Every self-respecting rancher needs a horse, Lisa Dunn." It hit her that it was the first time she'd heard her new name from her husband's mouth. She was now a Corrigan-turned-Dunn.

"I'm not quite a rancher yet, Lucas."

"Mount up," he told her as he mounted the grey stallion. "We need to take a little ride."

They rode for about ten minutes until they crested a low hill with an expansive view of the gentle grasslands spread before them. She couldn't believe what she was seeing. One, two, three…there were eight longhorns grazing on her farm…er, ranch.

Her jaw dropped. She looked from the longhorns to Luke and back again. "Lucas Dunn, you are an amazing man."

Luke uncharacteristically blushed a deep crimson. "I hoped you'd be pleased." He brushed his finger playfully aside his mustache.

She wanted to leap from her saddle and hug him. It was all so very real. She'd lost so much, but now her world had radically changed in a wonderful way. It taught her never ever to give up, so long as there was hope. Her dreams were becoming reality.

The only concern she faced was her brother Mike's prolonged

recovery. The snakebite had taken its toll, and it was possible the boy might never be quite right.

But, for now, there was wedded bliss to enjoy, to be free of life's realities for some finite time. They immersed themselves in their love.

Whelan coincidentally rode through Nuecestown, but later in the morning and well after the wedding. In fact, he had no idea that Luke and Elisa had wed. The streets were empty, which suited him and Scarlett just fine. They were striving to avoid encountering anyone who might bring up the gun battle with Perez's *Caballeros Negros* and the killing of Dirk Cavendish. Whelan was determined to forget the performance of his posse, plus the stigma of having allowed Scarlett to escape.

He was still conflicted about Scarlett. There was a fifty-fifty chance that the child growing in her belly was not his. But what if it was? They'd deal with it in Corpus Christi if they could manage to arrive there safely.

Whelan remained disconcerted by whatever had driven Colonel Rucker to pursue Scarlett. He had already asked her if she knew. Twice, she offered essentially the same answer. "I don't know. He seemed to know things about me before I even got to his ranch." Together, they wondered what in the recent past was so all-fired important that the colonel would risk life and limb as well as the lives of his sons.

Late afternoon, they pulled up in front of the Corpus Christi sheriff's office. A few folks noticed them riding in, and they couldn't miss her being in manacles and tied to the horse. Curious. Whelan dismounted and untied Scarlett. He took her out back to the privy before bringing her inside to the jail cell.

Once she was secured, he tipped his hat, turned, and stepped toward the door. "I'll be back. I must let the solicitor know that I've brought you back." He stopped before leaving. "Can I get you anything?"

"Water, food…a bit of whiskey?"

Whelan chuckled. He was relieved that they'd completed the journey from Austin. He'd rustle up some grub for Scarlett, but intuitively figured the whiskey was not advisable.

On his way to the solicitor, he debated about telling him that Scarlett was with child. He certainly dared not admit that it might be his.

He knocked and walked into the solicitor's office. "Bill, how are you doing? Busy?" He knew that there was very little going on as to legal matters other than minor offenses. "I've got an important case for you."

William Stokes prided himself on knowing just about all that was going on in Corpus Christi. What had he missed?

"I went up to Austin and recaptured Dirk Cavendish's partner in crime, that red-haired Laredo whore Scarlett Rose."

Stokes raised his eyebrows in surprise. "Seriously?"

"Yep, but there's a problem you should know about."

Stokes looked at him inquisitively. "What's that, George?"

Whelan chuckled, but quickly turned serious. "She's got a bun in the oven, Bill."

"Damn. We can't hang her." Stokes shook his head at this new dilemma. "That'd be sort of like killing two people."

"We could get that Apache witch women to get rid of it for us."

Stokes was amazed at Whelan's suggestion.

The sheriff had considered it as an option, but surprised even himself that he'd brought it up. "You're right, Bill. It might upset some folk."

"Let me think on this. As I recall, she helped rob the bank, shot and killed one of our citizens, and then escaped jail."

"I think Cavendish took the credit for the murder, Bill. As to the escape…" Whelan hesitated. "Bill, I must admit it was my fault. I let my guard down, and she took advantage."

Knowing Whelan as well as he did, Stokes quickly surmised what sort of advantage Scarlett had taken. "Okay, then she's an accessory to these crimes."

Whelan was relieved. He now knew that her punishment would be lighter. She'd avoid the hangman's noose. He thanked the solicitor and headed back to his office, stopping at the boarding house to dig up some grub for the two of them.

He knew intuitively that, as her pregnancy progressed, it might entail further needs for her care. He may have been a seemingly heartless slime when it came to the whores of Corpus Christi, but he wasn't a total lost soul. The possibility that he was responsible for her condition weighed heavily on him. Would the baby look like him or look like Cavendish? He didn't even consider the possibility of a third contributor to her pregnancy. Women seemed to know.

Carlos Perez groaned. He'd been given some water about the time Luke initially deposited him with Sheriff Stills. He pretty much was unable to eat, as he suffered from both the pain of his wounds and the accompanying nausea. His breathing was labored in large part thanks to the arrow still in his chest. The arrow had been there for several days now, and he was lucky major infection had not set in. He'd lost weight for sure.

Stills had one of the locals fetch the butcher. He was as close to a doctor as could be found in Laredo. The butcher was a Mexican-American who had chosen to stay in the U.S. after the Callahan incidents. Of course, he spoke Spanish, which was important, since Perez understood no English.

While Stills and two deputies stood guard, the butcher examined Perez' injuries. "*Qué lástima!*" he said to Perez in a low voice. Indeed, their seriousness was a pity. However, what he'd actually commented upon was that the wounds had not been mortal. The butcher had been a victim of the *Caballeros Negros* a couple of years ago. Perez's gang had beaten his wife and left her an invalid. She eventually passed away, leaving his three children motherless. The butcher would as soon have killed Perez right then and there.

He managed to get the arrow out of Perez by clipping one end and pulling it through. The untreated wound had begun to fester a bit, so he had to cut the infection out. He took perverse pleasure in causing Perez additional torment. The pain and loss of blood were terrible.

Then he had to deal with Perez's other problem. One of the guards held Perez down. The outlaw was already weak from the operation he'd endured to remove the arrow, so he put up almost no resistance. They cut off Perez' pants, revealing the full extent of damage to his privates. The butcher gagged uncharacteristically. The sight was not a very pleasant one.

"*Trataré de salvar to pene.*" Perez squirmed with the news of even the possibility of losing his penis. The butcher would do his best to save it, though he couldn't guarantee its functionality.

The specter of taking revenge on both the Texas Ranger and the Laredo whore were ever stronger. In combination, those memories were working to keep him alive. If he could get his hands on the Comanche chief, it would be the proverbial icing on his cake. His wounds might have killed men of weaker physical constitution. For a one-eyed, nearly-toothless bandit with a cut-up shoulder and no testicles, he was surprisingly durable. Ironically, his living through this nightmare could translate into yet fulfilling his dream of revenge.

He wasn't fully out of the woods just yet. In addition to his wounds, there was the inconvenient matter of being in jail and awaiting trial and probable execution. If he'd been jailed at the eastern end of the Nueces Strip, they'd likely just skip the trial portion. But, here in Laredo, there were enough folks of Mexican heritage that he had at least a possibility of getting a hearing. It might not be a fair one, but it'd be a hearing nonetheless.

Three Toes reached his people at last. Long Feathers welcomed him enthusiastically. He'd found some difficulty in dealing with the problems of leading. He was very happy to get Three Toes' wives off his back. They had been complaining ever since Three Toes left on his vision quest.

"My brother, welcome home. We have your teepee waiting."

Three Toes was tired. He gifted the horses in his string to Long Feathers and suggested they hold a council campfire that evening. He had much to share and wanted to learn about the soldiers and the reservation.

He dismounted and walked his pony toward his teepee. As he looked around, it occurred to him that his people did not look healthy. It was as though they weren't eating properly. Perhaps it was more than that.

His wives were either going to be angry or horny, or both. He was almost relieved to see that two were pregnant. He wanted to sleep, but that option was clearly not in his immediate future. He did his best with his wives before finding his way to a pile of buffalo robes in the teepee. He fell sound asleep.

He awoke in time for the council fire. Both he and Long Feathers were of a mind to leave Camp Cooper. The U.S. government was showing signs of not living up to its part of the treaty. Of course, that further incentivized the Comanche to periodically leave the reservation to hunt and deliver various forms of mayhem. The younger warriors were anxious for adventure, while the older men were tired of the white man's duplicity. There would be much discussion at the council.

Of great concern was the lack of a sufficient food supply as promised by the Indian agent. The warriors told of a man that occasionally arrived with wagons, but was seen taking buffalo hides while leaving very few foodstuffs behind. They felt that something wasn't right, but didn't fully understand what was happening. They sensed that they were being cheated. So long as warriors could get out and hunt, it was unlikely they'd starve, but neither would they eat well. Three Toes began to think more seriously about leaving.

He was conflicted over what the Great Spirit would have him do. He had developed a kinship with Ghost-Who-Rides, yet was uncertain whether his vision quest had been fulfilled. He found himself still searching for answers. The world seemed to be moving ever faster and the fate of the Comanche ever more inevitable.

The colonel made slow progress from San Antonio. He got ever more adept at mounting and dismounting without damaging his wounded arm as occasions necessitated. He even could start a fire one-handed.

The thoughts ruminating in his mind of recapturing Scarlett drove him beyond any pain from his wounds. He cursed the sheriff for being a just good enough marksman to inconvenience him. He'd spent far too much money and time to simply let her get away.

His superior officer, General Truax, had demanded utmost secrecy in having assigned him to keep Scarlett in Austin. If his secret were to be revealed, he'd pay for the rest of his life with the very worst field assignments conceivable. He dared not fail.

He finally wended his way along the Nueces River to the ferry, and thence to Nuecestown. He decided that, with Corpus Christi in his sights, it would do to get some rest as well as clean up for the final leg of his pursuit. With that in mind, he pulled up in front of Bernice and Agatha's boarding house. He dismounted and knocked on their door.

Bernice opened the door and peered out. "Can we help you?"

"My name is Rucker, Colonel Horace Rucker, and I'm looking for a room for tonight. I'm on my way to Corpus Christi."

Bernice welcomed him in. "Have you eaten, sir?" She noted that, save for the broad-brimmed blue hat with gold braid band, he wore no military clothes.

"I'd like to clean up and eat, ma'am."

"You can call me Bernice, Colonel Rucker. The stable boy will be coming by soon so, if you like, we can put up your horse for the night." She gave the colonel another visual once-over. "There's a water basin out back for washing."

"Thank you. I shouldn't be long." Little did he know that he'd be facing some of Bernice's over-cooked roast. Once he had taken care of his horse, settled into his room, and washed up, he found his way to the dining room and felt he could at last relax. He was curious as to what she might know of goings-on in Corpus Christi.

"So, Bernice, do you have any news from Corpus Christi?" He was necessarily taking his time eating, as the roast entailed extra chewing. "I understand Colonel Kinney returned from Austin."

"Why, yes, Colonel. I did hear about Colonel Kinney. You know, Corpus has endured quite a bit of crime lately, what with murders, rustling, and bank robbing."

"Is the sheriff bringing law and order back to the city?" he continued to question her.

"Sheriff Whelan is a good man, though, between you and me, he does have a weakness for women." Bernice wasn't someone you'd want to share any secrets with and she was right forthcoming. "He did catch that whore from Laredo."

"What happened to the murderers and bank robbers?"

"Well, we have a Texas Ranger that lives near here. Captain Dunn has got himself quite a reputation for bringing outlaws to justice on the Nueces Strip. Some call him Long Luke because of his height."

Bernice was turning out to be a veritable font of knowledge. "Where might I find Captain Dunn?"

"He and his new bride have a small ranch a bit south of here. It's likely as not along your way to Corpus. They named it Heaven's Gate."

The colonel was finding that, while Bernice's vegetables were wonderful, the meat continued to challenge him. His teeth weren't in the greatest condition, so it was actually a tiring exercise.

"Do you have particular business in the city, Colonel?" Bernice wouldn't be the town gossip if she didn't nose into her guests' business.

Agatha strolled in. She'd been listening from the adjoining room. "Good evening, Colonel. I'm Bernice's friend, Agatha. You can call me Aggie."

"Pleasure to meet you, Aggie." He smiled patronizingly. He'd managed to avoid answering Bernice's question about his business.

Bernice wasn't so easily put off. "What was that business, Colonel?"

The colonel thought fast. "It's U.S. Army business, ma'am. I'm not at liberty to discuss any specifics." Technically, it was military business, just not what might normally be expected.

"Well, Colonel, we hope you have a restful night. We have a quiet town here, so you shouldn't be disturbed." She turned to leave the room. "Will you be joining us for breakfast, Colonel Rucker?"

Bernice was listening to her intuition. Something wasn't quite right about this colonel. She wondered why he was not in uniform. She wished she could get word to Sheriff Whelan in Corpus Christi. She decided to ask Doc for advice. She put on her wrap and walked across the street.

The colonel watched from his window. Gossipers concerned him. He shrugged. Not much he could do about it.

The banging on the door of the sheriff's office was loud enough to have awakened the dead. Whelan sat bolt upright. The banging continued. He looked out the window and saw a well-lathered horse tied to the hitching post. He cracked the door open. "Dan?" It was the stable boy from Nuecestown. "Come in. What the hell are you doing out here in the middle of the night?" He shut the door behind the boy and offered him a seat. Scarlett awakened and was listening intently.

"Bernice sent me. She expects trouble."

"Don't leave me curious, boy. What sort of trouble?"

"Well, some U.S. Army colonel name of Rucker is spending the night at her boarding house. He said he's got business in Corpus, and Bernice had a feeling he was up to no good."

Whelan wiped his brow with his bandana. He and Scarlett exchanged concerned expressions. "You've done real good, Dan. You can tell Bernice that she's right about her suspicions." He gave the boy a silver coin. "On your way back, would you please stop at Luke Dunn's place and let him know about the colonel and that there may be trouble in Corpus Christi tomorrow." Whelan wished there was an Army fort nearby. "Is this colonel traveling alone?"

"Yes, sir, yes, he is. He is wearing some bandages. Bernice said he had been wounded."

The colonel was traveling alone. To come after Whelan without waiting for his wounds to heal spoke of some serious level of desperation. Something or someone was causing this behavior in the colonel. Whelan decided to visit Colonel Kinney first thing. If nothing else, he wanted greater security for Scarlett.

The colonel finished breakfast and left Bernice's boarding house. He was delayed just a bit, as he was told by the stable boy that his horse had a horseshoe problem and it would take a bit to replace it.

Dan was under instructions from Luke to buy time.

By the time the colonel was on the trail, it was nearly mid-morning. He was irritated at the delay, but no less determined. Bernice had given him directions to Luke's place, but it wasn't the most direct route. By the time he got to the ranch, it was late morning. As he approached, he noticed a young woman riding toward him to his left. He pulled up to the cabin and dismounted. Before he could head for the door, it opened and the imposing figure of Luke Dunn stepped toward him. "Welcome to Heaven's Gate. Can we help you?"

The colonel was momentarily taken aback by this larger-than-life lawman. "Yes, my name is Rucker, Colonel Horace Rucker, U.S. Army."

"Care for some coffee, Colonel?" About this time Elisa had ridden up and dismounted.

The colonel couldn't help but notice how downright beautiful the Texas Ranger's wife was. "Mrs. Dunn, I'm Colonel Rucker. I'm on my way to Corpus Christi on military business. It's a pleasure to make your acquaintance."

"Please pay me no never mind, Colonel. I was out checking on some of our cattle." She smiled friendly-like. She'd already been briefed by Luke as to the suspicious mission of this officer.

Luke emerged with cups of coffee and thrust one at the colonel. "My, it looks as though you've run afoul of some gunplay, Colonel. Are you all right?"

The colonel accepted the coffee. "Looks worse than it is, Captain Dunn."

"I need to head into Corpus myself, Colonel. Would you care for company?"

"I appreciate your offer, Captain Dunn, but my business is of a nature that requires me to travel alone."

This was telling. Luke knew from what Dan had passed along from Whelan that the colonel was after the Laredo whore, Miss Scarlett. "Suit yourself, Colonel. We hope you have an uneventful journey."

The colonel quaffed the rest of the coffee and mounted up. "Thanks for your hospitality. You have a beautiful home here. It's certainly not something you'd want to lose. Perhaps I'll see you on my way back from Corpus."

Luke was surprised by the not-so-veiled threat. The colonel must be quite confident in whomever he was taking his orders from. He determined to wait a bit and then take the trail to Corpus Christi. Whelan might need help.

The colonel had been visiting long enough to assess as to how much threat Luke might pose to his mission. He had a queasy feeling. He suspected the Ranger knew more about his trip to Corpus Christi than he was revealing.

"Lisa, sweetheart. I've got a duty here."

Elisa understood but wasn't happy about it. They'd had a couple of days of magical wedded bliss. The colonel had broken her idyll. "Be safe, Lucas." She packed some jerky for the ride.

Luke gathered his pair of Walker Colts, the Colt rifle, and plenty of ammunition. The guns were always kept in top working order. He would be ready, come what may.

He hugged and kissed Elisa, and was on his way. He was determined to keep sufficient distance behind the colonel to be out of sight. The wind was behind him, so he needed to be extra quiet.

He'd gone about halfway to Corpus when his intuition kicked in. He turned west and made a wide circle to a bluff overlooking the road. Sure enough, the colonel had doubled back to see whether anyone was following him. He might have been focused on his mission and nursing wounds, but he wasn't stupid.

Whelan talked Colonel Kinney into letting him relocate Scarlett to the bank. It seemed ironic, but the bank had better security than the jail. Colonel Kinney had vaguely heard of Colonel Rucker in Austin social circles. He recalled that the colonel's commanding officer was an up-and-coming brigadier general with considerable connections with the social and political circles of Washington, D.C.

"Scarlett, that fool colonel from Austin is still on our trail. He sent his sons home, but he returned and spent last night in Nuecestown. He's on his way. I sent a message to Captain Dunn, and he should be coming to help us. I'm moving you to the bank, as it's safer." He unlocked the cell door and placed the manacles on her wrists.

Scarlett was suffering from something women referred to as morning sickness. She felt poorly enough that where she was jailed at that moment didn't really matter.

Whelan deposited her at the bank and then went back to the jail to await Colonel Rucker. He made sure his arsenal was ready in case he needed to resort to gunplay. There was a tinge of regret that he hadn't aimed better when he'd met the colonel's charge a few days back. It was concerning that Rucker was so dogged in his pursuit. He wondered what this brigadier general that Kinney mentioned must be like.

Rucker felt confident that he wasn't being followed. He had played that old tactic he'd learned from Whelan about doubling back, and he'd seen no sign of anyone tracking him. Of course, he wasn't much of a tracker himself, so it was no surprise that he'd failed to see any trace of Luke.

As he entered Corpus Christi around midday, he couldn't help but notice that the streets weren't especially busy. It gave him an eerie feeling. Was it a trap? Had someone been tipped off? He felt a twinge of paranoia.

His first inclination was to stop at the sheriff's office, but he decided that a visit with Colonel Kinney might be a better first action. He noted that the city was considerably smaller than Austin or San Antonio. It had a reputation as a thriving port, but was not exactly overflowing with people. The colonel finally pulled up in front of Kinney's rather impressive house. He dismounted and surveyed the area. It was still eerily quiet. It was a bit warm and humid, but the citizens should be used to that.

He was about to knock on the door when it was opened by a black woman. "Hello, may I help you?" It was Colonel Kinney's housekeeper.

"Yes, I'm Colonel Horace Rucker and I'd like to visit with Colonel Kinney if he's available."

"One moment. Please come in." She stepped aside and then disappeared up the hallway. She was back in a few moments. "The colonel will see you in a few moments. He's finishing his meal. Please wait here in the library." She escorted the colonel into the library and motioned to a chair near a large desk. Colonel Kinney was putting this interloper in his place.

About twenty minutes later, Colonel Kinney stepped into the library. "Colonel Rucker, I presume. Pleasure to meet you, sir."

Colonel Rucker stood and accepted Kinney's proffered handshake.

"Thank you, Colonel Kinney. I've been looking forward to meeting the man that made Corpus Christi. I must say, it's quieter than I expected."

"It's a warm day, Colonel. How's General Truax these days?"

The colonel was only slightly alarmed that Kinney knew about his connection with the general. What else did he know? "He's fine, sir. He's soon to return to Washington to serve in the War Department." He mustn't be paranoid.

Colonel Kinney could sense that the colonel coveted an opportunity to travel in the elite circles of the nation's capital. "I'm sure he looks forward to that. I met him a couple of times in Austin." Colonel Kinney could have added that Truax was a sycophantic snob. "So, Colonel, what is your business here in Corpus Christi?"

Kinney had gotten right to the point. "It involves a woman, Colonel Kinney."

"And?"

"The general believes that a woman incarcerated in your jail may have committed treason, a federal crime. He's asked me personally to bring her back to Austin to face military justice."

Colonel Kinney noted the colonel's wounds. "It appears that you are quite committed to your mission, Colonel. Unfortunately, I'm unable to help you."

Colonel Rucker's eyes grew wide. He knew she was in Corpus Christi. "But..."

"We have no such person in our jail, Colonel." Kinney smiled. "It seems you're on a wild goose chase." Of course, Kinney was telling the truth. She was in the bank, not the jail.

The colonel knew he'd chased after her and Whelan. What was going on? He was momentarily dumbfounded. He collected himself. "Well, thank you, Colonel Kinney. I expect I'll be on my way."

Everything and everyone seemed to be conspiring against him. There'd been the delays in Nuecestown and now the obfuscation here in Corpus. It was clear he'd have to do his own detective work. He decided to pay a visit to Sheriff Whelan.

Scarlett feared for her life. She sat crammed into what amounted to a vault deep in the bowels of the bank. It was bad enough that the last time she'd been to this bank the situation had been quite different. It didn't bring back fond memories. Plus, the very thought of Rucker successfully abducting her and taking her back to some unknown fate in Austin was scary at best. Finally, the bank manager came by to check on her. "Are you all okay, Miss Scarlett? Can I get you anything?"

"I am hungry, thank you."

The bank manager went across to the nearby boarding house to get something for the prisoner to eat. As he entered, there was a newcomer signing in for a room. The man wore a military officer's hat, but was otherwise dressed as a civilian. He disconcertedly nodded at the man. "Donna, could you be kind enough to rustle up a bit of grub for our guest?"

The colonel gave the man a once-over. He wore a white shirt and a visor, along with a string tie. "Pardon me, sir, do you work at the bank?"

"Why, yes, I'm the manager. Do you need to make a deposit?" Only then did he realize he may have unwittingly revealed the secret prisoner.

Rucker thought it unusual that the bank manager would be ordering food to take back to the bank for a guest. The colonel was now thinking he might be making a withdrawal. He was rather glad he had stopped at the boarding house before visiting the sheriff. "Well, I'd very much like to see your bank, sir."

The bank manager nervously carried the tray of food across to the bank with the colonel following him. As they prepared to enter the bank, the colonel noticed a handsome grey stallion hitched in front of the place. He and the bank manager stepped into the foyer.

"I'll be right with you, sir." And the bank manager proceeded to head to the rear of the bank.

"Why, Colonel Rucker, fancy meeting you again."

The colonel scanned the room. They were alone, other than the Texas Ranger who stood before him larger than life. He had a Walker Colt holstered and a second in his belt. The Ranger's size was intimidating. Suddenly, the prospect of finding Scarlett was not nearly so attractive. "Uh, and good to see you, Captain Dunn." He tried not to look suspicious. "I see you have business in Corpus."

"Yes, Colonel. As I mentioned this morning, we're expanding our ranch so have purchased additional land. Were you able to complete your business?"

The colonel was seeing his Army career beginning to unravel. "I...I expect I'm pretty close to finished with my business, thanks."

"I'd be pleased to give you safe escort as far as Nuecestown, Colonel," Luke said.

Out of his peripheral vision, the colonel thought he saw someone... perhaps a woman...inside the bank vault. The bank manager had left the outer door to the vault open, though the inner iron door with its heavy bars remained locked. "I had planned to spend the night here, Captain Dunn, but my business appears to be finished and I may accept your offer after all."

"Happy to wait for you, Colonel, while you retrieve your belongings from the boarding house."

Rucker had to admit defeat for now. He wasn't about to start a bloodbath that he might be a victim of. He'd live to fight another day. He'd certainly absorbed enough of Sheriff Whelan's lead for now. He'd have a few days on the trail to conjure up an excuse to pass on to Brigadier General Truax.

Soon enough, Luke and Colonel Rucker were headed back toward Nuecestown. For now, Scarlett was protected.

As they silently rode northward, the colonel broke the ice. "Captain Dunn, I understand you're from Ireland. I've heard it's a lovely country but that many members of your family have settled here on the Nueces Strip."

"You've heard right, Colonel. We are a tightly knit family and are enjoying the freedoms and opportunities this land offers. The British were taking away our freedoms in Ireland. It was a far easier choice than you might imagine." Luke figured it was now safe to broach the sensitive topic of this day. "So, what did the general really want with Scarlett Rose, Colonel?"

Rucker wasn't surprised that Luke knew the purpose of his mission. "It was personal to the general, sir. It is apparently a family matter."

"Did you know that she's with child?"

The colonel pulled up his horse with an incredulous expression spread across his face. "No." This might change everything.

"I expect that happens in her business." The remark seemed cold, coming from Luke.

"Any idea who the father might be, Captain?" The colonel was genuinely curious.

Luke almost demurred, but chose to go on. "As I understand it, Colonel, it was either her outlaw lover Dirk Cavendish or Sheriff Whelan. Cavendish was shot and killed while trying to escape the law, so only the sheriff remains."

Colonel Rucker realized that, if the general was not going to be pleased over his failed mission, he was going to be especially unhappy over the pregnancy news. "I appreciate your candor, Captain Dunn." He paused thoughtfully, as humility was not exactly a virtue he was comfortable with. "I do thank you for keeping me from taking my intended actions in Corpus Christi."

"You're most welcome, Colonel. I hope you've reached closure on your mission...at least for the present."

Soon enough, they reached Heaven's Gate and Luke parted company with the colonel, who continued his likely fateful ride on toward Austin.

Luke waited at the arched gate as he watched Rucker ride off. He was grateful there'd been no gunplay. He turned the big grey stallion toward the cabin that he and Elisa now shared and stood tall in the stirrups so that he could see the roof and the smoke curling from the chimney. The setting sun painted the deep azure sky with a patina of gold dust.

He pondered his newly chosen future. Would it be as rancher? Texas Ranger? Both? No matter yet. He'd be husband to the most lovingly beautiful woman on earth. With that thought lingering, he settled into the saddle and gently applied his spurs just enough to move home at a fast trot. He'd only been away for a few hours, but his senses could already feel Elisa's touch and take in her fragrance. Would that this might never end.

Three Toes and a half dozen warriors left Camp Cooper and set out southwestwardly for the Balcones Escarpment deep in the Comancheria. They were of a mind to explore the opportunities for relocating to that region. The Comanche urgently wanted to be out from under the iron fist of the U.S. government. Once again, he'd left his three wives behind. He felt it was just as well, as they wore him out. It was easier in his mind to care for his horses, as they never complained. He appreciated a warm bed and good meals, but found himself needing escape. This mission afforded him that escape.

Having concluded with ever more certainty that he'd fulfilled his vision quest, Three Toes felt as though his life was complete. All the events that might follow would be by the good graces of the Great Spirit. They would be like a bonus. He thought often about Ghost-Who-Rides, and hoped the Ranger would find a happy life with Elisa and the possibility of peace on the Nueces Strip.

The nondescript old wagon pulled up across the street from the Laredo jail. It was early morning. One man stayed seated as he struggled to keep the horses steady. There was a nervousness in his manner that seemed to transmit through the reins. Another man walked over to the store next to the jail and leaned against a post. He tried to look casual as he lit a smoke. Two others hitched their horses and started walking toward the jail. Each man had a pistol in his belt and carried a rifle at the ready. Their sombreros were tilted low to partially cover their faces. One had a bandolier with rifle bullets across his chest. They were a gnarly bunch, to say the least.

The man at the store dropped his smoke and crushed it under his heel. He and the other two covered their faces with bandanas as they approached the front door of the jail. The man with the bandolier kicked open the door. Carlos Perez smiled groggily from his cell.

Luke rode up to the barn. He dismounted, unsaddled, and hastily curried the big stallion. As he began heading to the cabin, a tumbleweed rolled by on its aimless journey across the prairie. It gave him pause to consider again what journey lay ahead, certainly not an aimless one.

Lawman or rancher? A decision loomed before him. He stopped at the water basin and cleaned off a bit of the trail dust. He smelled her cooking before he even opened the door. Life was good.